A Cruel Trade

A Cruel Trade

Fergus Finlay

ANDRE DEUTSCH

First published 1990 by
André Deutsch Limited
105 - 106 Great Russell Street London WC1B 3LJ

Copyright © 1990 by Fergus Finlay
All rights reserved

British Library Cataloguing in Publication Data

Finlay, Fergus
A Cruel Trade
823.914 [F]

ISBN 0 233 98586 7

Typeset from disk by
Dublin Online Typographic Services Ltd.
Printed in Great Britain by
Billing & Sons Limited, Worcester

For Frieda,
without whom nothing would be worthwhile,
and for
Mandy, Vicky, Emma, and Sarah,
to whom the next four books will be dedicated!

"State business is a cruel trade."
                                    Lord Halifax

"Direct, we beseech Thee, O Lord, our actions by Thy holy inspirations and carry them on by Thy gracious assistance; that every word and work of ours may always begin from Thee, and by Thee be happily ended; through Christ Our Lord. Amen."
Prayer said at the start of Business in the Dail - the Irish House of Commons - every day.

"The head of the Government, or Prime Minister, shall be called, and in this Constitution is referred to as, the Taoiseach."
                Article 28.5.1 of the Irish Constitution.

CHAPTER 1

JUNE 29th - THE FOURTH DAY

THE REPORTER

"Murderer!"

It was a woman, and her shout had dropped into one of those silences that can happen at even the noisiest meetings. Because of the stillness, the shout had shocked everyone, prolonging the silence so that the word she had used seemed almost to leave an echo behind it in the hall.

People craned their necks, and started to mutter disapproval. Two of the stewards were already moving towards the woman, but even before they reached her, she was on her way out of the hall.

From the press table at a corner of the stage, I had been able to see the woman clearly. And I had been able to see Gibson's reaction to her. His face, which moments before had been animated, even passionate, had drained completely. There was no doubt about it - the look on that face, in that moment, was fear. Even after the woman had left the hall, it took him a moment or two to recover his composure.

He did, of course. The most seasoned political interrogator had never been able to disturb the famous Gibson composure for long. When the packed hall had settled down again, he said, "well, ladies and gentlemen, it looks as if the Opposition might get one vote in Kilkenny after all!" The remark nearly brought the house down, and after the applause had faded, Gibson continued with the rousing attack on the Opposition that the woman had interrupted.

Apart from Gibson's reaction to it, the other surprising thing about the woman's interruption was the fact that it had happened here. There were parts of Ireland where the very mention of the Taoiseach's name was enough to unleash a torrent of abuse, but here in Kilkenny, Andrew Gibson was king. It was his home town, and the Party he led had held sway throughout the county for generations. That was why Kilkenny had been picked as the obvious place to launch the campaign.

The Springhill Hotel's ballroom could accommodate nearly a thousand people, and many hundreds more were standing in the rain in the car-park outside, listening to the speeches being relayed over a hastily-erected loudspeaker. The meeting had been advertised, all that day and the previous one, as "Andy Coming Home", and clearly half the town had turned out to meet him.

And he was giving them their money's worth. He could dominate an audience at any time, with his great voice and that head of flowing hair that had been almost golden when he was younger, and was still impressive flecked with grey. Tonight, he was in especially good form, and was spell-binding them with the trick he did with his eyes.

It was a technique that never ceased to impress me, no matter how often I'd seen it. The only previous Taoiseach who had been able to do it was Haughey - and he had needed that kind of trick, because neither his voice nor his stature could impose itself on an audience. Gibson had all of the attributes of a powerful orator, and this use of his eyes never let him down.

He would let his eyes flicker over the audience until they came to rest on an individual. And if you were the individual in question, you knew with absolute certainty that for just that moment the Prime Minister of Ireland was talking to you - to you and to nobody else. And you knew that it was vital to him that you understood and agreed with everything he said. Very few could resist it.

He could do it on television too. He had a way of focusing on the camera as if it were a real person. The effect on people watching him was startling. The Taoiseach seemed to be looking directly at them. Even if they moved around their living-rooms, his eyes would follow.

It was all done with his eyes, just as he was doing it now. The audience in the Springhill were on the edge of their seats, each one hoping that Gibson's eyes would land on them. They were waiting, waiting to erupt in an enormous ovation as soon as he had finished.

"So there you have it," he was saying. "We face now the greatest opportunity this country has had since it was founded. We can resolve, almost at a stroke, the one great issue for which thousands of Irish men and women, in the generations that have gone before us, have fought and died. We cannot - and we will not - be deterred by the Opposition's snivelling doubts and fears from reaching out and grasping that opportunity. I know the risks - I think you know that our Party and our Government is well capable of dealing with any risks. I am leaving the choice up to you - the people of this country. This is your chance to make history - take it with both hands!"

It was a high note on which to finish and within seconds everyone in the hall was standing. They were cheering and stamping and waving. As Gibson stood to acknowledge the ovation, he beckoned one of the stewards over and whispered in his ear. I saw the man go down to the back of the hall and out the same door that the woman had used a few minutes earlier. After a couple of minutes, he reappeared and gave a thumbs-up sign towards the stage. The look of relief on the Taoiseach's face was obvious.

I was intrigued. What had the woman meant by calling the Prime Minister a murderer? Why had she chosen this forum to do it? And why did Gibson seem to be afraid of her?

Covering an election tour as a reporter isn't nearly as glamorous as it looks. Mostly, it's bloody awful boring - the same speeches every day, more time devoted to getting good photographs than to any analysis of what's being said. And the same phone call from your editor at the end of every day, wanting to know why you haven't got a fresh angle.

It was already the fourth day of the campaign, and I was still looking for an angle. Maybe there's an angle in this, I thought. Maybe it won't turn out to be the usual crackpot. I decided that if I got a chance tomorrow, I'd try to find out who the woman was.

THE PLAYER

The man came every day to play the same machine. A lot of people did that - they settled on one machine, the one that was going to make their fortune.

This was a straightforward one - three bars and you won the jackpot, three apples and you won a pound. It would never make anyone's fortune. But that didn't matter to the punters - as long as they were happy, they'd feed tenpences into a machine all day.

Many of them, just like this man, played the machines in total concentration. Feeding in coins, pulling the lever, barely waiting to see if a win had registered. If you didn't understand the compulsion, it didn't look rational. But if you were used to it, you wouldn't even notice the man.

Every day the same machine. He would stand there, the *Daily Mirror* he had brought in with him neatly folded and lying on the heavy metal table beside the machine. He was oblivious to the milling throng of holiday-makers and the raucous cries of the promenade barkers all around him.

He was waiting.

This day, like every other, he came in, placed his neat newspaper beside the machine, and started to play. He was invisible, just as he wanted to be.

Nobody saw the speed with which he had reached into the folded newspaper, and slid the parcel it had held under the slot machine. It fitted beautifully, and he was glad of that. It wasn't one of those situations where you could take measurements. When you do it by feel, it sometimes takes a couple of attempts to get it right, but he had guessed exactly.

Now that the parcel was in place, he would stop coming here. His companions could come in occasionally, just to check that it was still there. They would come in at random times - but he wouldn't come back.

That way, if anyone ever remembered that he had been here, his face would be fuzzy in their memory. It would be impossible to identify him clearly.

It was neat, and well done. He played on for another half-hour, then picked up his newspaper and left. The parcel would do its job all right.

CHAPTER 2

JUNE 26th - THE FIRST DAY

THE GOVERNMENT

In Ireland, even meetings of the Government don't start on time. Cabinet meetings are timed to start at ten-thirty every Tuesday morning. But Ministers are more likely to be found at that hour in the Cabinet ante-room, and in the Communications Room across the hall.

Those in the ante-room would stand around drinking the Bewleys' coffee that Jennifer, the girl in charge of communications, kept percolating constantly all day when the Government met. They were usually the Ministers who were not going to be under pressure at that meeting. There were three ways that Ministers could avoid pressure - either they didn't have anything on the Agenda that had to be sold to colleagues; or it was a non-contentious item, likely to go through "on the nod"; or - the best way - their business had been cleared with the Taoiseach in advance.

The Ministers in the Communications Room were usually those who expected pressure, and would be found huddled in a corner with some of their "officials" (civil servants are only referred to as civil servants outside the service - they always refer to themselves and to each other as officials).

The Communications Room was fairly quiet today. Despite its grandiose title, it was in fact a bare office, with a couple of tables and a number of telephones of various types - some equipped with direct lines to the outside world, others with scrambler attachments, and some linked to a system of tie lines that dialled Ministers' offices directly. The room was only used on Cabinet days, and its function was to enable Ministers to send or receive messages, because there were no phones in the Cabinet Room itself. In the case of incoming messages, these were transcribed by Jennifer or whoever else was in charge, who would then walk across the hall and press a button outside the double doors of the Cabinet Room. This would activate a light over the door on the inside, which would alert the Cabinet Secretary that there was a message for one of the Ministers.

When Gibson came down the back stairs from his own office he found most Ministers drinking coffee. There was no reason for any sense of urgency at this time of year, and several of them were discussing imminent holiday plans. Gibson smiled to himself at the thought that the announcement he was about to make would put an end to all thought of holidays, at least for the immediate future. Because he wanted to avoid any hint of what was to happen, it was ten minutes before the last member of his Cabinet had taken his place around the great Adams mahogany table that adorned the Cabinet Room itself.

Gibson called the meeting to order quickly, and issued the usual formal instruction to Bob Holloway, the Cabinet Secretary, who was the only outsider apart from the Attorney General allowed to attend meetings of the Cabinet, that decisions were to be recorded. There were occasional Government meetings, usually devoted to Party political topics, at which no decisions were recorded. At almost no Government meeting was the discussion leading to a decision ever recorded.

Then he announced, to the relief of one or two Ministers, that he was setting the prepared Agenda for the meeting aside.

It is entirely a matter for the Taoiseach of the day to determine whether his Cabinet is going to be the most or the least democratic forum in Irish politics. One of the complaints occasionally voiced about Gibson's predecessor Charles Page, when he was Taoiseach, was that he was so interested in seeking consensus around the Cabinet table that he often forgot that decisions were required. For his own part, Gibson was fond of repeating the old story about the time Abraham Lincoln called a vote in his Cabinet. Fourteen members voted "Aye", Lincoln voted "No". "The Nos have it," said Lincoln.

So no one was surprised, or complained, when Gibson set aside the prepared Agenda, even though some Ministers might have worked for months to get an item on to it. Such things were not discussed in Gibson's Cabinet - they were decided by Gibson.

"At approximately two-forty this afternoon," he began, "Mr Kinnock will tell the House of Commons that he intends to call an immediate General Election."

He paused, allowing the news to sink in. It was obvious that he had dropped a bombshell. Politicians everywhere are fascinated by politics, especially other peoples'. To an Irish politician the news of an election in the United Kingdom has a special interest, because always, to a greater or lesser extent, Ireland is an issue in that election. And there is nothing more interesting than an election in which you can feel involved, but in which your seat is not at stake. But there were questions on every face. If Mr Kinnock was prepared to dissolve the House of Commons a full year before he needed to, in order to seek a second term, how come the Irish Taoiseach was among the first to know?

"At about the same time," he continued, "I intend to dissolve the Dail and call an immediate election in the Republic."

If there was interest before, there was consternation now. Gibson thought that O'Flynn, the Minister for the Gaeltacht, was going to faint clean away. He remembered with amusement that it was O'Flynn, a first-time member of the Cabinet when Gibson formed his Government three years ago, who had announced at last week's Government meeting, "well lads, only six weeks more to go to the pension!"

It was a feature of Irish politics, much criticised by every Opposition but perpetuated by every Government, that three years in Ministerial office was enough to qualify the holder for a life-long pension based on the very handsome Ministerial salary. Gibson thought O'Flynn must have had a sudden vision of his pension going up in smoke.

It was Scally who broke the silence.

Joseph Scally was Gibson's most vociferous critic in the Cabinet - to put it more correctly, he was Gibson's only critic in the Cabinet. He had opposed Gibson for the leadership of the Party on two occasions in the previous six years, and thus was the only member of the Party whom Gibson felt he could not leave out of the Cabinet.

"Would you mind telling us, Taoiseach," he said, "what in God's name is going on?"

"Over the past three months or so," said the Taoiseach, careful to control his exhilaration as he came to the full drama of his announcement, "I have been engaged in virtually constant discussion with the British Prime Minister on the question of the unity of this country. We have reached an agreement on the matter, and that agreement is as follows."

Rapidly, he began to outline for his stunned colleagues the terms that would come to be known as the Gibson/Kinnock Agreement. They were simple enough, if dramatic.

Britain would, that same day, announce her intention to relinquish sovereignty over the North of Ireland, and to transfer that sovereignty to the Republic, under a Treaty to be signed under the auspices of the President of the United States of America.

In addition, Britain and the USA would make aid available, some of it to be repaid, to the tune of £6000 million over the next eight years, to facilitate the emergence of a unified State where the economies, social security systems, and infrastructural amenities were in harmony with one another.

In return, the Irish Government would publish a new Constitution, the outline of which was already prepared and agreed, guaranteeing equal rights to all citizens. The Government would also agree in that Constitution that for the same period of eight years (or two full periods of office, whichever was longer) at least one-third of the places in the Cabinet would be reserved for representatives of the Northern community, with a minimum guarantee of one Cabinet member from the Catholic minority and one from the Protestant majority - in practice, both sides recognised that the Catholic minority would hardly qualify for more than one, so that the Loyalists, or Protestants, would fill the other four (a third of the Cabinet represented five members in all).

During the transitional period, responsibility for security would remain vested in Britain, with some representatives from the South overseeing the operational details in tandem with their colleagues from the North. Finally, among the major points, a new Defence Treaty was to be drawn up. Under this Treaty, Britain and Ireland would commit each other to the joint defence of each other's countries.

Ireland, which for the previous seventy years had been a neutral country, would become a member of NATO, and three NATO bases would be located in the South, in addition to the one already in the North. One of these would be a submarine base, located in Galway, and precise details of the other two would be worked out in due course. And there would be a number of radar and other surveillance stations around the coast, under the operational control of NATO personnel. Because of the sensitivity of this proposal, it was understood that none of these personnel, at least during the transition, would be British, and that as far as possible, any construction contracts involved would be awarded to Irish firms.

There were a number of other minor matters, ranging from police integration to support for agriculture, that Gibson also outlined in the course of the next twenty minutes, reflecting to himself that he had never had a more attentive audience.

There were two final points that he intended to make, but he had already decided to keep them to himself until the discussion was under way.

He didn't have long to wait.

It was O'Flynn (as he had half expected) who was the first to speak.

"I think we must all congratulate you, Taoiseach," he began, "on a historic agreement that will place your name ..."

"Bullshit!" interrupted Scally, whose anger had been growing rapidly during Gibson's outline of the Agreement. "The only thing historic about this is the size of the sell-out! And from you, of all people, who has almost made a career out of attacking Britain in the name of our neutrality!"

Gibson had been waiting for this. Irish neutrality had been the cornerstone of his Party's foreign policy for generations. Because of it, the country had stayed out of the Second World War, and Gibson himself had built a reputation on his defence of neutrality in the past. Hanrahan in particular had been worried that the ending of neutrality would be a resigning matter for some of the Cabinet.

The Taoiseach knew he had to take this issue head on.

"Whenever I felt it necessary to defend our neutrality, I did so," he retorted. "And I don't ever remember getting much help from you."

"Damn right," said Scally hotly. "I never supported the way you went about it, and I never cared for the issues you chose. But I have always supported - and fervently supported - the commitment to neutrality. It's been almost an article of faith for me, and for a lot more of us as well, as you damn well know. And now you're offering to give it away - for something not one of us has been consulted about."

One or two nodded their heads at this last point. Hanrahan, Gibson's political adviser, had warned him about this. Some would be more offended at the fact that they had had no involvement in the discussions than they would be at the outcome.

"I'm not prepared to discuss the development and the history of the concept of Irish neutrality with you," he said to Scally. "You know and I know that the people who founded this Party always regarded it as an issue that would need to be reviewed, at least, when the question of Irish unity was settled. And as to the question of consultation - there was a reason for the secrecy, and all of you in this room who have ever spoken to a journalist about sensitive material know what the reason is."

By now Scally seemed ready to react more calmly. He realised, Gibson knew, that the Taoiseach had had a lot more time to prepare his answers than he had to prepare his questions.

"I'm sorry, Taoiseach," he said, "to appear to be the only one who is carping. But I have to disagree. The issues of neutrality and unity are two equally fundamental ones. I do not believe we have the right to change policy on one, even for the sake of the other."

This was Gibson's opportunity.

"I never said we did," he said. "I fully accept that only the Irish people have the right to make that choice, just as Mr Kinnock believes that he must seek a mandate for what he is offering. What we are proposing will in fact require significant Constitutional change in the Republic, although of course these matters can all be dealt with by way of legislation in Britain. But we cannot have a Referendum to adopt a new Constitution inside at least two months. That is why I have decided on this course now - to dissolve the Dail, as is my right, and to ask the people to endorse the Agreement in principle. When we are re-elected we will then immediately begin the process of asking the people to adopt the new Constitution."

"Furthermore," he concluded, "it is my intention that the last act of this Government will be to ratify this Agreement, to endorse my initialling of it, subject of course to the final determination of the Irish people. And I will insist here, in the privacy of this room, that that endorsement be unanimous and without any begrudgery."

In their reaction to the Agreement that Gibson had outlined, they had momentarily forgotten his intention to call a General Election. His reminder sent a small tremor of apprehension around the room. Nothing concentrates the mind of a politician like the words "General Election".

Already some of them were thinking about the things that would need to be cleared up quickly in their own areas. Holden, the Minister for Agriculture, was bitterly regretting the announcement of 200 job losses that had been made by the State-owned food processing plant in his own constituency; Ryan, in Transport, was thinking about the national bus and rail strike that was due to start the following Monday, and about which he had already issued a statement saying that the issue was "one of the deepest principle as far as I am concerned" ("why did Gibson let me issue that stupid fucking statement?" he was thinking); Barry, in the Department of Energy, was remembering his announcement made only a week ago that he was not going to proceed with the construction of a peat manufacturing plant only thirty miles from his own house (his thoughts were somewhat similar to Ryan's); and O'Brien, who was responsible for the Department of Justice, was thinking about some of the things he would not like to have discovered by any successor from the Opposition.

The members of Gibson's Cabinet had been carefully chosen. By and large, they fell into three categories. Some had been chosen because their local popularity enhanced the standing of the Party in their own areas - Barry, from Waterford, O'Brien and Ryan, both from the West of Ireland, were in this category. There were some who had a particular expertise, and because of their specialist status were unlikely to pose any threat to the Leadership. Expertise, in this sense, could mean skill at sniffing out sources of funds for the Party. Walsh, the Minister for Information, Deignan in the Department of Labour, and Kelly in Foreign Affairs (whose foreign affairs were legendary among his officials) could all be categorised as "specialists" of one sort or another.

The final category were those whom newspapers regularly referred to as Gibson's cronies. This generally meant that they were regarded as quite incapable of holding down a Ministerial portfolio on their own merits, and were seen as having been slotted into posts in which Gibson liked to have his own way a hundred per cent of the time. When the appointment of Brady as Minister for Finance had been announced, for instance, there was consternation in the Stock Exchange - "he couldn't give you the change out of a pound" was one of the kinder remarks quoted; and in the three years since his appointment, he had never given a single interview on the subject of his portfolio. O'Flynn, in the Gaeltacht, was another of the cronies. And so was Dawson in Health, who was known to spend a great deal of his time, and his Department's money, ensuring that Gibson's constituents in Kilkenny, and his own in Roscommon, wanted for nothing in the matter of health care and social security benefits.

They had one thing in common, all of them, with the exception of Scally: they were each heartily despised by the Taoiseach who had appointed them. He found it difficult, most of the time, to conceal this. Especially in the case of those whom the outside world regarded as his particular cronies, this difficulty often became an impossibility. Brady in particular, who held, nominally, the post second in importance to the Taoiseach, had been known to beg his officials to tell Gibson he was out of the country rather than answer one of the peremptory summonses to his office.

On his way up, over the years, Gibson had courted many of these men, and the way in which they had reacted to his flattery, his hints of advancement, his veiled threats, only made him despise them the more.

All except Scally. Scally was the one who made him work in Cabinet. He had been the favoured son of the old Leader, and for years had had a power-base of his own in the Party. Gibson had known, when he became Taoiseach, that to leave Scally out of his Cabinet would be an act of folly. "As Lyndon Johnson said," he remarked at the time, though not publicly, "if you've got to keep a camel, it's better to have him inside the tent pissing out than outside the tent pissing in."

Most of the time his majority in Cabinet was more than enough to prevent Gibson worrying about the arguments Scally was likely to put up. They were always worthy arguments, though sometimes tainted by a slightly "holier than thou" attitude. But on the big issues, such as this one, Scally had to be outmanoeuvred. One way or the other, Gibson had to pin him down.

That was why Gibson had decided to seek a formal Government decision endorsing his action in initialling the Agreement. In the circumstances, it was largely academic, since implementation of the Agreement would require Constitutional changes, which could only be brought about by a Referendum of all the people. Besides, it was a matter for the Lower and Upper Houses of the Parliament, the Dail and Senate, to ratify international agreements of any kind.

Discussion centred, not so much on the Agreement itself, but on the tactical questions surrounding the election. Most of them regarded the Agreement as a fait accompli, the major factor, but perhaps not the only one, in the election.

To all the questions about things which needed to be done before polling day, Gibson had only one answer.

"This will be a one-issue election," he said, "and the issue will be the greatest achievement of any Irish Government in the history of the State - the reunification of the country. That's what we have to keep hammering home - the historic opportunity we are being offered. If anything else crops up here in the Republic, it's your job to kill it. There may be violence in the North, and the British Prime Minister and I have discussed that possibility. He has given me his absolute assurance that it will be put down as firmly as necessary - and I don't think I need to remind any of you that he is well capable of delivering on that. Remember, anything else that crops up - it's your job to deal with it. You are all still going to continue drawing your salaries, after all, unlike your colleagues on the back benches."

"But Taoiseach," Ryan said, "there are some situations that could get out of hand ..."

"They had better not," replied Gibson sharply. "Let me spell it out very simply. If something needs to be fixed, then fix it. That strike of yours, for instance. I expect to see a news item in the papers tomorrow to the effect that you have invited the unions in for urgent talks - and that's the last news item I want to see on the subject until we have won this election."

He looked around the table.

"I wouldn't like to be misunderstood," he said. "If there are any of you who expect to be in this room after the election is over, you had better deliver now. Nothing - let me repeat nothing - is going to get between us and victory. You have the power to ensure that. Use it."

His words had the desired effect. For the remainder of the discussion, no one referred to the Ministerial tasks ahead of him. For two hours, they concentrated instead on teasing out all the ramifications of the Agreement that Gibson had brought them. There really was only one issue that some of them felt was difficult, the issue that Scally had highlighted at the start of the discussion, the question of neutrality.

Only a very small minority of Irish politicians had ever argued against absolute neutrality. There were those on the left who wanted to see the country's neutrality expressed in a different way - who wanted Ireland, for example, to become part of the non-aligned group of nations. But no senior politician in Ireland had ever before contemplated giving it up.

Gibson knew full well that if Charles Page had ever proposed yielding up Ireland's neutrality, or any part of its sovereignty, he himself would have led the attack on the proposal. But he had also realised, very early on in his negotiations with Mr Kinnock, that what he, and America, had to have was the strategically vital link that only Ireland, on the westernmost tip of Europe, could supply. It was the price he was going to have to pay.

And pay it he would. What he wanted was much too important for him to draw back, even though he would be reviled in some quarters for abandoning his country's neutrality, and even though it could well be an impossible decision to sell. Whatever the price of power was, Andrew Gibson would pay it. Like all great politicians, he believed that power had a value beyond price.

No matter how skillful the organiser of a meeting, it is impossible to keep a concentrated discussion going while people are eating and drinking. So Gibson waited until the sandwiches and coffee had been cleared away before putting the question to which he was determined to have a unanimous answer. Time was short, as the procedures of the Dail required his presence at two-thirty.

"I want a formal decision that the Government has ratified this Agreement, subject to the necessary Constitutional changes. When I get it, I will include an announcement to that effect in my statement to the Dail."

There were two dissenting voices - Scally's, which was no surprise, and Kelly's, which was. Gibson remembered that Kelly had contributed virtually nothing to the discussion, and he thought he knew the reason why. Of all the members of the Government, Kelly, because of his Foreign Affairs brief, would be expected to have been intimately involved in the negotiations. Gibson knew that Kelly would be feeling his exclusion keenly. The Taoiseach thought he had the answer to Kelly's problem.

The Foreign Affairs Minister was saying, "Taoiseach, with the best will in the world, I feel we have to suspend judgement until we have explored, at home and abroad, all the implications of the huge step you are proposing ..." when Gibson interrupted him.

"Look, Sean," he said, "I understand and share your anxiety that we do this properly. In fact, it was for that very reason that I insisted that the Agreement be properly signed under the auspices of the American President, as a public guarantee that there will be no reneging. He has agreed to preside over a formal signing ceremony next week in Washington, and it was my hope that you would represent the Government, and the Irish people, at that ceremony."

Kelly was almost bowled over at this vision of himself preening in the White House Rose Garden before the TV cameras of the world (and in the middle of an election campaign!), and Gibson had some difficulty preventing himself from chuckling aloud as the Foreign Minister said, "Of course, Taoiseach, if that is your wish, then you will not find me lacking in my duty."

Scally snorted in disgust. The ploy had been transparent, Sean Kelly's reaction equally so. Scally said: "What are you going to offer me, Taoiseach?"

"There's a place in history on offer here," Gibson said shortly. "Now, do we have to have a vote on this . . . or can we make it unanimous?"

Scally paused. All decisions of the Government are regarded as unanimous unless a vote is recorded. In the event of a vote, the names of those voting on both sides are recorded in the Cabinet minutes. Although these minutes are not a matter of public record, it was not unknown for dissent of the kind Scally had in mind to become public knowledge. Scally was thinking that if he were to cast his vote against the other fourteen, it would be in all the papers by morning, although he was fairly sure that his reasons would not be mentioned. His vote would be seen in the Party, if not in the country, as a vote against Irish unity. That would be something he was not prepared to contemplate, and Gibson knew it.

Scally made one last try.

"Look," he said, "what we are proposing is quite unnecessary, and I'm not even sure of its propriety. For a Government to ratify any Agreement, on the day it leaves office ..."

"You can stand where I expect Charles Page to stand on this, or you can stand with your own Party," Gibson said. "We don't have time for any more of this debate - I have to go to the Dail to make the announcement. We make our decision now. All in favour..."

"There's no need for a vote," said Scally.

Gibson had his unanimous decision.

THE LEADER OF THE OPPOSITION

Charles Page had always been the Irish politician who had the closest relationship with a succession of British Prime Ministers. He had always known, known absolutely, that when he had a full term of Government he would be able to turn that relationship to good account. He had worked out years ago the exact nature of the breakthrough in Anglo-Irish relations that was necessary, and the step-by-step approach to improving relations between the two divided communities in the North of Ireland that would lead inevitably to reconciliation across the whole island. He was stunned by Gibson's announcement that day.

That probably explains why he made the fundamental tactical mistake in the Dail, a mistake that left the members of his own Front Bench holding their heads in visible horror.

The Dail chamber was full. Gibson had allowed the Government Chief Whip to send out word that something big was going to be announced, and it had done the trick. The Opposition Front Bench would have been there anyway, as the Order of Business is their best opportunity each day to put the Taoiseach on his mettle. But the sense of anticipation was palpable.

The Press Gallery was full also - the antennae of the press around the Dail are very acute. But although they knew that something was on the cards, nobody anticipated what Gibson actually announced.

He addressed the Chair.

"A Cheann Comhairle, I wish to crave your indulgence so that I may advise the House of my intention to ask President Doyle this afternoon to dissolve the Dail, with a view to the holding of an immediate General Election."

There was uproar that it took the Ceann Comhairle three or four minutes to quell. Then there was ten minutes of intense concentration, while Gibson rapidly outlined his reasons for dissolving the Dail, and the purpose of the fresh mandate he was seeking. Every single deputy, whether Government or Opposition, was simply stunned by what they were hearing.

No one was more staggered than Charles Page. Because Gibson had used a parliamentary device known as "Statements" to make his announcement, Page would have a right of reply before the House was adjourned. He would be expected, he knew, to use it.

Government deputies are always alarmed at the news of a General Election, but opposition deputies usually greet the news with excitement. This is especially true of the Leader of the Opposition, who dreams of the day when his chance will come to replace the Taoiseach. A great deal depended on Charles Page's reply - and he blew it.

He blew it by standing up the moment Gibson sat down, and launching the most vicious personal attack on a fellow-politician in living memory. By the time he was finished, everyone present, and everyone reporting on the scene, was convinced that he was nothing more than jealous of Gibson's achievement. He spoke about Gibson's character, his money, his morals, his handling of the economy, his general lack of fitness for his office - he spoke about everything but the Agreement.

Page was jealous, of course. But to be fair, he had every reason to be. Not only had he done more than anyone else to foster good

Anglo-Irish relations, but he had participated in a number of the steps that had been taken over the years to break down barriers between Catholics and Protestants in the North. He had travelled North frequently, and had been instrumental in bringing about a measure of peace and understanding in a situation that others had despaired of. And he had done all this while Gibson, then on his way up in his own Party, was widely seen to be pandering to the most anti-British elements in that Party, and was even believed by some to be in touch with more sinister elements in the armed republican movement.

Gibson's response to Page's attack, when he was being interviewed on RTE television's "To the Point" that night, was simple and devastating.

"Mr Page, Leader of the Opposition and therefore a responsible politician - at least the holder of an office from which one expects responsibility - implies that I am neither fit nor capable of negotiating such an Agreement. But oddly enough, I have negotiated it. Since Mr Page has not bothered to comment on the Agreement, we cannot tell what sort of a judge he is where that is concerned. But he has at least helped us to form a view of what sort of a judge of character he is."

THE TAOISEACH

It was late that night before Gibson was finished. The Parliamentary Party meeting had started and ended with a standing ovation. The two appearances on television had led to the station being inundated by calls congratulating the Taoiseach. All in all, it was a gratifying start to an election campaign. There was a sense of history in the air, and Gibson was right at the heart of it.

The only slightly awkward moment occurred during his visit to Aras an Uachtarain, the home of the President of Ireland.

Under the Constitution of Ireland the role of the President of the country is largely to act as a figurehead. In recent years, the President's time was taken up with trade and tourism missions abroad, and with the promotion of youth and culture groups at home. But although the President's powers are limited, they are real, and among them is the power to dissolve the Dail: normally done on the advice of the Government of the day, the Dail can nevertheless not be dissolved without the consent of the President.

There was of course no question of the President refusing the advice of the Taoiseach in this instance, but she was a woman with a mind of her own, and she did refuse point blank to allow the camera crews who turned up to film her signing the dissolution document into the Aras. She had apparently decided that she was not going to be filmed in any situation that might be used as part of the re-election of Andrew Gibson. She received him coldly, formally, and in private.

This did not surprise Gibson, or upset him unduly. He had only assented to her nomination as an agreed candidate under pressure from his own Party, shortly after his own election as Taoiseach, because none of the political parties was anxious for another election. In theory the President of Ireland is elected by universal suffrage, but in practice, the nominating procedure is such that if the main Parties agree among themselves, they can select one person to fill the job without any other candidate being in a position to secure a nomination.

Almost the only victory Charles Page had been able to secure over Gibson in the last three years was forcing Mrs Doyle on him as President. Even that had been far from a total victory. Page had originally put forward a retiring Deputy from his own Party, but Gibson, knowing that he could not secure agreement for one of his own Deputies, had done a deal with Dan Horgan, the Leader of the tiny Labour Party that had shared in Government with Page. That was how Ireland came to have a woman socialist as President - an outcome considered so remarkable that she had been featured on the cover of TIME magazine. Although Page frequently claimed the credit for putting a woman in Aras an Uachtarain, the fact that she was a socialist as well grated sufficiently with some of his own deputies to take a good deal of the shine from the achievement.

From the moment Mrs Doyle was selected as President, Gibson ignored her entirely, as he was constitutionally entitled to do. Although a practice had developed over recent years of the Taoiseach paying occasional visits to the President to keep him or her abreast of developments, there was no obligation on him to do so. And Gibson simply didn't bother.

Today she had made it obvious that Gibson's neglect of her position had not gone un-noticed, but he was on a high, and couldn't care less.

The only thing that irked Gibson was having to ask Scally, whose job it was as Minister for the Environment, to issue the formal order setting the date for the election. The Taoiseach wanted the shortest possible campaign - twenty-one days was the minimum practical - and he was afraid that Scally would give him a fight over it ("if only," as he said to Hanrahan, "because he makes a principle out of being uncooperative.")

In the event, Scally put up no resistance.

"You name the date, Taoiseach," he said, "you've decided everything else."

"Make it July 17th," said Gibson, "three weeks from today."

Scally said to his Private Secretary that night, as he signed the Order: "It looks as if we might have to crown him High King of Ireland in three weeks' time."

For twenty days of that three weeks, it seemed as if Scally would be right.

CHAPTER 3

JUNE 27th - THE SECOND DAY

THE FOREIGN MINISTER

The great thing about being Foreign Minister, thought Sean Kelly, is that you always get a suite in your hotel, and you always get the girl.

Right now she was moving up and down on top of him, her hair brushing against his face and the little noises she made adding to his pleasure. He had been lucky to find her, he thought, and he was anxious that this wouldn't be the last time they would do this. It was one more incentive for winning the election, because he knew a girl like this wouldn't be turned on by a grubby room in a pension.

He had flown out after the Dail yesterday to what he supposed would be his last official engagement unless he was returned to his present post - except, that is, for the signing of the Memorandum of Understanding between the Irish and British Governments next week in Washington (it couldn't be called a Treaty until it had been ratified by both Parliaments after the elections). He was looking forward to the ceremony with keen anticipation - to be filmed on the Rose Lawn of the White House, with the President of the Free World between himself and Gerald Kaufmann. If that one piece of film didn't ensure his re-election, and a place in the incoming Cabinet, nothing would.

Perhaps it was the thought of his imminent future as a World

Statesman, but somehow Madeline riding him this way wasn't having the effect on him that it usually did. She sensed it and turned.

Slowly and lovingly she begin to lick and nibble at him. Sighing with pleasure, he gave himself up to thoughts of her.

They had met almost two years ago, when he was attending one of his first European Council meetings. She was an interpreter, and it was her voice, coming at him through the earphones he had to wear when anything but English was spoken, that had first attracted him. It had a quality, a depth that was overpowering, that had to suggest something magnificent behind it.

He had sought her out, and she was indeed magnificent. She told him later that he was not the first VIP who had been turned on by her voice, even though he was (or so she often assured him) the first to whom she had responded. She had refused the first invitation to dinner, although in a way that tempted him to ask again. And when she had finally succumbed to the little notes he had sent up to her glass booth, she had turned out to be a delightful companion - every bit the match of the sultry voice about which he had daydreamed.

In bed she was something else again. The first time, she had delighted him by taking the initiative, undressing him first, and then doing a strenuous strip-tease while he lay naked on the bed watching and playing with himself. She was strong, and her body would glisten with a fine coat of perspiration as she moved all over him.

It wasn't his fault, he often told himself. He was not a particularly demanding husband, but Ruth, his wife, had no interest in sex at all: she never seemed to want to do more than talk when they went to bed. She was a very good wife in every other respect, articulate and intelligent, and a perfect hostess at the official functions at which they presided. But a man had to have some relief, after all.

Relief was on the way now. Madeline's lips and tongue were moving more rapidly, and her hands were in on the act as well.

There was no stopping himself: with a heavy groan, he released all of the passion that he had in reserve into her willing mouth.

It was an unfortunate moment for the door to open. Madeline glanced up, and instantly leaped backwards, semen trickling down her chin.

"François!" she cried.

"Jesus Christ!" cried the Foreign Minister.

François was the name of Madeline's husband, Kelly knew. Madeline had spoken of him once or twice - of how jealous he was, of how he had threatened to kill her if he ever caught her with another man.

"You bitch!" screamed François at his wife (Kelly's French was terrible, but it was difficult to escape the meaning). And then he grabbed Madeline by the hair, and to Kelly's incredulous horror, he grabbed him by the hair too, and began dragging them out of the bedroom into the spacious sitting room of the suite. Kelly remembered afterwards thinking that that was the last time he was going to have an affair with the wife of a professional wrestler.

He never found out how François had got into the suite, or even what made him suspect his wife was there. What mattered, and what seemed at that moment like salvation, was that in letting himself in, he had left the door open. The Belgian TV crew whom Kelly had invited to the suite at three o'clock to talk about the Irish elections, and who had arrived early to set up their lights, had come straight in.

It was the Belgian TV reporter, and the sound man, who dragged François off them before he could do any real damage. They managed to restrain him while Madeline and the Foreign Minister crawled around the floor trying, with a total lack of success, to hide the mess they were in.

But what Sean Kelly didn't know was that the cameraman got the whole thing on videotape.

THE LEADER OF THE OPPOSITION

"I'll go to my grave," Pat Crowley said to Charles Page, "without ever understanding what came over you. There were a dozen different ways in which Gibson's Agreement was open to question. The whole neutrality and sovereignty issue - the involvement of terrorists, if there was any - the cost of it for us down here. You might even have got him by demanding that the House be given the right to debate such an Agreement before it was adjourned. But you had to go and attack the man. You just let him walk away with it - and in the process made yourself sound like a jealous kid. For God's sake, why?"

Page had known Crowley long enough to know that the question was largely rhetorical. They had served together in the Dail for many years, and when Page had been Taoiseach, Crowley had been his Minister for Finance. Crowley knew only too well how Page felt about Gibson, and he knew that Page had cherished the dream that he would be the one to advance the cause of reunification. He also knew something that very few others did. He knew that Page had himself turned down an overture from the British Prime Minister because of the explicit compromise to the country's neutrality that was involved. Crowley wondered if Page was regretting that now. If he had gone along with the idea when it was put to him, he could have presented an Agreement essentially the same as the one which now seemed likely to secure Gibson's place in history.

"The only worthwhile question now," said Page, "is where do we go from here."

"Yeah, that's the big one all right," replied Crowley. "That's why I asked some of the boys to come over with me. We have to get some kind of a strategy together this morning, because the Executive of the Party will be meeting at three, and they'll be looking for a way to fight this. But I have to tell you - the boys are looking for a bit of leadership as well. When I rang around last night, to ask them to come over, I got the strong impression that some of them were ready to throw in the towel already. O'Shea - you know how he thinks nothing is real unless he's seen it on television - he said he watched Gibson on the box last night, and that he's never looked more confident and convincing."

One of the differences between Gibson and Page was that, whereas Gibson had only a very small number of confidantes - essentially Hanrahan and one or two who reported through Hanrahan (Gibson had preferred it that way ever since his partner died) - Page had always surrounded himself with advisers. He believed you made better decisions by watching people tease problems out. "The boys" were a loose-knit group, some of them elected and some of them quite anonymous, who met frequently and informally to help Page handle a whole range of matters, from Party finance to public relations to the management of any current crisis. Although they had all, at one time or another, been privy to documents that should have been covered by the Official Secrets Act, none had ever betrayed Page's confidence.

"To be honest with you, Pat," said Page, "I spent most of last night feeling a bit that way myself. In the end I came to this conclusion: I could have had an Agreement like the one Gibson is running with four years ago. I rejected it then because it was wrong for this country, and if it was wrong then, it's wrong still."

"Maybe you should have said that to the House yesterday."

"But I couldn't, don't you see," protested Page. "There is no record of the discussions that took place - you remember, we took a deliberate decision that there shouldn't be. And even though I told some of the Cabinet at the time what was going on, which is more than Gibson appears to have done, I didn't tell everyone. There really wouldn't be any proof but my word and the British Prime Minister's - and I don't suppose he would feel that it was in his interest to get involved in that debate. No - if I was to try that tack, I'd sound twice as bad as I sounded yesterday."

Crowley had to agree that there would not be much mileage

in approaching the election along these lines. Besides, it would probably be wise to assume that Gibson had been forewarned by Mr Kinnock (in fact, he hadn't been, but the Irish Opposition were not in a position to know that).

"It's also true," continued Page, "whether we like it or not, that Andrew Gibson is not a fit man to trust with an ..."

"Look, Charles," interrupted Crowley savagely, "just knock off that bullshit. You may believe it, and I may believe it, but every time you say it, you sound like the kid whose ball has been taken away. Now, we're all agreed on that. You've got to get off this kick of attacking him personally. If you keep it up, you'll be inviting him to start comparing himself to Daniel O'Connell, or to Parnell. I can just hear him now - "the day that I am praised by Mr Page, it will be time to start examining my conscience ..." "

Page gave a reluctant grunt of laughter.

"OK, Pat," he said. "We'll leave that side of the issue out of it for the moment ..."

"Not just for the moment - for good." Page could see that Crowley was deadly serious. "I mean it, Charles - if you don't forego the personal attacks, you're not going to get your Party to keep a line on this Agreement. There were mutterings enough in the Dail bar last night, and some of our seats are very vulnerable to any kind of a Nationalist swing. So some of our people will climb on Gibson's bandwagon if you don't provide a bandwagon they can travel on. The more you attack him, the more you help him."

Page had to concede that Crowley was right. The papers this morning had already declared Gibson's performance yesterday a triumph, and Page's a disaster. If Gibson had not already scored a knock-out, he was already well ahead on points.

He sighed. "You win, Pat," he said. "I won't talk about the man's character again."

That was to prove a terrible mistake.

THE REPORTER

On June 27th, I was assigned to cover Gibson's election tour. I've always been a working reporter, and working reporters don't refuse an assignment. We go where we're sent, we report what we find as accurately as we can, and we file the story.

But an election tour! And for three whole weeks! Sometimes I think O'Byrne must have forgotten what a lousy job being a reporter can be. He just called me in and let me have the assignment right between the eyes.

"For fuck's sake!" I let him have it back. "Do you know what that means? Living out of a suitcase for three weeks, listening to the same crappy speech night after night, trying to write something different when it's actually the same old shit, day after day! C'mon Vincent - I deserve a bit better than that!"

O'Byrne tried flattery.

"I know you deserve better," he said. "But we discussed it this morning at the Editorial conference, and everyone agreed that you were the right one for this job. You are the only one on the political side that Gibson seems to have any respect for, and you might have some chance of getting him to cooperate, maybe with some exclusive thoughts on how the campaign is going or some off-the-cuff responses on any of the issues that come up."

If O'Byrne thought he was flattering me, he was doing a terrible job. Most reporters worth a damn consider it the kiss of death to be liked by a politician, and I'm no exception.

"I don't know how you figure that the Taoiseach has any time for me," I said, "but no matter who he is, I certainly don't see myself spending the next three weeks puffing him up on a daily basis."

"I'm not asking you to do that," O'Byrne said. "Just report it as you find it, and try to get a little colour into it."

"Can I appeal the assignment?" I asked him It would mean going to the management - usually a total waste of time.

"You can if you want to," said O'Byrne, "but I doubt if it will do you any good. A campaign like this one is going to take all the manpower we have. Besides, Andrew Gibson looks like being the uncrowned King of Ireland before long. Just imagine getting close to all that power!"

"Go and fuck yourself," I told him. "I'm lodging a formal appeal, and I'm only going to cover him until it's heard."

The only satisfaction I got was from demanding a big advance on expenses. O'Byrne had to approve it - a reporter couldn't be sent out to live on his own resources for three weeks if he wasn't prepared to do it.

But we both knew that those expenses would become a nightmare for him, as he tried to get me to fill in the forms that would account for the money he'd given me.

THE ADVISER

Hanrahan had brought the papers early that morning.

That was one of Hanrahan's jobs - at least it had developed that way. His nominal role was that of Gibson's administrative assistant, and his primary function the running of Gibson's constituency office. But his closeness to his boss was such, and the number of chores he was prepared to undertake was so great, that he had long been known to some of the other staff as "the Manservant". This particular manservant ruled a full-time staff of twelve, and was anything but humble where anyone but Gibson was concerned.

Not all members of his staff were paid by the State. Gibson himself, in his first year as Taoiseach, had ordered that each member of the Dail was to be provided with the sort of secretarial and research assistance that they had never had. The number of full-time staff available to each Minister to service his constituency office was increased to eight.

In addition to the eight, the Taoiseach provided an additional four out of his own resources. On a contract that would expire only when Gibson ceased to be Taoiseach, Hanrahan was employed as an Assistant Secretary of the Department, to ensure that these twelve people delivered the goods.

The fundamental rule about Irish politics is that life starts and finishes in the constituency. A politician who fails to deliver for the people of his own area, no matter how brilliant or gifted he may be in all other respects, soon ceases to be a politician. And delivery means everything from addressing the problems of an industry employing hundreds to getting a broken window in a council house repaired: the politician who is seen to have failed to fix the problem had better start looking for another job.

Politicians who want to regard themselves as national figures have railed about this system for years, but they created it, and they fight in fierce competition to sustain it. Almost without exception, they are paranoid about the small successes of their competitors, and gloat when they have put one over themselves. The Dail has always been full of deputies who have got where they are on the strength of their constituency "work" - work which often consists of being able to say that they attended more funerals, or sent more telegrams to more weddings, than anyone else.

Nobody understood this system better than Andrew Gibson. That was why he had Hanrahan. Gibson knew that Hanrahan would deliver. The reason had never been explored between them - it was just there. No matter what had needed to be done on the way to where they were now, it had been done. And done, often, without any explicit instructions.

There are people like Hanrahan in politics everywhere. Just as Kennedy had his Dave Powers, Harold Wilson his Marcia Falkender, and Nixon his H.R. Haldeman, Gibson had his Hanrahan. They understand what is required, and they deliver.

This particular morning, Hanrahan had brought the papers early because there was a great deal to be done. He had drafted, about three weeks ago, Gibson's itinerary for the duration of the election campaign, and now they needed to finalise it.

Hanrahan had expected that this would be a morning when Gibson would linger over the papers, gloating at the number of times his picture appeared, and savouring the editorial comment, which was universally favourable. But he hardly gave them a second glance.

"What can go wrong, Tim?" was the first thing he said to Hanrahan.

"Nothing, Andy," replied Hanrahan immediately. "At least, nothing we haven't already thought of. There may be trouble in the North; the Provos may reject the deal because it isn't a battlefield surrender by the Brits ..."

"The Provos," interrupted the Taoiseach. "If we had them on our side we'd be unstoppable."

"That may happen," said Hanrahan. "There's absolutely no reaction from them in the papers. They've obviously been caught on the hop. It may take them a couple of days to agree a reaction among themselves. I notice Paisley and his boys are talking about mobilising an army already - you appear to have brought him out of retirement!"

"Paisley!" Gibson snorted. "He's Kinnock's problem. The more he reacts, the more votes I'll get. No, the ones that worry me are the Provos - they could eat into our own support in some of the marginal counties if they go really heavy. How are we going to stop it?"

"I don't see ..." Hanrahan began.

Gibson interrupted him again.

"I've been thinking," he said, "and I want to meet Norton."

Hanrahan gasped. Padraig Norton was among the three or four most wanted men in Europe, and easily among the most dangerous. He could not be described as a household name in Ireland, but the Head of the Provisional IRA never has been. It has always been a matter of policy with them to ensure that those who lead the military wing maintain an extremely low profile. The pressure has tended to be absorbed by the titular heads of the political wing, Sinn Fein. Although there has always been a close link - the "political" head of Sinn Fein sits on the Army Council of the IRA, and has a say in all of the "military" decisions made - they nevertheless work hard at maintaining the fiction that they are two separate organisations.

Norton had served a prison sentence in the early seventies in connection with arms offences, and had then dropped out of sight. His reputation among the security forces, North and South of the Border, was awesome. He was reckoned to have killed up to thirty people himself (most, but by no means all, were soldiers shot in sniper operations), and of course to have masterminded the deaths of a great many more. There was little doubt that he was the Chief of Staff of the Provisional IRA, and as such the most powerful of the terrorist leaders in the country.

"You must be joking!" said Hanrahan to the Taoiseach. "There isn't any way of finding him - let alone guaranteeing your safety if you were to come into contact with him."

"I was never more serious in my life," said the Taoiseach. "And look - I know there isn't any way of finding him - Christ knows they've been trying to catch him long enough. But he might be willing to find me, if we can get the word to him that it would be safe."

"But how are we going to do that?" asked Hanrahan. "This sort of thing is a bit out of my league."

"Use Stafford," said Gibson. "If anyone has the contacts, he has. And it will be one way of making sure that the Commissioner knows nothing about it."

Hanrahan nodded. Once the question of how it was to be done was resolved, it was not his way to linger on why.

CHAPTER 4

JUNE 28th - THE THIRD DAY

THE TAOISEACH

Andrew Gibson had wanted to call the election today, to coincide with his sixtieth birthday. The only reason he hadn't was that the shifting of the Cabinet meeting from its normal day might have caused some speculation.

Sixty was a significant age for him - it signalled that he had been born and raised during the turbulent years when his Party was becoming established as a political force. Although the Kilkenny area had never been a specially republican area, the Party had taken hold there. Gibson's father, Norman, had served in the Dail for twelve years until his death, and Gibson himself was following in a time-honoured tradition when he had succeeded him.

His father had never made an impact in national politics. He had succeeded in winning and holding the seat by dint of two things. First, it was impossible to hold a funeral within twenty miles of Kilkenny city that Norman Gibson did not attend; second, it was widely believed that Norman Gibson had led a flying column during the Black and Tan war.

Many a political career in Ireland is built on rumours like that. The truth was that the only spell of military service that Norman Gibson had ever seen was in the British Army during the Second World War. That spell had lasted two years, and had ended when he secured a medical discharge because of a painful and recurring this, Andrew had to walk around the town for an hour in the dark before it went down again - he was frightened, thinking it never would.

Later, when he realised it was not going to stay hard forever, he didn't worry about it. It seemed to make Mr Boyd fond of him - and he became aware that it was a nice feeling. Besides, often after Mr Boyd had got red in the face and had to run into the little toilet at the back of the office, there was an extra threepence for Andrew, which didn't have to be handed up to his mother.

All that stopped when Andrew's father came back from the Army. From then on, things were not so easy. He grew to resent his father, and in time to hate him. For one thing, it became impossible to get Mr Boyd to part with the pennies and threepences that had accompanied their "little chats" in the evenings. For another, Andrew's father was determined that his son would be more than a book-keeper. He drove the boy hard, checking his homework every night, and punishing him as he imagined Andrew's teachers would punish him for mistakes. The worst feature of this was that he would never allow Andrew to correct the mistakes, so that the boy often got a second beating for the same mistakes in school the following day.

It paid off: Andrew came first in the county in the Leaving Certificate, and won a scholarship to University College, Dublin on the strength of it. But the hatred of his father that had been nurtured over all the years of his schooling never left him.

He graduated from college with a reasonable degree in law in the same year that his father was first elected to the Dail. The choice of law as a career was predetermined by the willingness of old Mr Boyd, now getting ready to retire, to take him into the practice as an articled clerk. This turned into a most convenient arrangement, especially as the old man never raised any objection to Andrew leaving the office around four in the afternoon, while Mr Boyd turned his attention to the latest young lad who was employed for errands and "chats".

that wasn't really a problem, because they were able to purchase land and property all over County Kilkenny at rock bottom prices. By and large, they made money because they were in a position to capitalise on the recession, and on the resulting tide of emigration. There was one deal in particular that happened to pay off very quickly, and it ensured that they were already wealthy when the property boom started.

It was that deal that first established Andrew as a public force in his own right - that, and his celebrated marriage. Maura Barrington was only eighteen when Andrew first asked her to go out with him. He was then twenty nine, and although successful, was not yet rich or famous enough to satisfy the Barringtons. They were one of the oldest families in the county, and very conscious of the fact. Colonel Barrington, Maura's father, took a dim view of the upstart who called on his daughter, and the relationship might never have got off the ground had Maura herself not been a determined young woman. She was completely smitten with the rising young solicitor, and gave her father no choice in the matter.

In order to woo Maura Barrington - or rather, her father - Andrew learned to ride a horse, and how to play bridge. He changed his little Triumph sportscar for something more substantial and sedate. He was never fully accepted, of course, but at least the Colonel did give his daughter away when the wedding took place. It was the social event of the year in Kilkenny, and Andrew was able to take savage pleasure in the spectacle of his father being tolerated by the aristocratic Colonel.

What clinched the Barrington family's grudging acceptance of Andrew was his sudden wealth. Almost a year earlier, he and Chris McDonald had bought a small farm just two miles outside Kilkenny, on the Callan road. Seven months after they bought the farm, they had sold it for a quarter of a million pounds to an Australian mining company which had discovered zinc on the land. That kind of money - even a half-share of it - represented staggering wealth in those days, and enabled them to increase the number of speculative investments which were to make them very wealthy men.

The Leinster Mines deal was the breakthrough for Andrew, and it had the added advantage of persuading Colonel Barrington that in Andrew Gibson he would have a son-in-law worth knowing. The Colonel, despite his reputation and his manners, hadn't a penny of his own.

Andrew's forty-third year should have been one of the best years of his life. Instead, it was almost the worst. He had been re-elected twice since entering the Dail seven years previously, and in February, in a Cabinet reshuffle, he was appointed Minister for Local Government. Despite the controversy surrounding the appointment of a man who was, to all intents and purposes, a property speculator, to a portfolio which at that time carried overall responsibility for town planning, he was determined that it would be the start of bigger things.

At forty-two, he was regarded as young to be in the Cabinet, but it was a period when young men were beginning to make their mark, and the brasher the young men, the better. It was an era when the country looked as if it was being run by tycoons, and the air of dynamism and confidence that was about was unmistakable.

Of course, he had to abandon any involvement in his own business, but Chris McDonald was more than well-equipped to look after his interests. Three weeks later, Chris McDonald died. It was not unexpected - they had known that time was running out - but it was a blow. Andrew had to put all of his property into a blind trust, and the possibility of expanding his property had to be postponed.

Less than a month after that, Maura died. That was bad enough, but then a post-mortem revealed that she had died by her own hand (through an overdose of sleeping tablets). And when the *Irish Times* reported that she had spent the last four years of her life in and out of mental hospitals, undergoing treatment for alcoholism and depression, it almost destroyed Andrew's career.

The Taoiseach, who only a couple of months previously had appointed him to the Cabinet, attended Maura's funeral, one of the biggest seen in Kilkenny for many years. Afterwards, he told Andrew that he was staying that night in the Club House Hotel, and asked Andrew to call on him later in the evening. The night his wife was buried, and less than two months after he had been appointed to the Cabinet, Andrew was gently, but firmly, asked to resign.

Lesser men would have gone under. Andrew almost did. In the seven years he had been a Dail deputy, he had seen how little the job was worth, except as a stepping stone to higher office. He had worked hard to get that higher office. He had made frequent speeches from the Dail benches, always carefully couched in the sort of colourful language that gets reported - and to make sure he was reported often, he had wined and dined the Parliamentary reporters for the newspapers. These were a neglected breed - their more illustrious colleagues, the Political Correspondents, were less easy to flatter, and were more interested in the doings and sayings of Ministers than of pushy junior deputies. But the Parliamentary reporters could guarantee you a satisfying quota of column inches, and Andrew was one of the few who recognised that fact.

One of the bonuses of getting his speeches reported frequently was that he was often invited to appear on radio, and then on television. Television, of course, was a brand new medium in those days, and Andrew was among the very first politicians to take its potential seriously - indeed, it was often said that he was the pioneer among politicians taking training courses for the box.

It had all paid off, with a Ministerial appointment at a young age; and now, before the seat of his Ministerial Mercedes was warm, he was being asked to resign. And all because the Taoiseach was unwilling to support him through a possible scandal, which would certainly blow over within a couple of weeks!

Of course he resigned - in Andrew's Party you did not rebel in public. In his letter to the Taoiseach he cited grief, and the need to get his personal affairs in order. Privately he vowed that he would be back, and that the Taoiseach would regret the day that he got rid of Andrew Gibson.

The scandal took longer than a few weeks to blow over, but not that much longer. The Barringtons, despite their prestige, had never been popular in Kilkenny, and soon it began to be believed that most of the family, and not just Maura, had been more than a little soft in the head. It was not long, indeed, until there was a perceptible feeling of sympathy for Andrew because of the trials he had uncomplainingly borne with his deranged wife.

In the period that followed - long and difficult years - Andrew worked very hard at consolidating his position within the Party. There was nowhere he was not prepared to go to address a gathering of the Party faithful, and there was no function of importance to the Party where Andrew was not to be seen in the front row. Outwardly, he remained intensely loyal to the leadership - always turning up to the airport to welcome the Taoiseach home from abroad, for instance. And when the Party was in opposition for a time during that period, even though he did not hold a front bench brief, he became one of the Government's staunchest critics, often outshining his senior colleagues in debate, and generally building a reputation as the defender of his Party's faith.

He also discovered republicanism in that period, at a time when the Party leadership seemed to be moving away from traditional approaches to the Irish question - and at a time of increasing violence in the North. Gradually a questioning began in the Party - a debate about the right approach to take in dealings with the British Government in relation to the North. And this debate began to spread, to cover wider issues. Two wings began to emerge - often seen as hawks and doves in relation to the North, and more vaguely, as "old men" and "young men" in relation to most of the other questions of the day.

Despite Andrew's denials, and his insistence that he was absolutely loyal, he was widely seen as the leader of the "young men" in the Party. And despite the Taoiseach's obvious distaste for Andrew - a distaste that had been fuelled by intelligence reports on some of the people with whom Andrew had had secret meetings - the pressure for a reconciliation became too great, and Andrew was reappointed to the Front Bench, emerging a couple of years later as Minister for Finance, and the undoubted heir apparent.

That was the year he chose to get married again. This time he was marrying someone who knew and shared her husband's burning ambition. Indeed, in the first interview she gave after becoming Mrs Gibson, Finola joined in the campaign against the "old men" of the Party. This campaign had by now the support of more than half of the Party's deputies, even though there was no formal way for them to express it.

The Taoiseach who had sacked Andrew eight years ago could read the writing on the wall better than most, and when he announced that the time had come for a well-earned retirement, Andrew's election as Party Leader and as Taoiseach was a foregone conclusion.

The only opposition came from Joseph Scally, who had at one time been seen as the likeliest successor to the Taoiseach. But the success of Andrew's campaign was so complete that Scally, because of his association with the old guard, received a derisory vote in the election.

Andrew Gibson had now been either Taoiseach or Leader of the Opposition for eleven years, and in that time he had strengthened his grip on the Party almost by the day. In the early years, to be sure, he had courted disaster once or twice, but certainly since the last election, there had been no voice raised against his. And his position in the country was as strong as his leadership of the Party.

In the long line of distinguished holders of the office of Taoiseach, Andrew Gibson was determined to be the one remembered longest. He often looked back at the careers of his predecessors - men like Lemass, Lynch, Haughey, Fitzgerald, and Page - and he knew that he was destined for the greatness that had finally eluded many of them.

Because today's birthday lunch was a special occasion, a table had been booked in the restaurant of the Shelbourne Hotel. Gibson had preferred the restaurant before its redecoration; the conversion had turned it from a room that belonged in a gentlemen's club, all old wood and smoky ceilings, into a room of pale pastel furniture and purple curtains. But the hotel still represented a certain style - it was the last of the great old Dublin institutions, and although its prices were beyond the majority of ordinary Dubliners, it was still a place to be seen in.

Over the meal Gibson told his wife of his plan to visit every county in the Republic, starting with their home constituency the following day.

"Is that necessary, Andy?" she asked. "After all, you're going to be on radio and television every day - and the Agreement is going to make sure that everyone knows your name."

"Yes," he said. "But when Page and his gang get their breath back, they are going to try to mount some kind of a campaign against the Agreement - and if Page gets his way, they're going to have a go at me on a personal basis. That's why I intend to be seen, not only standing over the Agreement, but also being available to every voter in the country. Hanrahan already has rallies arranged in all the key areas - and he is guaranteeing that we'll get big crowds and big welcomes. But the important thing is I want you to come with me."

"Why, Andy?" she asked. "Wouldn't I be more use to you at home? After all, there's always a danger when the constituency is left unmanned - you know how the Irish hate an absentee deputy."

Gibson disagreed.

"I don't think there's any danger of losing votes in Kilkenny. For once they'll have to understand that I have other things to do than knock on every door in my own home town," said Gibson. "I want you with me for a number of reasons. First, the fact that you're there will attract even more reporters to cover the tour. Every newspaper will feel obliged to make sure that the woman's angle is being covered. Besides, I want us to be seen together as much as possible in the next three weeks."

Finola knew what he meant - there was no need for elaboration. Gibson and his wife both knew that the Opposition would make an effort to resurrect any rumour about the Taoiseach that would hurt him. Gossip about his womanising was largely based on the fact that he was an undeniably attractive man; how much of it was true only he, and perhaps his wife, knew.

Certainly Finola Gibson was well aware that she was not married to a saint. In fact, their first encounter happened when he was married, and his wife was in a psychiatric hospital. Finola had been a successful model then, although coming to an age when thoughts of security and status had begun to be important.

Right from the start, she had realised that Andrew Gibson could provide both. She had known long before a great many others that he was going to be powerful, and that anyone associated with him would be famous as well. She was there the night he had been asked to resign from the Cabinet, and she had encouraged him to fight back against that decision. She would help him now too, in any way open to her.

After lunch, they were due at Party headquarters for a meeting of the National Executive Committee. The meeting had been arranged at short notice, in order that the Leader might outline the Agreement, and the plans for the General Election. The Chairman of the NEC had himself invited Finola to be present on this historic occasion.

The National Executive Committee of an Irish political party is a much over-rated body. In some of the smaller parties they do wield effective power, but in the larger ones they are essentially rubber stamps for leadership decisions. They exist primarily to give a semblance of democracy to the party's internal workings, and generally spend their time debating policy issues, in the certain knowledge that it is the elected politicians, and the needs of the day, that will dictate policy in relation to every issue.

They do have a symbolic importance, and Gibson had had occasion in the past to use the NEC of the Party to pass resolutions that were critical of the leadership, when he was on his way to that position, and supportive of the leadership in the face of any criticism thereafter.

Today's meeting was an unqualified success. The Chairman, Senator Mulrooney from Limerick (he had been handpicked by Gibson, who was looking for a total nonentity for the job and looked no further when Mulrooney's name had been mentioned) led the delegates in a standing ovation when the Taoiseach arrived. The Press, unusually, had been allowed in, and they recorded the happy scene that ensued.

"Prior to the commencement of business, Taoiseach," said Senator Mulrooney, "I have been asked by the members of the NEC to say a few words to you, on the occasion of your birthday. It is particularly gratifying that we should be meeting at this moment - when a great juncture in our history coincides with a significant event in the life of the person who has made that history."

For the next ten minutes, the Chairman regaled the company with a glowing account of the life and times of the Taoiseach: his upbringing in poor circumstances, his determination to secure a proper education, his life-long work for the underprivileged, his concern for the environment, his ambition to bring about a just and peaceful solution to the oppression of minorities everywhere, and particularly in the North of Ireland.

All of this, said the Chairman, had culminated in the Leader's greatest achievement - the Agreement they would be discussing later, an Agreement that would ensure that his name, and his Party's name, was written large in the history of our great nation. Gibson, listening, thought wryly to himself that if anyone on the NEC had harboured the notion of subjecting the Agreement to some critical analysis, they could forget it after an introduction like this.

The *pièce de résistance* was the birthday present that the NEC had commissioned from one of Ireland's leading painters. It was a portrait of Gibson, looking a good ten years younger, and set against a collage representing some of his achievements. Gibson accepted it gracefully, with frequent references to his humility at the honour that the NEC had done him, and to his inadequacy, but for the support and friendship of the many here present, for the tasks that still lay ahead.

After the last photograph was taken, and the Press had withdrawn, with the echoes of the last ovation still reverberating in their ears, the meeting proper began. It was a most gratifying occasion in every way. While it was to be expected that the NEC would endorse the Agreement unanimously, the fulsomeness of their praise of the Taoiseach was balm to him.

The clincher was the note that was delivered to the Taoiseach in the middle of the meeting, and which he took pleasure in reading to the meeting.

It said that the Leader of the Opposition, in a statement just issued, had announced that if elected, and despite some reservations about aspects of the Agreement, he would implement it in full, as it had been entered into by a duly elected sovereign Irish Government.

"That blows their whole campaign," he said to Finola, who was sitting beside him at the top table. "If they've decided they can't campaign against the Agreement, then nothing can stop us."

CHAPTER 5

JUNE 30th - THE FIFTH DAY

THE REPORTER

On the first Saturday of an election campaign, everyone involved takes stock. That means that very little actual campaigning happens, so that a reporter like me can get his laundry done.

There isn't any worse job in my book than being sent out to follow a politician on the campaign trail. For a start, nobody tells you anything. His plans are constantly being changed, and it nearly always happens when you're in the middle of a meal - usually the first meal you've had for hours. And you're never quite sure where he's going to finish at night, with the result that you can find yourself in the back end of nowhere, without a hotel room and with only a dirty shirt to wear the following day. Some politicians go out of their way to make sure that the press is properly looked after, but the bottom line is that during a campaign they know you have to follow them.

They didn't always have election tours in Irish politics. Part of the reason for that is that there is a history of even very senior politicians - Ministers, and in one or two cases Party Leaders - losing their seats. An Irish politician is never allowed to forget that he owes his status to the people of his own constituency first. The result is that unless the politician is very secure, he will spend as much time as he can in his constituency making sure of his seat. Sometimes when he is on tour he will finish the day by making a mad dash back to his home town to try to be seen in as many places as possible. If it's your job to follow, and if you have to provide your own transport (especially if he's being driven in a State Mercedes), the journey can take years off your life.

That's why it's such a relief to know that you can take a little time off. I knew that Gibson was spending the day at his home, meeting local constituency people. I had arranged an interview with him in the afternoon, which was to run in Monday's paper. So I had very little to do except to get my questions in the right order.

Over breakfast I caught up with the papers. The consensus was that Page, in accepting that the Agreement would have to be implemented, had more or less conceded defeat in the election before it had got under way. But there was general agreement as well that Page had very little choice. What he was trying to do was clear. He was hoping to turn the Agreement into a non-issue by accepting it, and to concentrate instead on other issues - probably economic ones, where Gibson should have been vulnerable.

And it was clear too that Page had decided it was pointless trying to fight an election about Andrew Gibson's character. In his statement about the Agreement, he had included a grudging tribute to Gibson's negotiating ability.

My guess was that the papers were right, and that Page's tactics wouldn't work. For a start, the Agreement was going to be an issue throughout the campaign - probably the only issue. Whatever Page wanted, the Labour Party was going to see to that. They had very strong views on the whole question of neutrality, and were already making it clear that they were going to oppose the Agreement tooth and nail. That wasn't going to affect the outcome of the election, I reckoned - the Labour Party had never commanded more than fifteen per cent of the vote in recent Irish elections - but it was going to make sure that opposition to the Agreement would be a feature of the campaign.

Secondly, Page was no more credible on the economy than

Gibson was. Both men in their time had espoused first one, then another, approach to basic issues such as public spending and whether or not the public or private sectors should be more favoured. In truth they were both total pragmatists, suiting their attitudes and actions to the prevailing climate. Although Gibson was normally seen as somewhat to Page's left, they were both so close to the centre that it was hard to tell the difference.

The Springhill Hotel, where I was staying until Monday morning, didn't stint on the breakfast, and I felt the need of a walk afterwards. I ambled into Kilkenny, and it was there, wandering around the city centre, with its narrow streets and attractive old buildings, that I met someone I knew slightly.

He was Shay Conway, one of the local Party stalwarts. I knew that he had been one of the people who had originally selected Andrew Gibson to succeed his father, and had been active in all of his campaigns ever since. He was a fairly old man now, and ran a small pub in the town. I had met him a few times in the past, while I was covering his Leader's local electioneering.

We stopped to exchange pleasantries. Conway was obviously delighted with the day's news about Page's announcement.

"That fellow is an awful eejit," he told me. "Imagine giving up before the election was even started. He's bloody lucky he's not the leader of our Party - there'd be men queuing up to look for his blood this morning. I wouldn't be surprised if even his own crowd drop him before this thing is over."

I agreed with him. There isn't much point in arguing with a Party activist about the wisdom or otherwise of the leader of another Party. He invited me to drop into his pub, which was just down the road, for a cup of tea, "or maybe something a bit stronger".

I accepted the offer of a drop of something stronger, and we were just on the point of entering the pub, when I saw her.

It was the woman I had seen shouting at the meeting in the hotel the night before. She was walking with another, younger, woman up the opposite side of Bridge Street. Now that I had a chance to have a good look at her, I could see that she was a good bit older than I had thought. She was perhaps in her mid-sixties, and dressed almost shabbily. Her face was pinched, and grey. It was obvious that she had been through some tough times, and that poverty had left its mark on her. She and the woman with her, who was a good deal younger, were just turning into a small café near the bridge.

"Who is that woman?" I asked Conway. "The older of those two, over there, outside the Bridge House."

He looked down the road, and snorted in disgust. "That old one!" he said. "That's old Annie Deane. She's as mad as a hatter."

"Isn't she the woman who shouted at the Taoiseach at the meeting?"

"Yes," he said. "She does that every time Andy speaks at a public meeting in the town. I told you - she's mad."

"I wonder does she have a thing about all politicians, or is it just the Taoiseach?"

"I couldn't tell you," he replied. The glance he gave me was a bit less friendly, and I remembered the look on the Taoiseach's face when Annie Deane had shouted at him. Something told me not to reveal too much curiosity. Instead, I knocked back the Paddy and water he offered me in the pub as quickly as possible, thanked him for his hospitality, and left to try to find the two women.

It didn't take long. They were still sitting in the café I had seen them entering. I bought a cup of coffee and sat down at the table next to theirs, pretending to read the *Irish Independent*.

"Oh Mum," the younger woman was saying, "can't we just leave it alone? It's been thirty years, and you've just wasted your whole life. Isn't it time to just forget it?"

"That's easy for you, Margaret," said Annie. "You were just a baby, and you never knew him. But he was my husband, and

I can't forget or forgive. Someday ..."

"Oh come on, Mum," said Margaret. "You know it's never going to happen now. You'll never get to him, and I can't bear to see the way it's made you so bitter. It hasn't been easy for you, I know that, but it wasn't easy for me either. Will you not reconsider, and come back to Dublin with me? There's room enough for both of us now, now that I've got the new flat."

"No, Margaret," her mother said. "Here is where I belong - and here is where I'm going to meet Andrew Gibson at every chance I get."

Margaret smiled at her mother. There was a lot in that smile - a great deal of love, and more than a little perception. With a start, I realised that I would not mind at all if Margaret Deane (if that was still her name) were to smile at me that way.

"If you were living with me in Dublin," she was saying, "you could meet Andrew Gibson every day of the week."

"Maybe I could," replied her mother, "but here is the only place he's afraid of me. He hasn't forgotten either, and he never will as long as I'm here."

They were preparing to leave. I decided that a direct approach was necessary.

"Excuse me," I said. "I couldn't help overhearing what you were saying. You were talking about the Taoiseach, weren't you?"

The younger of the two women looked at me sharply.

"We were having a private conversation," she said. "I don't know who you are, but what we are talking about has absolutely nothing to do with you."

"I'm sorry," I told her. "I didn't mean to be rude, but I'm a reporter, and I'm writing about the Taoiseach during this election ..."

At the mention of my job, Margaret stiffened even further. She told me that neither she nor her mother had anything to say to me about the election.

"It wasn't the election I had in mind," I said quickly. "I was at the Taoiseach's meeting last night, and I saw your mother shouting at the Taoiseach. And what's more, I could see that he didn't like it. I just wanted to find out what it was all about."

"Look," said Margaret, "none of this has anything to do with you. Just leave us alone!"

Her mother hadn't spoken up to now. Now she looked at me and said, "I've spoken to reporters about all this before, but they were all the same. They just laughed at me. It's never done any good."

I was starting to regret the whole thing. It was beginning to be obvious that these women had some kind of a chip on their shoulders. If they didn't want to talk about it, why should I bother? And yet there was something about Annie Deane. She didn't have the vindictive look of a crank. Her face was old, all right, older (I guessed) than her years. But her expression told me that she had suffered - it didn't tell me that she was malicious.

"I don't have any axe to grind," I said, "and maybe I will just laugh if you tell me your story. But I'm more than ready to listen, and I have an open mind. By the way, my name is Jim Flynn, and I work for one of the national dailies."

Annie Deane looked at me in silence. I couldn't tell - was she going to clam up, or was she deciding whether or not to trust me?

"Would you laugh, Mr Flynn," she said eventually, "if I told you that Andrew Gibson murdered my husband?"

I didn't laugh. Maybe I should have - it would have saved me an awful lot of trouble later on.

"That's quite an accusation," I told her. "I suppose you can prove it?"

"I could have proved it once," she said. "But the proof I had was stolen from me."

In every reporter's experience there are dozens of allegations, accusations, just like the one Annie had just made. Over the years, I had been told that the Cardinal who was the Head of the Irish Catholic Church was supporting a string of mistresses, that a well-known theatre director was a heroin addict, and that Shergar, the race horse who disappeared without trace, had been stolen by a Dublin businessman. All these stories had one thing in common - they were all told by people who claimed they had the proof, and they were all so impossible to stand up that they had to be lies.

And yet, and yet ... there was something about Annie Deane. And something more about her daughter, who was looking at me with a sort of quiet intensity - almost as if she was testing me.

"Would you be prepared to tell me the whole story?" I asked Annie. "I can assure you that I do have an open mind."

"Yes," said Annie Deane. "I'll tell you the story, but not here."

"Mum," said Margaret, "you don't have to do this, and it won't make ..."

"That's right," I interrupted, looking directly at Margaret. "Your mother doesn't have to tell me anything, but if she wants to, I'm willing to listen. And as to whether or not it will do any good, let's judge that as we go along."

I could tell that Margaret was a little surprised that I had anticipated what she was going to say. But I could tell too that she didn't trust me. She shrugged, and led the way out of the cafe and to a small car that was parked just down the road.

Annie Deane's house was a small terraced one just across the road from the County Council offices. Like Annie herself, it was poor but respectable. She and I sat in a small front parlour, while Margaret made coffee in the kitchen. And Annie told me how her husband had died.

Tom Deane was a small farmer. Annie knew when she married him that she was going into a life of poverty and hard work. But she didn't care about that. She had loved Tom Deane from the moment she first saw him, driving cattle into the mart in Kilkenny, only two miles from his farm. The day they got married was the happiest of her life until then, and it was surpassed only by the birth of a beautiful daughter.

Life was hard. The farm was big enough to support about fifteen cattle, barely enough to scratch a subsistence living. But the days were full, and Annie supplemented their income by making and selling cakes and jam in the neighbourhood.

Annie never forgot the day that Tom came home and told her that they were going to be rich. He wouldn't tell her why - only that their land was worth more than they had ever dreamed of. And she never forgot the day that the handsome young solicitor from Kilkenny, Andrew Gibson, came to the house to offer to buy the farm. Annie couldn't understand why Tom had turned down the offer - five hundred pounds an acre was an unheard of sum in those days.

But Tom virtually ordered Mr Gibson off the land, telling him he could keep his money, and that the farm was worth far more. But she trusted her husband, and anyway, she did not like Andrew Gibson. He had shouted at Tom, telling him he would be sorry if he wasn't prepared to do business with a local man.

The happiness ended for Annie the day her husband died. Margaret was three then, and it was she who had come running to tell Annie that her Dad was asleep on the ground in the lower field. Annie had found him, lying beside the overturned tractor, with a terrible swelling on the side of his head.

What Annie wanted most was an explanation. Tom had had that old tractor for years - it was too old to go more than a few miles an hour, and he had always been very careful. But there was no understanding it - and besides, Annie now had to make choices. She couldn't manage Margaret and the farm on her own, and it was too small for her to hire someone to work it. She was glad that she had known of Andrew Gibson's interest in the property, and grateful to him when he made her the same offer he had made to Tom. It gave her enough money to buy a small house in the town, with even a little left over. Annie saved every penny of that until Margaret was old enough to go to secondary school. Of course, she felt bitter when Gibson sold the farm again, only a few months after buying it from her, and for a fantastic profit. But after all, she reasoned, it was his good luck. He could not have known beforehand that one of the richest zinc mines in Europe was under her farm.

She believed that for ten years, until she got the letter from Christopher McDonald, Andrew Gibson's legal partner.

She told me what was in the letter, as if she knew it by heart. He was dying, dying of a cancer that had reduced him to an agonised, lonely wreck. But he could not die, he told her, with her husband's death on his conscience. He admitted that he had found out about the tests that were being carried out by the Australian mining company - that he had, in fact, advised them about local planning regulations. It was he who had encouraged Gibson to get hold of the farm, and it was he and Gibson who had killed her husband, very early one morning as he was driving on his tractor down to bring in the cattle.

They hadn't meant to kill him, he said. Andrew wanted to have another go at persuading him to sell, but a row had developed. McDonald had been haunted ever since by the sight of Andrew picking up an old fence post as Tom turned away, and bringing it down on the side of Tom's head as hard as he could. Tom had died instantly.

By the time Annie got this letter, Chris McDonald was already dead. At first she didn't know what to do. Together with the letter was a cheque for £10,000, and almost the first decision she made was to tear it up. When I asked her why she had refused to take the money, her answer shook me.

"Because if I had taken it," she said, "that man might have got some absolution for his sins."

Her second decision was to go to Andrew Gibson, to accuse him to his face. But he laughed at her, telling her that the pain in Chris McDonald's stomach had turned his brain, and that the letter was nothing more than the ravings of a dying man.

So she had taken the letter to the police, to the local Garda sergeant. She told me that his face had gone pale when he read it, and that he had told her he would have to bring detectives down from Dublin to deal with it.

But no detectives had ever come. The letter simply disappeared, and Sergeant Stafford told her three weeks later that she had never been to see him, that she had never given him any letter, that he had never met her before.

"I don't understand," I said to her. "How could he have denied the existence of the letter if you had made the complaint to him?"

"Don't you see?" said Margaret, who had joined us. "Stafford worked for Gibson. You can see it from the way he has risen as Gibson has."

I was staggered. "You're not talking about the Deputy Commissioner?" I said.

"Yes," said Margaret. "When Mum went to see him he was only a sergeant in Kilkenny. You see how important he is now."

She wasn't exaggerating. Deputy Commissioner Joe Stafford was the most powerful policeman in the country. Although nominally the Commissioner was in charge, everybody - certainly everybody in my business - knew that it was Stafford who ran the show. He was both hated and feared, not least among the criminal classes, a great many of whom he had put behind bars.

For five years after that Annie had tried to find redress. She had been to solicitors, to other politicians, to any new Gardai who came to the town, even to the local clergy. All told her the same thing, even those who said they believed her story - that without some proof, there was nothing that could be done.

And ever since then, for nearly fifteen years, she had tried to haunt the rising politician. No matter how many times she had encountered him, he had refused even to speak to her, and he had been instrumental in forging the impression among her neighbours that she was more than a little mad. Of course, there was no facsimile copy of the letter - women of her background didn't have much experience of photostat machines. But she had written out the contents of the letter herself before she had gone to the Guards, and now she went upstairs to get it for me.

It was all there - the nearest thing to a deathbed confession that I had ever read. Involuntarily, I shivered at the thought of the dying man, his body barely able to function, trying to clear his conscience in this way. But it was written in the spidery hand of a poorly educated woman - there was nothing to prove its origin.

As I read it, I felt their eyes on me.

"Mr Flynn," said Annie at last, "I have to ask you two questions. But the second depends on your answer to the first."

"Ask away," I said, trying to muster a smile. There was a long silence, while Annie stared hard at me. I found it hard to meet her gaze.

"Do you believe I have told you the truth?" she asked me at last.

I didn't answer immediately. The story I had been told was totally outlandish. I was being asked to believe that the Prime Minister of my country was a murderer, and that the Deputy Commissioner of the Gardai was an accessory. There was no proof, only Annie's word that a dying and tortured man had confessed to her. But there was something about Annie Deane. Something about the way she had told me the story, quietly, with total conviction. Something about the way she was looking at me now. Annie Deane was not mad, and she was no liar.

"Yes," I said. "I believe you."

"Then tell me, Mr Flynn" - I knew the harder question was coming - "is there anything that I can do?"

"I'm sorry," I said. "Without some proof - something that would stand up in a court - I don't see how anything can be done. I know you have been told this before, and I wish to God I could think of some way. But I honestly don't see any."

I don't think she was surprised at my answer. But I think too that she had been hoping, maybe this one last time, to hear something different. Annie's face began to crumple. I couldn't help it. I reached out to her, and tried to put my arms around her.

"I'm sorry, I'm sorry," she said. She was trying to regain her composure, and failing. As she half-ran, half-stumbled out of the room, I don't think I've ever felt more helpless in my life. Sitting there, my head slumped, I felt Margaret's hand on the back of mine.

"Jim," she said - it was the first time either of them had used my first name - "I'm sorry that I was so rude to you earlier on. And I want to tell you that I think you're a very nice man."

What could I say? I had just shattered the hope that her mother still clung to, and now I was off to interview the man who had murdered Margaret's father, and she picks this moment to be nice to me. It was all I could do to mutter my good-byes and to ask Margaret to apologise to her mother for my departure.

If Annie Deane's story was true - and I believed it - I was sitting on the biggest exclusive in history. And there was absolutely nothing I could do about it. No newspaper in its right mind would print a story like that, certainly not without having almost more proof than a court would require. The normal rules would not apply. It would not be enough to have two or three independent sources, and they certainly could not be anonymous.

A total jumble of thoughts was going through my head as I made my way back to the hotel to pick up my car, so that I could drive out to Gibson's house. Frustration, pity, anger - I find it hard even now to figure out what was my dominant reaction.

But there were other thoughts too. I couldn't shake off the look on Annie's face when I told her that there was nothing that could be done. I barely knew Annie Deane, but what I knew I admired. She had suffered at Gibson's hands, and she was entitled to some recompense. But there was nothing I could do to help her.

I couldn't face any lunch. On my way out to Gibson's house, I debated over and over again whether or not I should raise Annie Deane's accusations with him. In the end I knew there was no point. It was too easy to deny, and there was no point in pursuing something like that without proof.

I toyed with the idea of trying to construct a story around a denial by Gibson of the accusation of murder. That's an old reporter's trick - you can't make the accusation against some public figure stand up, but you put it to him anyway, and then print his denial, thereby getting your accusation into print as well. Sometimes the publication of the denial will bring sources forward that you didn't know about. But I knew that my paper wouldn't print a story like that when the accusation was so monstrous, especially in the middle of an election.

I found it hard to ask the questions I had prepared. Although I knew there was no point in challenging Gibson, I wanted to do it anyway. I was no fan of his, and the discovery that I had made that morning confirmed my worst suspicions of his character.

He, on the other hand, was behaving as if he was my greatest fan. He had obviously prepared well for the interview. He was able to refer fluently, and accurately, to points of detail in the British-Irish Agreement without any reference to notes. He was even able to quote historical references which were persuasive enough to counter the argument that he was selling his own Party's position on neutrality short.

When we turned to the economy he had answers for everything. When I asked him was he willing to debate the issues in the election on television with Charles Page, he said he was anxious for the opportunity to do so - with Page or anyone else. He even let me interrupt the interview to phone that piece of information through for Sunday's paper. It gave me an exclusive lead for the following day. I suppose I should have been grateful. But the more charming and capable he was, the more I found myself remembering Annie Deane.

He gave me two hours for the interview. It had been arranged in advance, of course, and the paper was going to run ads on the radio tomorrow, promising the first "in depth" interview of the campaign on Monday. But I had to admit it was a pretty good interview nevertheless. I had put him on his mettle, and he had given a superb performance.

Somewhat to my surprise, I was invited to stay for dinner, with the Taoiseach, his wife, and Tim Hanrahan. I knew Hanrahan well, and had met Finola Gibson several times. What I knew of her, I didn't much care for. Although she was a gorgeous looking woman, I had always felt uncomfortable in her company. She was like one of those salesmen that you meet at parties, always sizing you up to see if you can be any use to them.

This evening, though, like her husband, she was being at her most charming. They had obviously calculated that I was one of the relatively few journalists who were likely to be critical, and since I had been assigned to stay close to the Taoiseach during the campaign, had decided to disarm me with hospitality and kindness.

I hate being put in this situation. I knew it wouldn't influence the way I wrote up the interview, but I also knew that if the Taoiseach didn't like it, I would be treated to all sorts of expressions of hurt and betrayal the following day.

Still it was an opportunity to see them at close quarters. Since they were going out of their way to be hospitable, and since I hadn't had any lunch, I made the most of it. It was nine-thirty before I left, pleading that I still had work to do writing up the interview.

I didn't do any more work that night. The barman in the Springhill Hotel let me put a bottle of Paddy on the tab for my room number, and I took it up to my bedroom to try to figure the whole thing out.

The further away I got from Annie Deane's front room, the more outrageous her story seemed. The man I'd just had dinner with - the Prime Minister of Ireland - how could he be a murderer? But if he was not, Annie Deane was mad, or a liar.

Now, I'm a reporter, used to covering hard news, and I know I'm not an expert in anything. Stories come and go, and you learn whatever you need to cover the story. Unless you specialise, in business or tourism or motor cars or whatever, you get to know a little about everything and a lot about nothing. Except people. You do get to know a lot about people. You can tell a sane person from a lunatic, and you get to know when people are lying to you, and when they are telling you the truth. You may not know what it is that people have to hide, but you know if they're trying to hide something. Annie Deane was telling me the truth - I was sure of that. At least she was telling me what she really believed to be the truth.

But Gibson - a murderer? He was a calculating politician, and a man of very considerable charisma, with a glamorous wife and a fine house. After spending six hours with him I found myself doubting that he had any real commitment to the agreement he had negotiated - maybe he saw it as just another vehicle to help him become more famous, or whatever it was he was interested in. And I knew from his house, and the fine china on which we had eaten, that he enjoyed money. But would he kill for it? I couldn't say, but the more I thought about it, the more convinced I became that it was important to find out.

Around midnight I went for a walk around the hotel car park, to clear my head. At the front desk, while I was arranging to be called the following morning, the night porter told me that there was a note for me.

It was from Margaret Deane. It told me that both she and her mother were very grateful to me for the time I had given them. She hoped I didn't feel that they were just hysterical women with a grudge. Down at the bottom of the note was a Dublin address and telephone number. Margaret said that she had had to go back to work that evening, but if I would like to contact her when I got back to Dublin myself, she would be happy to hear from me.

I copied the address and phone number into my notebook, and tried to get some sleep.

CHAPTER 6
JULY 1st - THE SIXTH DAY

THE TAOISEACH

The crowd was pressing in; the people wanted to be close to their hero.

Although he had never been religious, Andrew Gibson had seldom missed Sunday Mass in his home town. It had become a tradition, to such an extent that a pew was unofficially reserved for him near the front of the Cathedral. He would arrive almost, but not quite, late, so that he could be seen by the entire congregation. Afterwards he would stand in the courtyard exchanging pleasantries with his constituents, and occasionally confidential whispers with those who needed his special favours. They all got the same response - "Come up to the house when you can, and we'll see what we can do."

And those who came to the house, still in their Sunday best, would be received as if their problem was the biggest in the Taoiseach's life. If he wasn't there, or couldn't see them himself, Tim Hanrahan would take down all the details, and they would be promised Mr Gibson's personal attention.

This Sunday morning was different. As soon as the Taoiseach and his wife entered the Cathedral, the applause started, and soon every man, woman and child was standing and clapping as they made their way to the front of the Church. The Bishop of Ossory, who had to stand holding the chalice until the Gibsons had taken their seats, was not amused. The frown on his face made Gibson chuckle inwardly. If only they knew, he thought to himself, that this whole agreement wasn't even my idea!

Gibson figured that he would never quite know why Neil Kinnock had initiated the discussions. He knew that their relations had been far from good in the past - there was the famous incident where there had been a public row in Milan, at a European summit, and he had managed to keep his temper in check only because Holloway had kept tugging at his jacket. And anyway, Mr Kinnock had always been regarded as having no real interest in Ireland. He'd been in Dublin a number of times, and always seemed at home there, but there had never seemed to be room on his agenda for anything but the economic revival he was masterminding at home.

Kinnock had said, in his usual blunt way, that despite everything he regarded Gibson as the only politician in Ireland who could pull it off, the only one with credentials that were adequate to bring in the harder-line republicans. But that didn't explain why Kinnock had started the discussions in the first place.

Perhaps, as Hanrahan, the only other person aware of all the details, had said, he had just decided to take on the biggest challenge of them all. The Irish question, after all, was the one great issue that no British politician felt safe with until there were no other mountains left to climb.

It had started quite simply. It had been in the course of one of the ritual tête-à-têtes that British and Irish Prime Ministers are expected to have during European summits (this one had taken place in the Hague).

"Andy," Kinnock had said (he insisted on getting on first name terms with everyone - Gibson had to restrain himself from telling him that no one outside his most intimate circle was allowed to call him Andy), "I would like very much if you would select one of your people - someone you trust absolutely - to talk to one of my people about certain ideas I have about re-uniting your country."

Gibson remembered that he had almost fallen off the elegant armchair he was sitting on. He knew that Kinnock was a man who chose his words carefully. He had never had even a hint from the British Prime Minister before that the word "reunification" had crossed his mind. He'd had to take a deep breath before asking him, "what ideas?"

Kinnock had declined to discuss them in any detail at that meeting, as it had been scheduled to last only half an hour and he was determined not to arouse the slightest speculation by allowing it to go over the allotted time. Gibson was able to establish only that there had already been some discussion between Kinnock and the President of the USA on the subject, before the meeting was adjourned.

Afterwards, the usual bland communiqué about friendly exchanges on matters of mutual interest was issued, and spokesmen for both Governments issued the usual rebuttals of paranoid outbursts from Loyalist politicians in the North of Ireland (which were never taken seriously anyway, since they were as regular as the summits) about an imminent sell-out of the Unionist birthright.

Outwardly, appearances were perfectly preserved.

Behind the scenes, negotiations were strictly confined to three people - Bob Holloway, representing the Taoiseach, Peter Clarke, representing the British Prime Minister, and later, when it became necessary, Nick Angleton, representing the White House. Gibson and Kinnock met only once in the course of the negotiations, at the next European summit in Manchester, although they spoke frequently by phone. They both briefed President Cuomo in Washington separately.

The complex ruses employed to maintain security had worked perfectly. Clarke had taken a holiday home in Glandore, in West Cork, and Holloway had rented a caravan in Castlefreke, about six miles away. These two locations were the base for about thirty intensive meetings that had taken place during the months of April, May, and June.

Finola had known some of what was going on, of course, but had not wanted any detailed information. As one of the most public "first ladies" that Ireland had seen, she knew that she would find herself in the company of journalists from time to time, and preferred to be in a position where she was unable to let slip hints of what was going on.

She was, anyway, much more interested in the fact of the Agreement, and in the sense of history that was in the air, than she was in the content of the Agreement. Finola Gibson wanted power just as much as her husband. She believed absolutely that the getting and keeping of power justified anything. And now she knew that real power was soon going to be theirs. The atmosphere in the Cathedral was unmistakable. They were on their way.

And she knew that the things she had done for him, on his way back to favour, tied him to her for all time. Now that he had arrived, they would share power together.

"Hey!"

Startled, she glanced at her husband, who was grinning at her. It was he who had whispered.

"You're squeezing my hand," he whispered again.

She hadn't realised it. The knuckles on her own hand were white, she had been squeezing so hard.

"I'm proud of you," she said to him. "Nothing can stop you now."

THE MINISTER FOR TRANSPORT

Joe Ryan sighed. It was going to be a very rough day. It was bad enough having to work on a Sunday, and it was worse when he should really be in his constituency trying to get himself re-elected. But it was the nature of the job he had to do today which filled him with dread.

Ryan was a coward. He was afraid of anyone who raised his voice or made a threatening gesture. And today he had to deal with a whole room of people who had already shouted at him more than once. Today he was going to fix a transport strike.

The thought of it made his piles itch.

The first thing that Joe Ryan's officials learned about him was that he suffered terribly from piles. On his first day in the Department, an old granite building in Kildare Street that had last seen an internal decorator in the Second World War, he had rejected the chair placed behind the Ministerial desk, and had gone himself to the furniture store in the basement to pick one out that was soft enough. And a substantial sum of taxpayers' money had to be spent to provide a personal toilet for the Minister next to his office, where he spent hours wrestling with problems of state and with his bowels.

The Taoiseach had told him last Tuesday to fix the strike. The same Taoiseach had told him - had roared at him - only a few days before that "There's no way we're going to give in to those bastards!". That was why he had issued a statement which had had the effect of putting the strike beyond any hope of an easy settlement. And that was why, on top of his other problems, he was now looking forward to a large dose of humble pie for his Sunday lunch.

And however much he ate, the strike would still be devilishly hard to fix. It had been caused by money, and it would take money to settle it. There were two problems. First, there was no money in the Exchequer, and a settlement that looked as if it was achieved at any cost would generate adverse publicity, especially for the Minister who had done a U-turn just because there was an election on.

And secondly, there was Bill Browne. Unlike many Trade Union officials, Bill Browne had no politics. He had only two convictions that anyone knew about. One was that transport workers were seriously underpaid, and the other was that the only way they could do anything about it was to put themselves in a position where they could hold the entire country to ransom if necessary.

From the moment he had been appointed as General Secretary of one of the smaller Unions representing bus workers, that had been his message. And he preached it at every opportunity. He was particularly anxious to reach an agreement with the unions who had members in the airports, so that his aim of a Transport United Front could become a reality. He spent the four years it took to reach that goal fighting a sort of guerilla war with CIE, the bus and rail company. In the process he became a well-known and intimidating public figure, and the Minister for Transport stepped up his visits to the toilet. When the Unions eventually agreed to the formation of TUF, Browne emerged naturally as the spokesman. In this capacity he led TUF into battle, by lodging a claim for a twenty-five per cent increase, and by declaring the intention to strike within one month "unless realistic negotiations, based on a recognition of the under- privilege among TUF members, were concluded before then."

No Government could give in to this, of course. "Blackmail," said the Taoiseach. "Issues of deepest principle involved," said the Minister. Even the Leader of the Opposition, while calling on the Government to facilitate the processing of the claim through the normal channels, acknowledged that it could not be conceded to tactics like this.

And then the election was called, and everyone realised that Bill Browne had the power to cut the country off from the outside world. The Taoiseach had decided it had to be fixed.

The Minister's officials were not so sure. Officials are seldom persuaded by such minor imperatives as General Elections. Governments come and go, after all, but administration goes on for ever, and administration has its own imperatives. Chief among them is the commandment "thou shalt not set a precedent". And a settlement of this dispute would undoubtedly set a precedent if there was any cash involved.

At the meeting with the Minister on Sunday morning, before the Unions came in, they explained this to Joe Ryan, slowly and painstakingly. They showed him how transport workers' pay, although admittedly small, had in fact kept pace in relative terms with that of other, better-paid public servants (like themselves) over the previous few years. They told him of all the other grades whose relative position would be disturbed by an offer to the transport workers - the hospital staffs, the local authority workers, the technicians, the engineers, the clerks. And they showed him how the knock-on effects of a settlement would cost hundreds of millions of pounds, once the settlement had spread throughout all these other grades. And worst of all, when all that had happened, the transport workers would be no better off in relative terms. They would catch up with the others, only to see the others passing them out again. The process would be unending.

The Minister didn't want to know any of it.

"What am I going to tell the Taoiseach," was all he could say, "if I can't fix this damn thing? He'll skin me alive! It's your job to help me sort it out!"

That's when the officials unveiled their master stroke. A Committee. They proposed the establishment of a Committee, equally representative of the TUF unions and the transport companies, under an independent Chairman. It would have terms of reference that would enable it to examine the whole problem of low pay in the industry, and to make appropriate recommendations to the Minister. In order to convey the required sense of urgency, and to impress the Unions, the officials suggested that the committee should not be called a committee. It would be a Task Force, instructed by the Minister to report in three months. Its findings would be made public - the Minister, after all, had no interest in seeing the legitimate sense of grievance of workers swept under the carpet. The officials suggested that the Minister keep one ace up his sleeve. He would retain the right to accept the Task Force recommendations or not - but if put under enough pressure, he could graciously concede that he would be prepared to accept the findings of the Task Force in advance.

The Minister, though, was doubtful.

"Are you sure they'll buy it?" he wanted to know.

"Trust us, Minister," the officials chorused. "This man Browne is a realist. He knows how far he can go."

The trouble was, the officials were absolutely right. Bill Browne *was* a realist. He knew that the only reason he and his comrades had been invited in to meet the Minister was because of the General Election. And he knew that if he didn't make the most of his opportunity, there might not be another. So his mind was made up. The calling of the General Election was the best thing that could have happened to him. It was going to be twenty five per cent or nothing, and he didn't beat about the bush.

"We're here to see the colour of your money, Minister," was his opening statement.

The Minister was uneasy at having to attend meetings in the Department's Conference Room, on the floor below his office. It was a long corridor and two flights of stairs (twenty-four steps - the Minister had counted them) away from his toilet. Browne's truculent opening stirred uneasiness into the beginnings of panic.

And even he could see that the intervention of Seamus Byrne, his Assistant Secretary in charge of remuneration, did not help matters. Byrne was one of the most pompous men in the Civil Service, who took exception to trade union officials coming to see him without wearing a tie. The tone of Browne's opening remark had made him bridle.

"There's no need to take that tone, Mr Browne," he boomed. "The Minister has gone to considerable trouble to see you today - a certain amount of courtesy would not be out of place."

Browne grinned. "Relax, Seamus," he said (Ryan could almost feel the Assistant Secretary's horror at being addressed by his first name by this person), "The Minister isn't going to any trouble on negotiating committee began to join in. For fully three minutes they laughed, clapping one another on the back, shaking their heads, dabbing at their eyes with handkerchiefs.

Ryan had never seen anything like it. He didn't know what to do - should he join in, should he be offended? He looked up and down the table at his own officials. They were all stony-faced, except one, an irreverent Principal Officer who had been drafted in from the Department of Labour to help with the negotiations. Ryan couldn't even remember his name, but he was smiling. The Minister decided to follow his lead, and forced a very tight chuckle from his dry lips. Eventually Browne, with what seemed like a great effort of will, began to get himself under control.

"A committee, Joe?" he said at last, still wiping his eyes. "To *really* look at our little problem?"

Ryan could feel the mood changing by the second. He hadn't realised how afraid he was of this man until now, as he watched him, much like a chicken would watch a fox. Browne leaned over the heavy oak table, staring directly into the Minister's eyes.

"For fuck's sake Minister," he said, "what do you think we are? Innocents from your fucking constituency?"

Nobody present, on either side of the table, had ever heard a Minister spoken to like that before. Ryan could only think of two things. The first was that if he let this man get away with it, he would never again have the respect of his officials; the second was that he had to go to the toilet - immediately. It was that overwhelming urge that saved him, for the moment at least.

"I'm going to give you five minutes to think about that remark, Mr Browne," he said, pushing back his chair. He left the room quickly, followed by his officials.

It was twenty minutes before the Minister and his team returned. The Minister had spent most of that time locked in his the Taoiseach's words, and the threat that his Cabinet place hung in the balance if the Taoiseach read any more about this matter in the newspapers. His heart sank as he heard Browne's response.

"There's no go," he was saying. "We've been waiting too long for decent progress on our members' behalf. It's money on the table, or there's nothing doing."

"But don't you understand?" Ryan said, "it would only have to take a month. You wouldn't have to call off your strike, just postpone it for a little while."

Browne laughed again. The Minister nearly fainted, thinking he was going to be subjected to more united hilarity by the union side. But this time the laughter was short-lived.

"I know I'm only an ignorant trade union official, Minister," Browne said, "but even I know that the election will be over in a month. And whichever side wins, the TUF claim won't be very high on the agenda. Your party mightn't win, and even if they do, you mightn't be in office. So anything that's agreed today has to be in force before the whole thing is over - and the only thing that will work, for that reason, is money."

He leaned over the table, speaking directly to the Minister, with his voice lowered as if he wanted to tell Ryan a secret.

"Look, Minister," he said, "we're not unreasonable people. We don't expect the whole lot to be paid immediately - we know the cost of that would be substantial. I think we'd be prepared to agree to a phased commitment - say ten per cent now and the balance next year. It would have to be in writing, you understand, but it would save the taxpayers a few bob, and sure, aren't we taxpayers too. And look at it from your own point of view - you'd be able to go back and tell the Government that you'd beaten a big concession out of us."

For the first time, Ryan saw a gleam of hope. But hope has a funny way of disappearing just as fast as it materialises. It was Seamus Byrne, the Assistant Secretary, speaking before Ryan could gather his thoughts, who put paid to it this time.

"You just don't understand, do you, Mr Browne?" he said. "Money has nothing to do with this. There are principles involved here, and procedures. The Minister is willing to stretch a point by inventing a new procedure for your claim to be dealt with, but he will never agree to abandon his principles."

Ryan would have abandoned his principles like a shot, but now he had been deprived of the opportunity.

"Right," said Browne, "you'll have to suit yourselves of course, but I have more to do than to hang around here wasting a Sunday afternoon. I have a strike to organise."

With that he gathered up his papers and walked to the door. At the door he stopped, and turned to grin at the Minister.

"We'll see you on the picket line, Joe," he said.

Ryan was close to tears. When the TUF delegation had left, his officials gathered round, assuring him that there was nothing more he could have done, that the strike would only last a day or two, that the TUF people would see sense, that they'd be back with their tails between their legs. All he could say, again and again, was,

"Jesus Christ! What am I going to say to the Taoiseach?"

CHAPTER 7

JULY 2nd - THE SEVENTH DAY

THE REPORTER

Proof was easier to come by than I had ever expected.

On Sunday morning I had an idea. I telephoned Vincent O'Byrne at home, and told him that the Taoiseach had given me permission to write an in-depth profile of him, and had assured me of the utmost co-operation. I told O'Byrne that what I had in mind was a sort of "Andrew Gibson as the public had never seen him" article, to run over two days maybe, and to appear before the election. I even added that Gibson had agreed to talk about such taboo subjects as the death of his first wife, and his wealth.

O'Byrne was excited about the project - I thought he would be. I thought to myself that he would be even more excited if he knew what I was really going after. But I had learned from long experience that you don't ever tell an editor what you've got until you're in a position to write the story. If it's a good story, his first reaction is to put others on it to help you. Then he keeps interrupting you to know when you're going to have it finished. He may even decide that he can write it better than you. By the time an editor is finished interfering with a good story it may still be good, but it isn't yours any more.

He agreed readily to allow me to concentrate on the new project for several days, so that I didn't have to follow the campaign around the country.

That was the easy bit. The hard bit was that I now had to approach Gibson himself. I was going to look a bit silly if, having assured my editor that he would co-operate, the Taoiseach wasn't prepared to go along.

As it happened, I needn't have worried. When I rang him from the hotel, he answered the phone himself. I thanked him for his hospitality of the previous night, and added, in what I hoped was a suitably ingratiating tone, that I felt sure he was going to like the interview that appeared on Monday.

"Well now Jim," he said (obviously he was trying to be hearty as well), "I wouldn't expect anything other than your usual professional job."

Since we were being so chummy, I asked him if I could see him for a moment or two that afternoon to talk about a different project. He immediately invited me up to the house for coffee.

On the way I rehearsed, as I had done the day before, the things I was going to say to him. In the end I decided to repeat exactly what I had said to Vincent.

To my surprise he agreed to co-operate with the project almost immediately. He even agreed to talk about his first wife.

"There's a skeleton in every cupboard, Jim," he told me, "and Maura Barrington was mine. I wasn't very good to her, you know. Mind you, I was very young then, with all the callousness of young people. But when she died, I was overwhelmed with guilt. I like to think that I learned from the experience - at least that I learned how to treat people a bit better."

He only wanted to lay down one condition for agreeing to co-operate fully.

"I know I hardly need to make the point, Jim," he said, "but I've put up with an awful lot of muck-raking in my life. I'm not afraid of a balanced picture emerging - one that shows me warts and all - but I'm not walking myself into a straightforward muck-raking job, am I?"

There was no way I was going to say yes to that, whatever the truth. We parted the best of friends, with my assurances of balance and fair play ringing in his ears. We agreed that I would meet him again on Thursday night, to ask him anything I wanted to about his personal life and background, and I assured him that if I found out anything that was less than flattering, he would have an opportunity then to straighten out the record from his point of view.

It was fairly easy to figure out why he had agreed so easily to co-operate with such an in-depth profile. From his perspective, how could he lose? For a politician, publicity is his life's blood, even bad publicity if it puts him on the front pages of a newspaper.

That's how I came to be in the offices of Boyd, Gibson & Sons (whose sons did they have in mind? I wondered), early the following morning, in Patrick Street in Kilkenny. It was like all the solicitors' offices in all the towns throughout Ireland, dark, dusty, with a harried middle-aged woman in an outer room, surrounded by long narrow files and with only an old manual typewriter to keep her company.

She showed me in to the office of Mr Brendan O'Keeffe, who I had been told was now running the firm. I had taken the precaution of asking Tim Hanrahan to ring ahead of me, so O'Keeffe had already been told that I was researching a major article on the Taoiseach, and that he was to facilitate me in any way possible. I was curious about O'Keeffe's status in the business.

"Andrew Gibson and I are partners," he told me. "I was employed by the firm, specifically by the Taoiseach's former partner before he died. But after his death and especially when the Taoiseach began to move up in politics, Mr Gibson offered me a full partnership. Now I look after the business full-time - he cannot have any involvement, of course, while he holds public office. We employ three other solicitors, but they are all on a salary."

"Is it a very successful business then?" I asked him.

"We are quite busy, of course," he said, with a slight frown. He might be willing to help me, but asking a solicitor to tell you what he earns is going too far.

"I understand that a substantial part of the business is concerned with property development," I said.

"Not really," he replied, "not any more. The Taoiseach does own a certain amount of property, of course, but a separate company was established to handle all that. He and Chris McDonald were the only shareholders in that company. Now the whole company is in a blind trust, which I administer. But the Taoiseach cannot do any buying or selling of property while he holds office - that means that the trust merely holds the property, and we collect rent on some of it. The rent, of course, provides some of the Taoiseach's income - but it will remain fixed for as long as he is in office."

"So I suppose it could actually be said that his holding office is costing him money," I asked.

"Indeed it could," said Mr O'Keeffe. "I often think how little the people of this country appreciate the sacrifices made by people who leave businesses behind them when they go into public life."

"And I suppose," I asked, "the value of Mr Gibson's property was halved when his partner died?"

"Well, no," O'Keeffe told me. "Chris McDonald died intestate, and without next-of-kin. We advertised for a long time to try to find a relative but none turned up. So the shares in Leinster Resources - that's the name of their holding company - reverted to the Taoiseach. In any event, even though they were equal partners, most of the capital originally invested was Mr Gibson's."

I made a written note of some of this information. If Annie Deane had been telling me the truth, it was important to find out as much as I could about Christopher McDonald.

"What about McDonald's personal estate?" I asked O'Keeffe.

"There really wasn't one," he said. "McDonald was a strange man in many ways. I was the one who tried to tidy up his affairs when he died, but there was very little to tidy up. He didn't even own a house of his own, although he could have bought half a dozen. All that was left was a small bank account, with about twelve thousand pounds in it. It wasn't an inconsiderable sum in those days, but it was nothing like one would expect. The bank account is still there, incidentally, and the money has been earning interest all this time. So if a relative ever materialises, there will be quite a windfall."

"It's a strange story, isn't it?" I asked him, "you'd imagine a man of substance like that would at least own his own house."

"You'd want to have known Christopher McDonald personally," he replied. "He was a very odd man. I hadn't been working here very long when he died, although I knew of his reputation before I joined the firm. He was a brilliant lawyer, you know, quite brilliant, but he could be very difficult personally. We all tended to make allowances, because we knew he was suffering from stomach cancer, and he was in considerable pain a good deal of the time. As he became more ill, he came to be something of a recluse, refusing to see anyone, even Andrew -" he coughed, and corrected himself, "excuse me, I mean the Taoiseach. I gather he was an atheist most of his life, but towards the end, he became very devoted to religion. We've always believed he gave most of his money to the Church before he died."

"It sounds like a fascinating story in its own right," I said. But I was anxious not to stir any suspicion in his mind, so for the next hour, while the lady from the outer office served us coffee, I asked him about Gibson: what kind of a lawyer he was, what he was like to work with, what kind of cases he preferred to deal with, how he had mixed politics and his practice in the early days.

Although O'Keeffe assured me several times that he was going to answer my questions as objectively as possible, his answers described a paragon of virtue. Gibson was the best employer, the most considerate partner, the most effective lawyer that Brendan O'Keeffe had ever met. It appeared that none of the famous outbursts of temper, or any of the vindictive acts that had been attributed to Gibson, had ever happened in his solicitor's office.

After an hour of this recital, during which I took copious notes, I stood up to take my leave. At the door I paused, as if a thought had struck me.

"It's a pity Chris McDonald isn't still around," I said. "After all, he knew the Taoiseach better than anyone else. I'll bet he could give quite an insight into his character. If he'd kept a diary, it would tell us a lot."

It was a very long shot, of course - I don't think I expected anything to come of it. So it was amazing that he failed to notice any sign of excitement in me at his reply.

"All that was left was an old box of papers," he said. "It was a terrible jumble of stuff, all stuffed into an old iron chest. I probably should have gone through it carefully, but I'm afraid I never had the heart. It was mostly old school reports, photographs of his parents, stuff like that."

"I suppose you threw it out?" I asked him, my heart pounding. He smiled.

"You don't know solicitors," he said. "We never throw anything away. But I'm not sure that I could put my hands on it easily. And I'm sure that there would be nothing of interest in it."

"I'm sure you're right," I said quickly. "But you never know - and it might give me a better feel for one of the central characters in the Taoiseach's career."

"All right," he said. "But I will have to ask you only to look at the documents. It wouldn't be proper for me to hand over someone else's belongings to you - even if that person is already dead."

He pressed a button on an ancient intercom on his desk.

"Miss Joyce," he said, "could you help Mr Flynn to locate Mr McDonald's old box in the strongroom?"

Turning to me, he explained that he had to go out for a couple of hours. He told me to feel free to use his office, and that Miss Joyce was at my disposal.

O'Keeffe's "strongroom" was in fact the basement of the building. Miss Joyce made it plain that she did not enjoy venturing down there with a perfect stranger, and I found it hard to blame her. It took a bit of rummaging around among what she referred to as the "obsoletes", which all appeared to be stored in a particularly dank corner of the basement, before we found the iron chest that contained whatever was left of the private life of Christopher McDonald.

Even though it was heavy, and I was out of breath by the time I had lugged it into O'Keeffe's office, I was grateful that it was made of iron. Nothing could have survived for twenty years in that smelly basement unless it was contained in a box as sturdy as this. It wasn't locked, but it still took me a few minutes to force the lid open, so rusted had it become.

My heart fell when I saw the contents. It was filled almost to overflowing with old envelopes, photographs, year-books of a boarding school in Roscrea, County Tipperary, files, and loose scraps of paper. I thought to myself that I had little chance of finding anything in this lot, and no chance at all of finding it before O'Keeffe came back.

I piled up the year books on a corner of O'Keeffe's desk. They might have been interesting in themselves, but I didn't want to know about McDonald's academic career just now. Then I began sorting through the papers in the box, putting photographs on one side and scanning, as rapidly as possible, the contents of the envelopes. At the end of two hours, I had found no evidence of murder.

I jumped when Miss Joyce opened the door. There was no particular reason why I should have felt guilty, but somehow the mission on which I was engaged had made me feel more than a little furtive.

"Would you care for a cup of coffee, Mr Flynn?" she asked. "I was just making some."

I thanked her. I hadn't realised how quickly time was passing. O'Keeffe would be back soon, and whatever hope I had of finding incriminating evidence in the old iron chest, I would have no chance at all while O'Keeffe was sitting at his desk watching me.

Miss Joyce came back, carrying a small tray with cups and saucers. It was when she was putting it down on the desk that she knocked off the pile of year books, scattering them all around me on the floor.

One of them fell apart. It wasn't a year-book, but a handwritten notebook. I knew immediately I saw it that it was what I was looking for. I could feel the hairs rising on the back of my neck as I assured Miss Joyce that there was no harm done, hoping that she would not bend down to start gathering up the scattered documents. I was almost trembling, more with the effort involved in hiding my excitement than with anything else.

When Miss Joyce had left the room, I picked up the notebook. It took me a second or two to realise how gingerly I was handling it, almost as if I was afraid it would be hot to the touch. I looked at it for a long time before opening it. The loose pages had been scattered when the notebook fell on the floor, and they were out of order. I recognised the hand-writing immediately - I had, after all, been looking at it for the past two hours.

I resisted the temptation to read the pages. The priority was to get them out of O'Keeffe's office. That would be easy enough provided he suspected nothing. So I put the notebook in one of my inside pockets, and tidied up the contents of the box. As it happened, I was only just in time, because O'Keeffe returned shortly afterwards.

He smiled when he saw me sitting on the floor, surrounded by Chris McDonald's memorabilia.

"Well, Mr Flynn," he said, "I take it you've discovered how hard it is for lawyers to part with even useless information."

I tried to laugh - my lips and throat were so dry, with tension and with the fear of discovery, that for an instant I was sure that he could see how forced it was. I told him that I had learned a little about Christopher McDonald's school days, but nothing at all about Andrew Gibson.

"That often happens to reporters," I said, "but if you're not prepared to do the spadework, you'll never dig up anything."

We exchanged a few more pleasantries while I finished putting the papers back in the box. Then, feeling like a heel, I thanked him for his help, and went back to the Springhill.

I shuddered as I read. It was hard to believe that I was sitting in a hotel bedroom on a sunny afternoon towards the end of the twentieth century. The notebook had been written by a man possessed, possessed with a medieval sense of fear and guilt.

Christopher McDonald had died a convert. He had made a confession to a priest, but not content with that, he had written it down as well.

The trouble was, most of the names in it had been shortened to initials. AG was easy enough to decipher. There was almost a hint of madness in the things McDonald said about Gibson in the notebook.

"AG has sentenced me to hell. I have committed crimes for him which I have been afraid before now to confess to a priest, and for which I'm certain there can be no forgiveness anyway. I am only a couple of days away from hell, and the only consolation I can find is that sooner or later he will join me. We will both burn there, for what he made me do, for the rest of time."

AD was also easy to interpret - Annie Deane. There were a number of references to her, and they confirmed that he had written to her, trying to explain, and sending her half of all the money he had left. His notes proved to my satisfaction that she had been telling the truth all along. As I read them I felt a twinge of shame for having begun to doubt her - and for doubting my own instinct that she was telling me the truth. One of the things that was now abundantly clear to me was the role played by Deputy Commissioner Stafford in covering up Gibson's crime.

But who was MB, who had been sent the other half of McDonald's money? There were references to MB throughout the notes - he seemed obsessed with her, and with whatever he and Gibson had done to her. He had sent a letter to MB with the money, pleading for forgiveness. The only person I could think of whose initials might qualify was Maura Barrington, Andrew Gibson's first wife. But she was dead, and if memory served me, she had died around the same time as McDonald. That seemed to rule her out.

Taken all in all, McDonald's notebook confirmed implicitly that everything Annie Deane had told me was true. But I would need more. McDonald's handwritten confession conveyed a powerful sense of his own guilt, but it did not go far enough in implicating Andrew Gibson. The Taoiseach's initials would not be enough. I knew I needed more - if MB were Maura Barrington, and if she were still alive, maybe she could give it to me.

On impulse, I picked up the local telephone directory and leafed through it. There was still a listing for a Maura Barrington in Kilkenny. The address was less than a mile away.

Maura Barrington's mother was an old lady, the last of the family left. She lived not more than three miles from the Gibsons, in the sort of house generally associated with the old ascendancy in Ireland. But whereas Gibson's house was perfectly looked after, with manicured lawns and carefully tended flower-beds, the Barrington place had clearly seen better days.

I had explained over the telephone that I was working on a major series of articles about the Taoiseach, and that I was hoping she would help me to fill in some of the background about his first marriage to her daughter. She had agreed to see me readily enough. As I picked my way through the ruts and rotten branches on the driveway, I reflected that the Barrington ancestors, who had owned much of the land for miles around, would be turning in their graves if they could see it now. The land on both sides of the narrow, poplar-lined, drive had obviously been sold off for housing. The effect made the old mansion, rather than the modern bungalows surrounding it, look sadly out of place.

Mrs Barrington herself had more than a touch of the old world relic about her. A small, stooped woman, with untidy grey hair, she was heavily wrapped in what had probably once been a very fine shawl. I had time to observe the way in which the house was crumbling around her as she led me to a very large, and very cold, drawing room. The sherry she served me, although it was from a Waterford decanter, tasted cheap. We sat in front of a small fire, which needed to be bigger to get the chill out of the room, even though it was mid-summer.

"Mr Gibson has always been very good to me," she said. "I'd never have been able to keep on this house if it wasn't for him."

"How do you manage here?" I asked her. "It must be a very expensive house to maintain."

"Indeed it is," she said. "And I certainly wouldn't be able to manage on what my husband left me. I suppose I should have given up the house when I was left on my own, but somehow I can't bring myself to leave it. But at least I don't have to pay any taxes on it, since Mr Gibson helped me to have it classified as a historic monument. And he pays me a small allowance. With that and the interest from Mr McDonald's money, I just about get by. Mind you, it's the least they could do in the circumstances."

"Do you mean Christopher McDonald?" I asked her. Immediately she looked furtive. She had told me something she hadn't meant to. Now she debated whether or not to answer my question. I could tell even before she spoke that she was going to lie.

"Yes," she said. "Mr McDonald was a good friend of the

whole family - he used to hunt with my husband, you know. He left us some money in his will."

"Oh, I see," I said, as casually as possible.

She was relieved that her lies had worked. Christopher McDonald was not from Kilkenny, and he was certainly not the huntin' and shootin' type. Besides, he had died intestate. I knew where the money had come from. I needed to know why.

I asked her another question.

"When you said it was the least they could do in the circumstances, what did you mean?"

She looked at me again, and this time I detected more than furtiveness. There was a kind of crazy cunning there.

"It was just a figure of speech," she said. "Mr Gibson did very well out of the arrangement with my daughter."

It struck me as an odd way to describe her daughter's marriage, so I asked her what she meant.

"Well," she said, "I should tell you first of all that my husband did not entirely approve of Mr Gibson. Not quite our sort of person, you know. He tried very hard to persuade Maura not to see him - but she was absolutely determined. A very spoiled child she was - nobody had ever said no to her before. Everyone else in this house had always taken second place to her - there was nothing her father wouldn't do for her. But she still insisted on having her own way where Mr Gibson was concerned."

"But after they were married," I said, "something went very badly wrong, didn't it?"

"I don't know what you mean," she told me. "Maura was always a little mad, you know - it ran in her father's side of the family. He was a very heavy drinker himself - it killed him in the end. But as I said, Mr Gibson was always very kind to me. I never believed the things Maura used to say about him."

"What kind of things?" I asked her. But she just shook her head.

Her dislike of her daughter was as clear as her partiality for Gibson. She was not going to say anything against him. I decided to change the subject.

"How long had Maura been ill before she died?" I asked.

"She didn't die!" she snapped. "She killed herself, and brought shame on this family and scandal on her husband."

"But she must have been very unhappy to have done that," I said as gently as possible. "I'm told she was very unhappy in her marriage?"

"She made her bed," her mother retorted, "and then she didn't want to lie in it. Other women have had to put up with a great deal worse."

"You didn't like your daughter very much, did you?" I said. "What do you know, young man?" she snapped. "She made a brilliant match, but nothing was ever enough for her. She wasn't content with killing herself - she broke her father's heart as well."

"I'm sorry," I said. "I didn't mean to offend you. I wasn't aware that she had made her father suffer."

"Well, she did." Old Mrs Barrington was angry now. "He only began drinking really heavily when she started sending him those letters from that awful mental hospital."

More letters! I could hardly believe my luck. I could hear my heart beating as I asked her if she had kept them.

"I never read them," she said, "they were filthy, horrible letters. But my husband would never let me throw them out. And he kept them, locked in that bureau over there."

It was an old walnut chiffonnier with a series of small drawers. "May I see them?" I asked. But she was suddenly cautious.

"Why should I show them to you?" she said. "Nobody else has ever seen them."

I lied, hoping against hope it was convincing.

"Andrew Gibson and I have talked a lot about his first marriage. We both agree that if I'm to present a full picture of him, I can't leave that out. He has told me how disturbed Maura was, and I believe him. But I do need to get the fullest possible picture. You understand that, don't you?"

Still she looked doubtful. I decided that I would have to risk everything.

"Look," I said, "I've given Mr Gibson my word that nothing will appear in print that he doesn't agree with. If you like, you can ring him yourself to check."

She glanced towards the telephone, and for an awful moment I thought she might actually pick it up. But she was convinced, and got up to shuffle towards the cabinet. I decided to try one last throw.

"By the way," I said, as casually as my heartbeat would let me, "Andy told me that Christopher McDonald had written to you just before he died. You wouldn't have kept that letter as well, would you?"

She stopped.

"Surely Mr Gibson wouldn't want you to see that?" she said.

"I already know, more or less, what's in it," I lied again. "That whole period was specially difficult and traumatic for Andy, and all the letters that his sick partner wrote just added to it. He particularly mentioned that you were one of the people who had got a letter, and he's always been grateful that you never held it against him."

"I never knew he knew," she told me. And then she handed me all the proof I needed.

I stood up immediately.

"I've taken up too much of your time already," I said. "I'll read these later, and return them to you in a couple of days if I may."

As I turned to go, it occurred to me that she could still ring Gibson.

"I'm sorry," I said. "When I mentioned to Andy that I was coming to see you, he asked me to give you this."

Her eyes lit up when I handed her most of the advance I had received from my expenses. My instinct had been right - her relationship with Gibson had been based for years on his regular payments of conscience money. There was little danger she would check with him now.

Maura Gibson had been a virgin when she married, and in the more than two years of their courtship, Andrew had never given her the slightest hint of what was to come. On their wedding night, which they spent in the Gresham Hotel in Dublin before flying to London, she discovered that he was a violent and unpredictable man. He left her in her wedding bed, bleeding and sobbing as if she would die, and spent the remainder of the night in the bar downstairs.

Later, after a fortnight in which he was by turns tender and savage, they returned to Kilkenny to settle into a rented house in Patrick Street, while they waited for the big house which he was restoring on the outskirts of town to be finished. As time went on, Maura realised that Andrew had never wanted anything from her but her name and her status. He frequently stayed out all night, and made no secret of the fact that he was far more interested in other women than he was in her.

Her situation improved for a time when his father died. Although Maura knew in her heart of hearts that she had never meant anything to her husband other than the society wedding she had given him, she was thankful that from the moment Andrew entered the Dail, he stopped appearing in late-night pubs and making it obvious that he had no responsibility towards his wife. It lasted until they established that Maura would never be able to have children.

After that, Andrew resumed to the full a life that Maura believed was designed to humiliate her in public. The only consolation she had was that he confined his activities, for the most part, to the three or four days a week that he spent in Dublin as a member of the Dail. At home, he began to beat her with increasing regularity, and to threaten that he would be rid of her whatever way he could.

The letters from Maura to her father were heart-rending. They revealed a little of the torment she must have suffered, and a lot about the man she was married to.

McDonald's letter to Mrs Barrington revealed another crime, perhaps even more horrible than the murder I already knew about.

McDonald had written to the old woman to confess that he and Gibson had conspired to have Maura Barrington certified as insane. Gibson had signed a certificate which had the effect of ensuring that she could only be released from hospital with his consent, but it was McDonald who had forged a doctor's signature on the same document.

I had a vague memory that it was possible, before the reform of the Health Acts in the early seventies, for such things to happen. Obviously I would have to check out the technical details, but the extent of Gibson's abuse of innocent people was becoming clearer all the time.

And, I reflected, Mrs Barrington wasn't going to come well out of the story when it was written. Another £10,000 cheque had been enclosed with the letter to her. She had not only cashed it, but had gone on defending Gibson even after she knew the truth about him. McDonald knew her price, I thought.

I knew I had to get out of Kilkenny.

I had a story, and it was a story that would destroy the Prime Minister of the country. I knew the paper would publish it - the signed letter I had would authenticate McDonald's notes. The lawyers would want to be satisfied that the signature was McDonald's, but they would be able to establish that themselves - even though he was dead a long time, his signature would be accessible. They wouldn't have to look any further than the Land Registry Office. There might be a slight problem over the way I had come into possession of the material, but nothing could stop a story like this from being published.

The other thing I knew was that the Taoiseach would do anything to stop the letters, both McDonald's and Maura's, from seeing the light of day. It's not often I get paranoid, but the more I thought about it, the more certain I became that I was in a very dangerous situation. Everything I had learned of the Taoiseach persuaded me that he would stop at nothing to prevent my story appearing. That meant I had to make decisions.

First, I had to protect my documents. I decided to ask if I could use the hotel's photocopier to make copies. When I had them, I'd send them to myself at a number of different addresses.

Second, I had to go underground until the story was written. I'd never done that before, but I'd never had a story like this before. I decided not to tell anyone where I was, not my editor, not anyone, until the whole thing was typed and ready to be submitted. That would have the effect of protecting me - and everyone else in the management of the paper - from any pressure to try and stop the story.

But where was I to go? Where can you hide from the Prime Minister, if he's determined to find you? My own flat would be the first place anyone would look. I had a brother who lived in Meath with his wife and children - but my brother and his address were well-known in the paper. I'd easily be traced there.

I thought about it for a while. There was one place I felt reasonably sure I could go, one person I thought I could trust in this situation. I dialled the telephone number she had given me a couple of days ago.

Margaret Deane's flat was in the basement of an old Georgian house in Mount Pleasant Square in Ranelagh, about fifteen minute's walk from the centre of Dublin. It was an area which had been run down and neglected, but had become fashionable in the last few years, with many of the old houses turned into trendy homes by younger professionals.

That, it transpired, was what Margaret Deane was - not a couple, but a woman with a profession. She was a doctor, working in a geriatric wing in St. James' Hospital. She told me when I rang that she was due to go on duty in an hour's time. But she believed me when I said it was urgent that I see her as soon as I could get to Dublin, and she arranged for someone else to take her shift.

It was eleven by the time I got there, and I was exhausted. Before I had left the Springhill Hotel, I had made three copies of everything. The hotel's machine could hardly be described as new technology, but the copies, and the signature, were legible enough. I had posted them to myself at three different addresses, marking the envelopes "private and confidential" in each case - one to the paper, where I knew it would lie in a pigeonhole until I died or retired; one to my brother in Meath; and one care of Margaret Deane. The originals were in the bottom of my suitcase, wrapped in a dirty shirt.

I had decided to tell Margaret everything I had found. She listened without interrupting while I described my conversations with Gibson, Brendan O'Keeffe, and Mrs Barrington. It was only when I got out the documents, and gave them to her to read, that she reacted.

I don't know what I had been expecting, but I hadn't expected her to cry. She cried silently at first, and then with huge, racking sobs, much as her mother had done.

I didn't know what to do, so I sat on one side of her fireplace, while she sat crying on the other side. I wished, not for the first time, that I possessed whatever instinct it is that tells you how to handle these situations. If someone is lying to me, or trying to bully me, I generally know what to do, but if they are distressed, especially if it's someone I like (and I was acutely conscious that I liked Margaret Deane very much), I'm out of my depth.

Eventually her crying stopped. She stared for a long time into the fire, and then turned to me, with a smile that was incredibly sweet, even if it was still a little watery.

"I'm sorry, Jim," she said. "Every time you meet Mum and me, one of us breaks down on you."

"I'm the one who's sorry," I told her. "It must be a shock to see the whole thing written down like that."

"I don't really think that's why I was crying," Margaret said. "I think, to be honest, I was crying because of all the times I've doubted my Mum, all the times I began to wonder if maybe she had made the whole thing up. And I was crying for my Dad - I never missed him as much as when I read that notebook just now, even though I've known the story for years. Maybe most of all I was crying for Maura Barrington - how could anyone do what they did to her?"

"I don't know," I replied. "I've been having a lot of trouble figuring out what makes people like that tick. It doesn't seem possible that a bastard like that could rise to the top the way he has."

She looked at me again, fiercely this time.

"You can get him now Jim, can't you?" she asked. "You can make him pay - for the things we know he's done, and maybe some things we don't know about?"

It wasn't a question - it was a demand. This time I could give her the answer she wanted.

"We can get him," I said. "We can get them all - the Taoiseach and the policeman who helped him and anyone else who was involved. When I start this ball rolling, it will bury him, and anyone else who was mixed up in it."

It was my turn to ask something of her.

"I need your help," I told her. "Specifically, I need a place to stay while I write this story. It will probably only be for a couple of days, but I am not going to feel safe until the story is published, and that means I need somewhere where I'm not likely to be found."

"There's plenty of room here," she said. "I got this flat in the hope that I could persuade Mum to come and live with me. You wouldn't have to go out - anything you need I can get for you."

With that issue settled, we talked for a long time about what was likely to happen once the story was published. As we talked, I felt the tiredness lifting from me. I wanted to know a great deal about Margaret Deane. And so I asked her, and we talked about her childhood, and the sacrifices her mother had made, and the years she had spent in London after her training to gather experience. I even asked her why she hadn't married ("Why haven't you?" was the only answer I got).

At two in the morning, the tiredness returned, and Margaret showed me to the room she had decorated for her mother. Although pink isn't my colour, I had to admit that the room was a good deal cleaner and more comfortable than my own dingy flat. She said goodnight, and I fell into the bed.

I must have slept. I had no awareness of Margaret coming into the room, or of how much later that was. I only knew that she was there, sitting on the edge of my bed, touching my shoulder.

"I couldn't sleep, Jim," was all she said.

I held out my arms to her, and she came to me immediately. I don't know how long after that it was before we finally slept. All I can remember thinking was that I never wanted to sleep alone again.

CHAPTER 8

JULY 3rd - THE EIGHTH DAY

THE POLICEMAN

When most of the other Deputy and Assistant Commissioners of the Garda Siochana had moved to their new headquarters in Harcourt Street, in the centre of Dublin, Joe Stafford had stayed put.

There were two reasons for this. The first was a simple one - he loved the Phoenix Park, where the old Headquarters had been. Nothing gave him greater pleasure than being driven to the Park early in the morning before the city traffic had begun to build up. The deer were out then, often right at the side of the main road.

The second reason - the reason the Commissioner had consented to leaving Stafford behind - was operational. Joe Stafford was the Deputy Commissioner with overall responsibility for crime investigation. In that capacity he directed the operations of more than a thousand plain-clothes policemen, and under his direction, they had become an extremely successful force. But Joe Stafford also directed another force of men, a much smaller force, even though it took up a great deal more of his time than the Criminal Investigation Division. Those few people who knew anything about it called it P3. Those few did not include a great many people who should have known more. The present Taoiseach was aware of P3's existence, for instance, but the previous one was not. Neither was the previous Commissioner, and only one or two of the most senior Garda Officers had more than a vague idea of what it did. Which was, basically, whatever was required.

The thirty or so members of P3 were paid very high salaries - the lowest was paid the equivalent of a Chief Inspector. They did not ask questions, and questions were not asked of them. Because it was so little known, P3 was not a section that ordinary Gardai applied to join. Those who were in it were hand-picked by Stafford, and several of them had been recruited from outside the force.

P3's brief was State security, as defined by Deputy Commissioner Stafford and those he collaborated with. By this definition, it meant a number of things. No less than three of the senior lieutenants of Padraig Norton, the Chief of Staff of the IRA, were members of P3. But P3 also had a member on the Administrative Council of the Labour Party, and one of the drivers assigned to Charles Page's State car (he was entitled to one as a former Taoiseach) was also in P3.

They had access, through Stafford, to all of the resources available to the Gardai, although they did not always return the compliment. Anything on the huge computer in Harcourt Street was available to them, and in addition there were parts of that data bank which could be opened by using codes known only to Stafford and one or two others. They carried out their own bugging and surveillance operations, and their Chief could requisition the results of other Sections' more orthodox arrangements. As a result, there were few problems that Joe Stafford couldn't solve if he wanted to.

That was why Tim Hanrahan, who had only an inkling of the power wielded by the Deputy Commissioner, had been sent by the Taoiseach, who knew a great deal about that power, to ask Stafford to arrange a safe meeting with Padraig Norton.

Although Stafford wouldn't be prepared to admit it to Hanrahan, it had been a slightly ticklish problem. He had three high-level contacts in Norton's organisation, and as long as they knew where Norton was, so did Stafford. But Norton trusted nobody - even his most senior men did not know where he was and what he was doing all the time.

Stafford's three plants knew enough to have had Norton arrested on several occasions in the last few years, had Stafford chosen to give the order. The reason he had not done so was that he had never yet felt it necessary and was confident that he'd be able to catch the man as soon as he did. In addition to which catching Norton would only mean the emergence of a new leader, with new structures around him and a different sense of who was loyal and who wasn't. If that happened, Stafford would have to begin all over again, building up contacts within the organisation.

Putting Norton away would have prevented a number of murders, of course. But Stafford didn't believe in prevention of crime. It suited him considerably better to be dealing with a man he knew. And if Norton murdered a British soldier or two, what was that to Stafford? The sooner the British got out of the country the better - he believed he could run a much better operation in the North anyway than any of the British security people he had had to deal with.

So Stafford had decided he could not risk blowing the cover of any of his men by using them to get a message to Norton. In the end, he had decided to try a simpler route.

He had established that Norton, who seldom stayed long in the same place, was spending three nights in a guest house in Rathmines. Since his purpose there was to meet a number of members of the IRA Army Council, to discuss a reaction to the Kinnock/Gibson Agreement, he would find it impossible to trace any leak of his whereabouts.

It would have been a simple matter to have him arrested there, but since the Taoiseach had said he did not want to meet him under duress, Stafford had simply sent him a letter. It was delivered to the guesthouse by hand, addressed to Norton under the assumed name that Stafford knew he was using.

The letter invited him to ring "Pearse" for information of fundamental importance to "the armed struggle", and quoted a telephone number. The number led directly to a telephone on Deputy Commissioner Stafford's desk.

Two days elapsed before Norton rang the number. He would have had it checked out, of course. The Provisionals had more contacts in the telephone exchanges than any other organisation. It would be a simple matter for them to gain access to the computer in Andrews Street that contained the reverse directory, the one that identified the subscriber when the telephone number was punched in.

Stafford smiled to himself at the thought of how intrigued Norton would have been when the computer failed to turn up any listing for that number. That wouldn't have happened to him before - there were only five numbers in the whole country that had been kept off that computer. Stafford's was one, and he knew the other four. As far as he was aware, he was the only person who knew all five.

When the call came, Stafford was not very direct. He refused to identify himself as anything other than Pearse. For one thing, he couldn't be sure that it was Norton on the other end of the line. He reasoned that Norton might well have instructed one of his men to make the call, in case some trap was involved, and he wasn't going to identify himself as an equal to anyone other than Norton himself.

He told Norton (or the messenger, if it was a messenger) that a very important person wanted to meet him. This person would be prepared to meet in a location of Norton's choosing, or alternatively would be prepared to guarantee Norton safe passage to and from a meeting. The meeting would be to Norton's benefit.

"Who are you asking me to meet?" Norton asked.

"I cannot identify the name of the person at this stage," was all that Stafford would say. Norton had hung up, and Stafford was left wondering had he been too careful.

An hour later the phone had rung again.

"There will be no meeting unless the person is identified," the voice said.

"I'm sorry," Stafford answered. "All I can say is that it is a very important person."

This time Norton did not hang up. There was a silence on the other end of the line (if I was tracing this call I'd have him by now, Stafford thought). Eventually, Norton said,

"Is there a more important person?"

Stafford hesitated for only a moment. "No," he told him, "there isn't."

"O.K. then. Tell him to go to number 162, North Circular Road, tomorrow night, eleven o'clock. Ordinary car, and he's to be alone."

"No," said Stafford quickly. "He will be in an unmarked car, but he won't be alone. He will have one bodyguard, and you can have one. And the house is to be vacant for the whole day tomorrow. Nobody from either side is to go into it before 10 p.m."

There was another pause, and then, "Agreed," said Norton, and hung up.

Joe Stafford smiled to himself. Padraig Norton has style, he thought. When we're on the same side, we'll make them jump.

THE ADVISER

Stafford reported to Hanrahan, and Hanrahan confirmed with the Taoiseach that he would be at the meeting. But Hanrahan had had other problems that he needed Stafford's help with.

That morning the Taoiseach had been angrier than Hanrahan had ever seen him.

"Jesus Christ!" he had exploded when his chief of staff had brought the papers. "I've just had the Ambassador to Belgium on the phone, and you won't believe what that stupid bollocks Kelly has done. Our fucking Foreign Minister - our holier-than-thou asshole of a diplomat - has got himself filmed by a Belgian television crew!"

Hanrahan was puzzled.

"I don't follow..." he began.

"How could you?" interrupted the Taoiseach. "The stupid bastard was bollocks naked at the time. He had a hard-on. He was rolling on the floor with some tart who was as naked as he was. And the bastards in Belgian TV are going to show the film tonight! They've told our Ambassador as a matter of courtesy. Courtesy! They're going to make a laughing stock out of us all over Europe!"

Hanrahan was horrified.

"But surely they wouldn't be allowed?" he asked.

"Why the fuck not?" raged the Taoiseach. "They show fucking porno movies on their television all the time. Do you know what their fucking Prime Minister told me? That because the news is broadcast during prime time, they're going to put an X over Kelly's prick!"

Hanrahan didn't know whether to laugh or cry.

"You've been in touch with the Belgian Prime Minister then," he said.

"Yes," said the Taoiseach. "You know what that bastard did? He didn't quite remind me that I had told him to fuck himself during the Agricultural Policy negotiations last month. But I could hear it in his voice. He told me he'd look into the matter, and then he came back in an hour to say that he could not interfere with the freedom of the press, but that he had asked them, as a favour to the Irish people, to cover the Foreign Minister's private parts. The miserable bollocks!"

Hanrahan wasn't sure whether the last remark was a reference to the Belgian Prime Minister or to Sean Kelly's genitals. Just at the moment, he didn't care.

He knew that the film would never be shown on Irish television, but he was fairly sure they would report the incident. Even if they didn't, the British television channels were available in most parts of the country, and they would never be able to resist a glorious Irish joke like this. And the newspapers, both Irish and British, would have a field day. The full implications of Kelly's incredible stupidity were horrible to contemplate.

Hanrahan looked at the Taoiseach, who was pacing his office like an alsation on guard duty.

"We'll have to do what the Americans would do," the adviser said.

"What do you mean?" said Gibson, stopping to look at him.

"You know," said Hanrahan, "remember last year, when the Russians kicked out a few American spies. So the Americans kicked out twice as many Russians, and so on, until no one could remember who had discovered spies first."

"Have you gone raving mad?" the Taoiseach asked him. "There aren't any Belgian spies in Ireland. What the fuck would they spy on?"

"I know there aren't any spies here," Hanrahan said. "But there is a randy Ambassador ..."

The Taoiseach stopped pacing, suddenly.

"That's brilliant, Tim!" he said. "You mean the little fat guy - what's his name - De Vries, that's it. I've seen him myself, at State receptions, groping everything in sight."

He paused for a moment.

"Tim," he said, "when you're with Stafford, find out what he has on the Belgian Ambassador. Then we'll see if we can't do a trade with M. De Vries's sanctimonious Prime Minister."

Stafford did indeed have a file. He and Hanrahan had driven over to the computer complex in Harcourt Street. Stafford had his own access codes, and punched them in himself. Then he consulted a small black notebook, and punched in a series of numbers.

What came up on the screen was fascinating, and rapidly translated into print at another touch of the buttons by Stafford.

M. De Vries was more than randy - he had had a string of liaisons that covered three closely printed pages of text. Among the women whom he had squired around Dublin were some of the city's best-known society names. The houses he had slept in included the homes of a High Court judge (the file noted the judge's absence, on a trip to Brussels, of all places), and of a leading member of the Opposition, who, it was noted, was also away at the time.

To Hanrahan's amazement, the file also noted the restaurants and department stores in which the Ambassador maintained accounts, and the amounts of money involved.

But of most interest were three complaints that had been made against the Ambassador. On three separate occasions, two of them involving staff of hotels in which the Ambassador had stayed, and the other involving a girl who had been employed as a typist in the Embassy, M. De Vries had apparently conducted himself in such a manner as to inspire complaints of indecent behaviour to be made to the Gardai.

It had not been possible to proceed with any action against the Ambassador because of his diplomatic status. However, he had been visited on all three occasions by a Superintendent of the Gardai, and all three complaints had been withdrawn after the Ambassador had written profuse letters of apology to the girls involved. Only after it had happened a third time had any report been made to the Department of Foreign Affairs, and it appeared from the file that no further action had been taken by them.

Hanrahan did not stop to wonder why Stafford had maintained so detailed a file on the Ambassador - nor was it important to ask who else was covered by Stafford's little notebook. Not for the first time, the only thing that occurred to him was how useful Stafford was.

The Taoiseach chuckled as he read the file. When he was finished, he issued instructions that the Minister for Foreign Affairs was to be sent for urgently, and that he was to be given no inkling of why he was required.

When Sean Kelly arrived Hanrahan thought he had never seen him so haggard - he looked as if he hadn't slept for a week. The pompous manner was missing, and the normally florid complexion was pale.

Hanrahan was right - Sean Kelly was not a well man. Ever since the episode in Brussels he had been in an agony of fear. He had had to call the Embassy to get him a doctor, because he thought François had broken one of his ribs (luckily, nothing was broken, although the Belgian doctor had strapped him up as a precaution). No comment had been passed by the First Secretary who had come over from the Embassy, even about the enormous row he had witnessed in the lobby of the hotel between an enraged Frenchman and his very attractive, though still very dishevelled, wife. But Kelly was convinced that everyone knew what happened, and that it must by now be the talk of Brussels. He also had an uneasy feeling that the cameraman who had come into the room must have got some of the fight on videotape, even though he did not know just how good a cameraman he was.

That was why, when the call came to attend on the Taoiseach urgently, Kelly had almost fainted with fright. He was trembling now, not knowing how much about the incident was known in the Taoiseach's office. If it was known, Gibson would surely fire him without the slightest compunction. Then Ruth would find out - and Ruth was the only person in the world who frightened Sean Kelly more than Andrew Gibson.

But to his enormous relief, it was a smiling Andrew Gibson who greeted him.

"Sean," he said, "there's a minor diplomatic situation that I feel requires some urgent attention. I've more or less decided to deal with it myself, just to get it over and done with. But I wanted you to be involved, just so that I would have the assurance that I was doing the right thing."

The words almost tumbled out of the Foreign Minister's mouth.

"Certainly Taoiseach, anything at all I can do to help, I'm sure there's no situation that we cannot resolve between us, any resources I can put at your disposal ..."

The Taoiseach smiled. "I was sure I could count on you," he said. Then he pressed the intercom button on his desk, and told his Private Secretary that he wished to speak by telephone to the Belgian Prime Minister.

Kelly stiffened. What had the Belgian Prime Minister got to do with anything, unless ... But no, he thought, if Gibson had heard about his difficulty with Madeline and her husband, he wouldn't be sitting there smiling at me.

It took ten minutes for the call to come through. It was the longest ten minutes of Sean Kelly's life. While they were waiting, the Taoiseach made copious notes in the margins of a document he seemed to be terribly interested in. Hanrahan stood at one of the windows with his back to them, looking down at the students coming and going in the grounds of the University College School of Science, which was located next door to Government Buildings.

Kelly longed to ask the purpose of the phone call for which they were all waiting, but he hadn't the nerve. Instead he sat in one of the easy chairs in front of the Taoiseach's desk, his hands clasped between his knees. Small white flecks formed at the corners of his mouth, and his throat became painfully dry.

He jumped when the phone rang on the Taoiseach's desk.

"Henri," Gibson said (Kelly knew that Henri Van Escher, the Belgian Prime Minister, had fluent English), "it was so good of you to spare a moment of your time. I'm afraid a situation has developed with which I must acquaint you, even though I find it painful to do so."

There was a pause while Gibson listened to Van Escher.

"No, no, not at all. Where our earlier conversation is

concerned, you must do what you believe to be best. What I have to say to you now concerns a quite different issue. I am afraid that certain complaints have been made against your Ambassador to our country, and I am afraid I am going to have to authorise the taking of action on them."

Another pause. What is going on, Kelly wondered.

"Well, Henri, to be blunt, I wish I could spare you the details of these complaints, but my fear is that they will become a matter of public knowledge very quickly - possibly within a day or two, maybe less. It seems that our police - our Gardai, as we call the police force - have received three separate complaints which all involve indecent exposure, accompanied by suggestions of a most improper kind. You can see the position that places me in."

The Belgian Prime Minister evidently asked a question.

"Oh," said the Taoiseach, "the immediate decision I must make is to authorise the Ambassador's arrest. Normally I would not even be consulted - arrest would be immediate in the case of complaints of this sort - but I was in this instance, as it is so delicate. Of course, I haven't yet examined the implications of the Ambassador's immunity. It may well be that instead of seeing him tried, and perhaps imprisoned, I may be able to organise things so that he can leave the country to return home. But the publicity will be enormous, and that is why I felt obliged to consult you."

By now Hanrahan felt that the Taoiseach was laying things on a bit. He's obviously enjoying himself, he thought.

"Oh, of course," Gibson said eventually. "I wish it were possible to help" - he was now grinning broadly at the two men in the room - "but you must understand that to interfere in the course of justice would be a very difficult procedure. And the rights of three Irish citizens have been violated - I would find it very difficult to stand idly by in that situation ..."

From the wink that Gibson threw Hanrahan, it was obvious that the Taoiseach's Belgian counterpart had capitulated.

"Well," said the Taoiseach, after another silence, "I will of course do whatever I can to avert this dreadful situation. You can rely on my very best efforts. I would be more than hopeful that it will be possible to avoid any embarrassment. And let me say in return, Henri, how grateful I am to you for your offer of help" - and now, for the first time since the conversation began, the Taoiseach looked directly at Sean Kelly. "I can readily appreciate how unfortunate it would be if the Ambassador of your country were to find himself in the dock in our courts, and I know you realise how embarrassing it would be if our Foreign Minister were to appear naked on your television news!"

The Taoiseach hung up, and turned his gaze on Sean Kelly. Hanrahan chuckled. Sean Kelly thought he would wet himself.

Gibson stood up from his desk, and walked around it to where Kelly sat. His right hand shot out and grabbed the Foreign Minister's tie. He yanked Kelly half out of the chair, until the tie was so tight around his neck that the Foreign Minister's face began to bulge. Hanrahan was horrified. He had never seen the Taoiseach so violent.

"Do you know what I've just done?" Gibson screamed into Kelly's face. "I've just blackmailed the Prime Minister of another country into letting you off the hook. You worthless bag of shit!"

He released his hold on the tie, and Kelly slumped back into his chair, coughing and choking for breath. Then, to Hanrahan's amazement, Kelly began to cry, his head in his hands.

"Cut that out!" the Taoiseach barked. But Kelly couldn't stop. He had thought he was going to die, right there in the Taoiseach's office. He had never seen a look like the look that had been in Gibson's eyes a few moments before.

Gibson said it again - "Cut it out!" Then suddenly he kicked the Foreign Minister, hard, just below the knee. Kelly gave a little shriek of terror, and stopped.

There was a silence in the room, as both men collected themselves. Hanrahan didn't know what was going to happen next.

Gibson went back to his desk and sat down. He was breathing heavily, and there were two bright red spots high on his cheeks. Otherwise it was as if nothing at all had happened.

The same could not be said for Sean Kelly. He sat slumped forward in the armchair, nursing a leg that was going to be badly bruised. His tie was twisted around his neck, his shirt was pulled almost out of his trousers. His normally handsome face was almost purple. He didn't know how Gibson had found out, or even how much he knew. He only knew that his career was over. He would walk out of this office a nobody.

Then, to his astonishment, the Taoiseach smiled at him.

"Well, Sean," he said, "you appear to have made a bit of a fool of yourself. But I think we've managed to prevent any damage being done. So I suggest we put the whole business behind us and get on with winning this election. What do you say?"

Kelly didn't know what to say. He was staggered. How could the Taoiseach, after what had just happened, be prepared to let bygones be bygones? But even as he tried to find his voice, a new hope was beginning to form in his mind. Maybe the good life wasn't over after all - maybe there was a future. Gibson came round to his chair again, but this time patted him on the shoulder.

"Look," he said, "I think maybe you'd better use my private bathroom to freshen up before you leave. And take the lift down to the North Road. I imagine your car will be parked there."

Kelly almost felt honoured. Since Andrew Gibson had become Taoiseach, nobody else had ever used the small private lift that went directly from his office to the side road that ran between Government Buildings and Leinster House, where the Dail sat. And certainly nobody had ever used Gibson's private bathroom.

As Kelly almost backed out of the office through the side door that led to the private bathroom, Gibson stopped him.

"By the way, Sean," he said, "you'll be off to the States in a couple of days to attend that signing ceremony. Perhaps you might ask your people to send me over a copy of your speech before you go, just so I can have a look."

"Of course, Taoiseach, of course," blurted the Foreign Minister, "whatever you say, whatever you say."

"Oh, and one more thing, Sean," smiled the Taoiseach, "while you're over there, keep your trousers on, OK?"

Hanrahan was amazed. Like Kelly, he had assumed that the Foreign Minister would be fired.

"Why the change of heart, Taoiseach?" he asked, after Kelly had finally bowed his way out of the room.

"What change of heart?" said Gibson. "That stupid bollocks is finished. He will never serve in any Government of mine again. But he's not going to know that until the election is over. I didn't go to all those lengths to cover this thing up just to have him weeping all over the papers because I fired him. We still have a job for the stupid bastard to do, and I'll fire him out on his ear as soon as it's done."

"I see," Hanrahan said. "For a minute there I was a bit confused. To be honest with you, I'm not sure he deserves to be left in his job. Could you not have asked him to go on health grounds or something?"

Gibson looked at him.

"By the time I'm finished with Sean Kelly," he said, "he'll have plenty of health grounds. Nobody puts me through all that shit and walks away from it. What I want you to do is to get me two copies of that videotape."

"Why two?" Hanrahan asked.

"I want one for myself," Gibson replied, "and I want one for Sean Kelly's wife."

Later, Hanrahan would remember that as the moment he began to be afraid of Andrew Gibson.

CHAPTER 9

JULY 4th - THE NINTH DAY

THE TAOISEACH

When you climb the twenty steps through the front door of Government Buildings in Merrion Street in Dublin, you have to wait outside a glass door into the hall until the porter at the reception desk presses the electronic control. Visitors are usually not allowed in until the person they are here to see comes down to the hall to collect them.

The building, an impressive granite structure that is linked to some other Government Departments (particularly the Department of Finance) by means of an underground tunnel, houses the Taoiseach of the day and his Junior Ministers. It also accommodates a battery of usually very able civil servants who have two main functions.

The first is to ensure that the Taoiseach is adequately briefed on every issue that might come up, and equipped to deal with it. The second, particularly of those employed in the Cabinet Secretariat, is to service the Government as a whole - which is another way of saying that they run the arcane system of transferring paper backwards and forwards which is designed to prevent the Government from taking too many decisions, and especially decisions that the civil servants regard as hasty.

They have other responsibilities as well - some of the staff, for instance, are employed in the Attorney General's Office. Not only do they have the sensitive job of making sure that everything the Government does is legal, but they are also entrusted with the drafting of all legislation, and are privy to vast amounts of confidential information. And some of them look after areas which are the Taoiseach's responsibility only because no one else wants them, such as arts and culture.

Because the Taoiseach works here, security is as tight as it ever gets in Ireland, which is to say that it would take a determined terrorist about ten minutes to figure out how to get around it. Just inside the hall door there is a small glass cubicle in which sits an armed soldier. He is there to stop intruders from forcing an entry, but he has another task as well, that of saluting important personages who pass him by. In the normal run of things, these are the Taoiseach, the Tanaiste, or Deputy Prime Minister, and the Minister for Defence (he is not obliged to salute other Ministers).

Charles Page disliked being saluted, so the practice had gradually fallen into disuse, but Andrew Gibson was different. When he was appointed Taoiseach one of his first acts - virtually on his first day in office - was to order the removal of a soldier who was reading a newspaper as Gibson passed the cubicle.

Thereafter, not only was the soldier on duty expected to salute as the Taoiseach walked past, he was expected to be standing in the hall waiting to salute as the Taoiseach mounted the stairs. The soldiers, the porters in the reception area, and the guards outside had to develop an elaborate tick-tack system to let each other know when the Taoiseach's car came into view.

Today, since a Cabinet meeting was expected, they were well prepared for the arrival of the Taoiseach anyway. Not that it mattered, as it turned out. Gibson was lost in thought as he came into the building and almost ran up the great brass staircase to his office.

Private Jackson, who had presented his crispest salute, thought to himself that he might as well have been picking his nose for all the notice the Taoiseach took.

As soon as Gibson had reached his office, and was seated in front of the elaborate intercom system he had installed, he pressed the button which connected him directly to the Secretary to the Government. There were forty such buttons, each one directly connected to a senior civil servant. Each caused a peremptory buzz on the desk of the civil servant concerned. It was understood that when you heard that buzz, you dropped everything and went to the Taoiseach's office immediately, even though you might then be kept waiting for twenty minutes in the ante-room outside.

The only exception to this was Bob Holloway, whom Gibson had just buzzed. Holloway, like the others, came immediately, but unlike the others, he was never kept waiting.

Bob Holloway was a perfect civil servant. He had entered the Service as an Administrative Officer twenty-five years previously, armed with an impeccable degree in Political Science from University College Cork, and had risen inexorably to the position of Cabinet Secretary, which combined the responsibilities of Secretary to the Government with those of Head of the Civil Service. His discretion, his attention to detail, and his self-effacing nature were legendary among his colleagues. Today the Taoiseach wanted to discuss the Cabinet agenda with him.

"I'm only dealing with issues that are absolutely current, Bob," he said. "Some of them will be political, but I want you there anyway. Tell me what you think are the priorities."

Holloway outlined rapidly his two principal priorities. First, there had been a small but perceptible increase in the level of violence in the North, and particularly in the Border counties. In the days since the Agreement had been announced, there had been six murders and more than two dozen explosions. What was alarming about them was that it was obvious that in most cases the destruction was the work of Loyalist gangs, rather than the IRA. These Loyalist gangs had been quiescent for the last couple of years, and the general assumption was that they were incapable of mounting any counter-offensive.

Gibson wasn't unduly worried about Loyalist violence. He regarded it as a problem for Neil Kinnock, even though he always issued the usual ritualistic statements of horror and condemnation whenever anyone died. But he was seriously concerned about the possibility that the IRA would take it on themselves to sort out the Loyalists before the election was over. A massive increase in IRA violence now would turn people in the Republic off in their thousands, and if they turned their fear and anger on him, it was bound to affect his chances of winning the election.

He had already decided to deal with the possibility of IRA violence himself, which was why he had arranged to meet Padraig Norton later that night. He was fairly sure that he would be able to handle him, and maybe turn the IRA into a vehicle for winning, rather than losing, votes.

The second priority Holloway dealt with was the transport strike, which had now been going for three days, and was already beginning to bite hard. Management in the various transport companies was trying to keep a minimal service going, but passengers who had to wait more than an hour for a bus to get to work were more frustrated than if they knew there would be no buses at all. There had already been some ironic comment in the papers about the fact that the Foreign Minister, in order to get to Washington, would have to fly by military aircraft to London to connect with a British commercial flight. This move had been labelled as strike-breaking by Bill Browne, and he had vowed that they would seek the support of their British counterparts to ensure that the Minister was prevented from making his journey.

The Transport United Front, even though it had an effective strike going, did not have a great deal of public sympathy. But Gibson knew that the public would change its mind on the matter once things began to get really rough. That was always the way whenever there was a strike that caused inconvenience to the public at large. Before it started, politicians would be urged not to yield to pressure, but after it had been going a week, people were interested only in seeing the dispute fixed and the inconvenience to themselves ended. So even though there was no sign yet that the strike was affecting the Government's popularity, Gibson believed that there soon would be. So when the first Cabinet meeting of the election campaign began that morning, the focus of discussion was the transport strike. Two things were apparent from Joe Ryan's report to the meeting: first, Ryan had screwed up the negotiations badly by conceding that TUF had a case while refusing to do anything about it; and second, neither he nor his Department had any idea what to do next.

Gibson snorted in disgust as the report was read to the meeting, especially when Ryan hesitantly read out the paragraph which indicated that the dispute had become difficult to resolve when the Minister, "after consultation with the Taoiseach", had issued a statement declaring that there were issues of major principle involved. Typical of that weakling Ryan, the Taoiseach thought, to try to blame me for his cock-up.

It quickly became clear that if the Department of Transport had no ideas, nobody else had any either. Scally proposed bringing in the army, a step that had been taken before when the buses had gone on strike. But it was not a practical solution on this occasion. For one thing, the Army could probably only keep the buses running in Dublin and Cork. They could do nothing about provincial buses, and still less about cross-Channel ferries and airports. There just wasn't the manpower or expertise. Secondly, the possibility of Border violence meant that it might be necessary to increase Army patrols in that area.

Still, the seeds of an idea began to grow in Gibson's mind.

"What do we know about this Bill Browne character?" he wanted to know. "Is he open to persuasion?"

"No," Ryan said quickly, "he's very tough, and very single-minded. When he's gone this far, he's not going to back off."

"Why do you ask, Taoiseach?" asked Scally. "Had you something in mind?"

"I was thinking," said the Taoiseach drily, "that I might appeal to him in the national interest."

The Constitution of Ireland is an unusual document. The rights of free speech, free assembly, and free association are enshrined in its fifty Articles. The right to form Unions is explicitly recognised. But all of these can be set aside "in time of war" or if an armed rebellion exists. The Constitution even defines a "time of war". Essentially, it is whatever Parliament says it is.

The Irish Parliament declared that a state of emergency existed at the start of the Second World War in 1939. That involved both Houses of Parliament passing a resolution. It was mainly because of that resolution that the Second World War has always been known in Ireland as "the Emergency".

Because the Constitution is worded in a particular way, the State of Emergency declared in 1939 cannot end until Parliament passes another resolution declaring it over. Not only has that never happened, but Parliament actually renewed and confirmed the State of Emergency in the mid-70s. As far as its national legislators are declared, Ireland is still in the grip of a war in which it remained neutral.

Occasionally this absurdity is referred to by outside commentators, but it is almost never mentioned at home. That's because the condition suits the legislators. It has ensured that they have had the power to pass a range of legislation which would have been repugnant to the Constitution if a state of emergency did not exist. Generally speaking, legislators on all sides have comforted themselves that they did not abuse this power - the Acts that they passed were confined to dealing with the outbreak of violence that accompanied "the troubles" in Northern Ireland, and to combatting more modern phenomena like drug pushers and young vandals. Most legislators, in their hearts, were sure that the emergency provision would never be used against "legitimate" free speech, or "responsible" free assembly - so if the state of emergency was perfectly harmless as well as totally spurious, why should they bother to think about it?

Maybe because they didn't realise what a resourceful man Andrew Gibson was. Bill Browne had been asked to attend on the Taoiseach at three in the afternoon. By three-thirty the strike was effectively over. He had come alone, as requested. The Taoiseach had put it to him, fairly and squarely, that he was prepared to make a concession in order to end the strike.

"What have you in mind, Taoiseach?" Browne asked.

"Three per cent," said Gibson. "Effective immediately. That's to help you save face. And I'll set up the Committee that Joe Ryan promised you, to see if any more is warranted in due course."

"I don't think you understand, Taoiseach," Browne replied. "If I was to take an offer like that to my membership, it would make the situation worse. They're not in a mood to be insulted, and they know they can win this dispute."

"There's just two things I intend to say to that," the Taoiseach said, looking steadily at Browne. "First, nothing more will be offered. Second, your members will not win this strike."

Up to this point the negotiations had been conducted almost like a friendly chat. Browne had known before he came in that tactics that had frightened the wits out of Joe Ryan would not work on this man. He had decided to treat him in a businesslike, man-to-man way. But Gibson's cool arrogance, in a situation where Browne knew he had the upper hand, had got under his skin almost immediately.

"Why don't you tell my members that," he said, and stood up to leave.

"Sit down!" Gibson barked. "You'll leave when I tell you to."

Browne, startled at the sudden ferocity in the Taoiseach's

voice, sat down. He wasn't a man who frightened easily, but there was something about Gibson that unsettled him.

The Taoiseach continued.

"The offer I'm making you is a fair one," he said. "I'm offering you something now, with the possibility of something else in the future. Now I'm going to tell you the alternative. In 1941, the Parliament of this country passed legislation to enable the Government of the day to introduce forced conscription if necessary to deal with the emergency at that time. That legislation was never invoked. If this strike is still going on twenty-four hours from now, I'm going to invoke it. Within twenty-four hours more, every one of your members will be a member of the Army, and subject to military discipline. That means if they fail to turn up for work, they're absent without leave. If they refuse to carry out an order, they're insubordinate. And if they remain on strike, they're involved in a mutiny. And the appropriate penalty for such offences will be applied in each case."

"Now," he continued, "you might still win, but only after the greatest crisis this country has ever seen. Lives will be lost, on your side and mine. Because believe me, if there is a mutiny, I'm going to use all the force at my disposal to put it down. You and I, here in this room, have the power to decide whether we have a crisis of democracy or not. As I say, you might win - but if you lose, you're going to lose more than a little face. You'll be a criminal, and you'll be hunted down with any of your members who stay with you."

The Taoiseach stopped. Browne was staggered. He had had no idea that such an approach might be possible.

"You're bluffing!" he said eventually. "You wouldn't dare! We wouldn't even have to fight you in the streets, because we'd win in the courts. The Constitution guarantees us the right to act as a Union ..."

"Read your Constitution again, friend," the Taoiseach interrupted him. "Ever since the State of Emergency was declared in

1939, the rights of trade unions are subject to the vital interests of the State. Here - read this ..."

He pushed a sheet of paper across the table for Browne to read. It was headed "*Memorandum from the Attorney General*", and it advised the Taoiseach, in clipped legal wording, that the State of Emergency created under Article 28, Section 3, Sub-section 3 of the Constitution was still extant. Accordingly, the Attorney General had written, whatever the merits of invoking the Defence Forces Act of 1942 might be, it was both legally and technically possible to do so. No person or association involved could claim the protection of Article 40 of the Constitution (which set out the basic rights normally accorded to citizens) for as long as conscription was declared to be "in the vital interests of the State".

Although the document did not say so in so many words, Browne formed the impression that the Attorney General, in offering legal advice, was also trying to convey his disapproval of the course of action the Taoiseach had outlined. But the document was quite clear - Gibson had the power to do it.

"Think about it," the Taoiseach said. "You can get off the hook now, or you can impale us both on a bigger hook."

Browne thought about it. For perhaps the first time in his career, he didn't know what to say. He knew - and he suspected that the Taoiseach knew as well - that if he accepted the offer, the strike would crumble. Even though he would have to report to a Strike Committee, who were nominally in charge, his would be the final word. He had not spent the last few years building TUF into a united front without acquiring a lot of authority along the way.

The choice facing him now was stark - if he walked out of this room without accepting what the Taoiseach was offering, and if Gibson's threat was serious, he was going to lead his members into a confrontation beyond their worst nightmares. They couldn't hope to win a confrontation like that - they couldn't even hope to maintain a degree of unity in the face of a threat like that.

He looked at Gibson, whose large frame dominated even the

huge oak desk at which he was sitting. He had never been this close to the Taoiseach, and it was not hard to imagine how the man he was dealing with had developed such a reputation for inspiring both fear and respect. Gibson was a huge, handsome man, who radiated physical strength and power. And he was holding a lot of cards.

The Taoiseach was ignoring him, apparently writing busily on a sheet of paper in front of him. The large office, with its marble fireplace that had been recovered from a basement in the Board of Works building, its modern paintings counterpointing the antique conference table and chairs in the centre of the room, its deep pile carpet and comfortable armchairs surrounding a television and video in one corner, was quiet.

The two men sat there, one writing, the other in an agony of indecision. Was Gibson serious? Did he have the nerve to embark on a course whose outcome was totally unpredictable? It was possible, and Gibson must know it, that the conflict could engulf the whole election campaign, relegating every other issue to second place. It was possible that Gibson couldn't deliver on his threat, and that the threat could cost him the election. So it was possible, if Gibson knew all these things, that he was just bluffing.

But the more Browne thought about it, the more convinced he became that Gibson wasn't bluffing. He had the power, and Browne decided he had the nerve as well. Everything he knew about this man persuaded him that he was not used to being beaten, and that if his bluff was called, he'd go all the way. Increasingly, Browne felt like a man with a lot to lose.

After ten minutes of silence, ten minutes in which Gibson never glanced once at the man sitting opposite him, ten minutes in which Browne felt he had aged a year, the trade union official said, "I'll tell you what I think, Taoiseach. I think you're fascist enough to do what you say you will. So I'll take your offer, because I'm not going to see you put my members in jail in pursuit of their legitimate rights."

Gibson looked up at him, and smiled. It occurred to Browne that maybe had taken what he had said as a compliment. He pushed the sheet of paper on which he had been writing across the table to Browne. It said that the Taoiseach had fully considered the case made on behalf of TUF, and was impressed that they had a very strong case.

TUF, in return, had agreed that their case should be processed through more normal channels, and were prepared to suspend their dispute to enable a Commission of Enquiry to examine their case. In return for an immediate return to normal working, and as an earnest of its good intentions, the Government was prepared to implement an immediate increase of three per cent, together with a flat, once-off payment of £150 per member.

"£150?" Browne asked, raising his eyebrows at the Taoiseach. "You never mentioned that."

"Yes," said the Taoiseach. "Perhaps I should have. But that payment only applies if you take that press statement out of here. If you feel obliged to tell the press that I blackmailed you into accepting three per cent, then three per cent is all it is."

Browne grinned. He knew when he had met his match, and he had the grace to admit it.

"You're a bastard," he said, "but you have style!"

He took the sheet of paper, and left the office without looking back. Gibson sat back in the huge brown leather swivel chair. He let out a long, deep sigh.

He had called Browne's bluff. Gibson knew that if Browne's nerve had held, the trade union official would have won. There was no way that the Taoiseach would have been prepared to go through with his threat - Gibson never willingly entered into any course of action whose outcome he could not predict with reasonable confidence. But the bluff had worked, and he was fairly sure that he wouldn't be troubled by Bill Browne again.

He smiled to himself. Bill Browne hadn't been as tough as

he had expected. The mistake was to ask a coward like Joe Ryan to handle him. But would the Chief of Staff of the IRA be as easy?

The house on North Circular Road was a tall, red-brick one quite close to the Phoenix Park. It was one of several dozen in a long terrace, all of them bringing in a regular income as guest houses, offering bed, breakfast and evening meals at reasonable rates to businessmen. At weekends they made extra money offering accommodation to people who came up from the country to follow their county teams to matches in Croke Park.

Number 162 was for sale. Stafford's check had revealed that it had been owned by an old woman, a Mrs O'Brien, who had died a month before. It was her children, who obviously had no interest in the catering business, who had decided to sell it. The auctioneer handling the sale had been on Stafford's books for years as a Provisional IRA sympathiser - that was how they had access to the premises. It was easy to see how, if the back of the house only was used, it would not attract any attention: at night no light would be visible from the road.

Of course, Stafford had arranged to place the house under total surveillance within minutes of making the arrangement with Norton. He had two men positioned near the front of the house in a van normally used by the phone company, Telecom Eireann, and two at the back, in the upper window of a pub that overlooked the lane leading to the back gate of the house. From their vantage points, they were able to report that there was no activity within, and nobody coming or going all day.

What made Stafford feel comfortable about the rendezvous was the telephone call he had got during the day from Joe Maguire, who was one of his own men working within Norton's inner circle. Maguire had been chosen to act as Norton's bodyguard!

He was able to reassure Stafford that Norton was not planning any trap, and was nervous of being trapped himself. Although they weren't certain, they were fairly sure they were being asked to meet the Taoiseach. And Norton had ordered an investigation into how Stafford had found him.

Stafford intended to accompany the Taoiseach himself. He was going to carry a gun, a 9 mm Mauser automatic that he had bought in America - his favourite among his collection of handguns. He had tried it in the past, on the Special Branch practice range, with both ordinary cartridges and soft-nosed ones. The soft-nosed cartridges had a most satisfactorily destructive effect on the targets, and his gun was loaded with them tonight.

It had been agreed with the Taoiseach that he would come to Stafford's office in the Phoenix Park, which was close to the house, and that they would drive over there in an unmarked Special Branch car. While they waited for the men staking out the house to tell them that Norton and Maguire had arrived and gone in, Stafford briefed the Taoiseach with everything he had learned during the day. Gibson was suitably impressed.

As they had expected, the house appeared to be in total darkness when they arrived, promptly at eleven. Despite the hour, there was still a fair bit of traffic around, so the two men walked quickly up the short drive and climbed the steps to the front door, huddling in the porch until their knock was answered.

It was Maguire who opened the door. Silently he led them down a dark hall to the kitchen at the back of the house.

Gibson hadn't quite known what to expect. The recent photographs of Norton on file were either fuzzy, or taken from a considerable distance. Somehow, he was disappointed that the man was so slight, and looked so ordinary.

No introductions were necessary, and no surprise was expressed that it was the Taoiseach who had come. Gibson shook the hand that Norton held out.

They sat around the kitchen table. It contained a pot of coffee, milk, sugar, and four mugs.

"What do you want of me, Gibson?" Norton asked, in a voice that belied his reputation.

Like his frame, the voice was an ordinary, rather gentle one, with only a slight Northern accent. Gibson recognised the insult implicit in being addressed by his surname, but decided to ignore it. He knew that the IRA was committed to a policy of refusing to recognise the institutions of State, both North and South, for as long as the country was divided. He chose to regard Norton's ignoring his title as an expression of policy.

"I think you know what I want, Padraig," he replied, his tone as matter of fact as Norton's had been. "I want this Agreement given a chance. I want a truce from your organisation, and as many of the factions as you can influence. I want a public statement that arms are going to be laid down, so that the people can speak. And if they vote for the Agreement, I want your war ended, and open negotiations on terms."

"Is that all?" smiled Norton. "Is that all you want? You want us to agree that British imperial interests can be replaced on this island by American military influence? You want us to agree that we should regain our sovereignty, only to sell it again immediately? I don't think you understand us too well, Mr Gibson. That's not what we are about. I don't see how this quisling agreement of yours is going to bring a socialist republican state forward one inch. And that's my aim and objective - it's certainly not part of any plan of mine to be providing aid and comfort to any capitalist collaborators with NATO."

"And how long have you been pursuing this objective of yours?" the Taoiseach asked him.

"What do you mean?" said Norton. "As you know very well, I've been pursuing that objective all my adult life."

"You haven't got very far, have you?" asked the Taoiseach, as casually as possible.

It was a calculated remark. Gibson wanted to see how easily the Provos' Chief of Staff would be annoyed. He needed to know what it would take to make Norton walk away from the table. That would be a good indicator of how badly he wanted to stay there.

The remark caused a slight frown, no more, to crease Norton's forehead. Then he smiled.

"I'm a young man yet," he said. "I've got lots of time."

"Only if we don't catch you first," Gibson said. They all joined in the laughter, and Gibson knew that Norton was not in a hurry to get away from the table.

For the next two hours, they talked about Norton's objectives, while Maguire and Stafford refilled the coffee pot. Gibson found that he liked this man - he had a passion and a conviction that took a while to draw out, but when it came, it exceeded anything that Gibson was used to in the politicians around him. We have a lot in common, Gibson thought. This isn't one of your mediocre time-servers. This man believes in what he's doing, and he's prepared to take risks for it, even the ultimate risk of putting his own life on the line.

Gibson's plan was a simple one. He wanted to persuade Norton that they had shared objectives, and that Norton could trust him. That would be necessary if the next phase of the discussion was to work.

He had known before he went in that neither Norton nor the IRA would be likely to be impressed with the principles that underlay the Agreement. And he had known too that they would oppose its essential NATO elements. Despite all the money that the IRA had got from their American sympathisers and supporters over the years, the organisation was as fiercely anti-American as it was anti-British.

And so for two hours he worked on gaining a measure of trust from the man sitting across the kitchen table. He told him that he didn't expect Norton to share his politics; that he knew Norton regarded himself as a socialist, and that he respected him for the conviction with which he practiced his beliefs. He applied all of his considerable skill to the task of projecting sincerity. And still Norton did not leave the table.

At one o'clock in the morning, Gibson said: "Look, Padraig, I know there are elements of this agreement that are unacceptable to you in principle. I knew that before I asked you to meet me. But have you considered that there may be good tactical reasons why you should give it a chance?"

"How do you mean?" Norton asked him.

"Well," Gibson replied, "we may not know as much about your organisation as we'd like to, but we do know some things. We know that you're not beaten, and not likely to be in the near future. But we also know that you've had a lot of set-backs in the last couple of years. You've lost men, both killed and captured. A lot of the American money has dried up. The supplies of arms that used to come from the middle-East are much more difficult to get now. You're threatened, and so is your money, from a number of directions. I think you need to buy some time. I think you know people who need to be cleaned out of the organisation, and people who need to be got back on the streets - out of prison."

Norton looked at him for a while, before asking, "Are you suggesting an amnesty?"

"Would it help?" asked the Taoiseach. "Would it make a difference to your capacity to win through to your objectives?"

Norton didn't answer. The kitchen became silent, except for the dripping of a tap in the corner. After a few minutes, it was Norton who got up to twist it tightly off. Then he turned to the Taoiseach.

"What else?" he said. "What else are you offering?"

"I'm not necessarily offering anything else," Gibson told him. "You know what I want - and I'm interested in hearing what you want."

"What if we ask for too high a price?"

Gibson smiled. Once you start wondering about the price, you're past the issue of principle, he thought.

"I think you'll find I'm prepared to pay for what I want," he said.

Norton stood up suddenly.

"Will ye wait here?" he asked.

"How long?"

"Until I come back," Norton said. "And you must make no effort to contact anyone while I'm gone."

He was asking them to agree to be his prisoners. If the Taoiseach had asked Stafford's advice, the answer would have been no. But Gibson didn't ask Stafford. Instead he told Norton that he was prepared to wait for three hours.

After Norton and Maguire had left, and before the Taoiseach could say anything, Stafford put a finger to his lips. Then, while Gibson watched in silence, he began to search the kitchen. It didn't take long to find the bug: a small round metal object, attached to the inside of a drawer. As Stafford explained later to the Taoiseach, you could tell from its size that it wouldn't transmit very far, which meant that the listeners were probably in a nearby house - maybe even the same house, although Stafford was fairly sure that his surveillance would have spotted them going in.

He was equally certain that it was Norton's own people who had planted the bug. For two reasons - first, for security; if any attempt were made to take Norton a prisoner, they could be on the scene very quickly. And second, the transmission was undoubtedly being recorded - they would have figured that it was highly unlikely that Gibson would agree to minutes being taken. This way, whatever they wanted in writing, they had.

There was of course a possibility that someone else had planted the bug. But Stafford thought that unlikely. He knew that, like him, British Military Intelligence had agents within Norton's organisation - they had exchanged information often enough in the past to make him sure of that. But the quality of their information had always convinced him that the MI5 people were not as well placed as he was. And they would need to be very well-placed to have learned the location for this meeting in time to bug it without being spotted.

No, on balance it was far more likely that either Norton or Maguire had carried the bug in with them. Gibson wasn't disturbed by the discovery. He had not expected to be taken on trust by the Provisionals. He knew what he was prepared to put in writing - and what he couldn't. But he also knew that if he was going to make an agreement with the Provos, he was going to have to go pretty far out on a limb.

Besides, knowing that the bug was there gave him one advantage. The fact that he was going to be listened to for the next three hours, without the listeners knowing that the bug had been discovered, gave him an opportunity to display his trustworthiness.

So they carried out Norton's instructions. They waited in the kitchen, chatting about the meeting and how it had gone. Gibson took the opportunity to tell Stafford, with much gesticulating in the direction of the bug so Stafford would know for whose benefit the remark was being made, that he believed he could trust Norton, and that the most important thing was that any agreement made must be fully honoured on both sides.

It was a long wait, so long that Gibson began to be seriously worried. He knew that he would have to follow through on his statement that he would wait three hours. If he waited longer, he would be betraying too much anxiety to make an agreement at any price.

Fortunately, just as the time was almost up, and as Gibson and Stafford were getting ready to leave, Norton and Maguire returned.

"I'm sorry for keeping ye," Norton grinned. "Sometimes, in democratic organisations like yours and mine, it takes a bit longer to get things done."

Another man might have objected to Norton's description of the IRA as democratic, but Gibson was amused by it. Besides, he knew what Norton meant. How often had he felt the same frustration himself at having to consult people within the Party, especially when he was only looking for vindication for a decision he had already made?

Norton gave them a sheet of paper.

It contained the Provisional IRA's terms for a ceasefire, and it was in two parts. The first set out what the Provos wanted, the second what they were prepared to do in return. As Gibson read the document aloud, he realised that Norton was even cleverer than he had given him credit for. The demands were high, but not so high that they could not be met. They had been pitched at just the right level to test him.

Firstly, they wanted a full amnesty for all prisoners in Irish jails who had been convicted of membership of the IRA, and those who had been convicted of possession of firearms. Secondly, in the case of about thirty named individuals who had been convicted of more serious crimes, they wanted sentences commuted so that none of them would still be in jail in eighteen months' time.

Thirdly, they wanted one million pounds in cash, to be paid into a nominated account. And fourthly, they wanted Gibson's assurance that on the night of the 10th of July, no ships or boats in Irish waters would be molested or interfered with by the Irish navy.

In return, if these demands were met, the Provisional IRA would declare the following day that they were calling a ceasefire, with immediate effect, for six months, in order "to evaluate the impact of the Anglo-Irish Treaty on the achievement of the goal of unity". During that period they would initiate no military actions, although they reserved their right to respond to any provocative actions from any other source. They would support political and democratic campaigns against any diminution of Irish sovereignty that might arise from the Treaty.

It was a sophisticated set of demands.

They were not asking him to release the more murderous of their members immediately, because they knew as well as he did that such a move would be very unpopular, and could be counter-productive. The amount of money they were looking for, although substantial, was not so big that it could not be hidden (and Gibson already knew the budgetary sub-head that he could use to hide the money).

The fourth demand, although couched in somewhat mysterious language, was also easy to understand. Obviously the Provos had a big shipment coming in on the 10th of July, probably of arms, and probably from America. Considering the small coasters that they had used for that kind of shipment before, it might already be on the high seas.

More than one of their arms shipments had been intercepted in the past, and they had obviously decided that it was worth their while using this opportunity to see that this one got home safely. They knew that it would be easy enough for the Government to organise a blind eye in relation to activity of that sort.

One other thing was clear to Gibson. What was on offer here was not a truce, not an end to the killing and the maiming of the last twenty years. They were offering him a chance to get on with winning his election, while they took the time to regroup and re-equip themselves. Then the killing would start again, with weapons that he had paid for, and all but supplied.

Of course, he reasoned, after his re-election he would be in a good position to declare war on them if he found it necessary to do so. He did not see any reason why the men he was being asked to release could not be recaptured and put back in Portlaoise Prison once he was back in office.

And besides, the only bit of all this that would become public knowledge before the election - provided he held his nerve and did not renege - was the ceasefire. That would give a tremendous boost to the Agreement, and virtually guarantee his victory.

"There is one problem," Norton said. "We've had a cell under deep cover in Britain for nearly two years now. There are three people, and they are on a job that is one of the biggest we've ever carried out. The British establishment will be shaken to its roots when it happens, and it could happen any day."

Gibson was aghast.

"Can you not stop it?" he asked.

"No," Norton said. "We put them under the deepest cover possible - we cannot even make contact with them. We're trying to overcome the problem in other ways, but I had to warn you that someone could be killed ..."

"Stop!" Gibson barked. "I don't want to know who the target is. Will it be traceable to you when it happens?"

"The assumption will be made, of course - but we won't be claiming responsibility on this occasion."

"Then the less I know about it the better," said Gibson crisply. "I'm willing to accept your terms. But I cannot implement the amnesty and commutations until after the election. Neither can I organise the money until then. I will look after your shipment next week. But there is a condition: no publicity about my side of this agreement. Your announcement of a ceasefire must be kept simple - it is not necessary to mention the time limit in that announcement. The whole thing should look like a spontaneous decision by you. As far as I'm concerned, this meeting has never happened."

For a moment he thought he had gone too far. Norton stood up and leaned over the table to look directly down at him.

"Then why should I trust you?" he wanted to know. "What's to stop you reneging on everything you've just agreed to if I go along with all that?"

Gibson returned his stare, coldly.

"You have bugged this whole meeting," he said. "And I have no doubt that you recorded everything, including your own attempt to make me an accessory to an assassination plot. For as long as I co-operate with you, it's not in your interest to publish that tape. The moment I renege, you can destroy me by broadcasting what I have agreed to every journalist in Ireland."

Norton laughed.

"You've got a deal," he said.

Daylight was already breaking over the city as they made their way back to Mount Merrion. Stafford was driving.

"We've travelled a long way together, Joe," said Gibson, after they had driven in silence for a while. "But I reckon we could go a lot further after this night's work. If the Provo ceasefire doesn't copper-fasten the election, nothing will. And once this election is over, I'm putting you in charge. I think it's time the Commissioner retired!"

Stafford glanced over at the Taoiseach, who had reclined the front passenger seat. They exchanged a grin.

"And the first job you'll have to do," said Gibson, "is to get me back that tape."

CHAPTER 10

JULY 5th - THE TENTH DAY

THE REPORTER

There were two stories to be written: a news story, which would go on the front page of the newspaper, and in which the whole history of Gibson's crimes had to be compressed into about eighteen short paragraphs. And a feature piece, which would occupy (with photographs, I imagined) perhaps two full pages in the centre of the paper. This would be the piece that would stand on the record, so it had to be written carefully and in considerable detail. I had started with the feature piece.

My first three paragraphs read like this:

Christopher McDonald died alone. For most of his life he had been a wealthy and successful lawyer, with a partner who was destined to hold the highest public office in the land. But now all he had left was two days of intense pain, before he shut his eyes for the last time. In that two days, he had a confession to make.

Because Chris McDonald was an accessory to murder. He had watched while his partner had beaten a man to death. He had helped that same partner to have his wife committed, fraudulently, to a mental institution, where she had taken her own life. And now, unless he confessed, he was going to die with these crimes on his conscience.

And so he confessed, in writing, to his part in two murders. His confession has never come to light until now, because it was covered up by a policeman. The man who suppressed Chris McDonald's deathbed confession was Joe Stafford, who is now Deputy Commissioner of the Garda Siochana. And the man who stands accused by his partner of two terrible crimes is the Taoiseach, Andrew Gibson.

It took me a long time to get those first three paragraphs right. There were a dozen different ways I could have written them, but the more I thought about it, the more it seemed to me that Christopher McDonald was the character around whom this story had to be written. I remembered the feeling I had had when I read his notebook, just the day before, in my hotel room in Kilkenny. I decided to try to recapture that feeling in my story.

The news story, of course, would be written in a totally different, sparer, style, concentrating on the facts, and putting Gibson's name into the first paragraph. But I was determined that the full horror of what Gibson had done would be felt by everyone who read the inside story. It had never taken me two days to write a story before, especially one that I already had in my head. But it's hard to write when all you want to do is to make love to a woman you've only just met, and harder still when she wants to make love to you.

We made love on Tuesday morning when we woke up. I don't know whether we made love for hours or whether we woke up late but it was lunch-time when I eventually looked at my watch. Margaret went down to the delicatessen in Ranelagh to buy vegetable soup and sausage rolls while I had a shower.

And when she came back with the food we made love again. It's amazing how good cold vegetable soup can taste.

I'd never known anyone like Margaret Deane before. Oh sure, I've met a lot of women, even some who thought being a reporter was glamorous. And maybe that was part of the appeal for Margaret as well. Not only was I a reporter, but I was the reporter who was going to deliver the justice that she and her mother thought would never come. Even now, I'm fairly sure that was what she fell in love with at first.

I wasn't complaining. Margaret grew on me very fast. She had a quality, in the way she moved around the flat, in the way she talked about her patients, that made me feel on that first day that I had known her all my life. I remember thinking, before Tuesday was over, that I couldn't conceive of moving back to my own flat in Blackrock. And I'd never felt that way before - it wasn't much of a place, but I'd always felt comfortable surrounded by piles of old books and newspapers. And eating late at night out of the Chinese takeaway in the Main Street had never bothered me. Now, even the thought of going back to that - essentially, of being on my own again - seemed intolerable.

That was what made me slow to start the story, I think: knowing that when I had it written, and when I handed it over to my editor, that Margaret would have a choice again. She was committed now - but I wasn't sure what she was committed to. Was it me, or was it my story?

Anyway, between one thing and another, it was late on Tuesday night when I sat down at the table in Margaret's flat. I had the portable typewriter that travelled everywhere with me, and some paper, and I had spread out the originals of the McDonald letters on the table.

I didn't wake up until eleven on Wednesday. There was a note beside the bed from Margaret, to tell me she had left for work at eight and would be back by four o'clock. There were three postscripts with the note. The first said I wasn't to worry - she wouldn't be mentioning the fact that I was in her flat to anyone. The second said that she had read the story in my typewriter, and that it was brilliant. The third was only three words: "I love you".

When I had dressed and had eaten some brown bread, I made an effort to tidy up the flat. Somehow, when Margaret wasn't there, it seemed just an ordinary flat. Although there were lots of touches of her around, it needed her presence to give it life.

I had only begun to work on the news story when she came back. She was calling me as she came in. Even before she had her coat fully off, she somehow managed to get her arms around me. When we disentangled, a few minutes later, I asked, "What was that in aid of?"

"I just missed you, Jim," she said. "I thought about you all day, and I couldn't wait to get home. When I wrote you that note this morning, I had an idea that you mightn't be here when I got back, and I had butterflies in my stomach just at the thought of it."

"Well, I'm here," I said, "and I intend to stay for a while."

As I spoke, she was unbuttoning her blouse.

"I hope so," she said.

I worked late again that night. Margaret had agreed with me that the manner in which Gibson ended up as sole owner of Leinster Resources seemed suspicious. She didn't regard it as a particularly important element of the story, until I explained that what I was anxious to do was to pile up the questions that Gibson needed to answer. She had agreed to contact her own solicitor and ask him some hypothetical questions.

His answers were definitive enough for me. If a man who is part owner of an enterprise dies intestate, his share must lie there, accumulating profits or losses, until next of kin is found to claim it. The only circumstance in which things might be different would arise if there was a contract between the various owners of the business which specified that on the death of one partner, his shares would revert to the others. Such a contract would be unusual, and it could be open to challenge by the next of kin of the dead man.

O'Keeffe had never mentioned any contract to me, so I was able to say in my piece that serious questions arose about the way in which Gibson had acquired ownership of the whole business, and about the part his existing legal partner might have played in facilitating that ownership. The more I thought about it, the more certain I was that O'Keeffe must have known that there was something odd about the whole affair. It had struck me as strange that he had not made a thorough search of McDonald's iron chest - was it possible that, knowing there were no obvious next of kin, he didn't want to find a will? I finished writing the whole thing at about one o'clock on Thursday morning. As I re-read it I realised, for the first time, that it was going to be very difficult for anyone to believe it. After all, I had had difficulty coming to terms with it myself, and I felt I knew all of the people involved very well. How was someone reading it for the first time going to react?

As it happened, when I rang Vincent O'Byrne early on Thursday morning, he was already reacting to the fact that he hadn't heard from me for four days.

"Where the fuck have you been?" was his opening remark.

I knew he'd be a bit upset. After all, I was out on expenses, and hadn't filed anything, or even rung the office, since Saturday. Even though he had given me permission to concentrate on the "profile" of Gibson, he would feel entitled to be getting regular progress reports. We worked for a daily paper, after all, and didn't have the luxury that our Sunday colleagues had of only popping in once a week. I understood how he felt.

"I have a story, Vincent," I told him. "It's the biggest story I've ever had. I'm afraid of it myself. That's why I've been - well, hiding. I think you'll see why when you read it."

There was a silence on the other end of the line. I knew he was impressed. It wouldn't be my normal form to make exaggerated claims for my stories. When he spoke again, the irritation had gone out of his voice.

"When are you coming in?" he asked me.

"I don't want to come in," I said. "I want you to meet me in town. I don't want anyone else to see this until you do."

"Jesus!" he exploded. "What have you got - the start of World War Three?"

"Just trust me," I said. "I've never let you down before, and I know what I'm doing. Meet me in the bar of the Dergvale Hotel at twelve o'clock, and I'll show you what I've got."

There was a slight pause.

"O.K.," he said, "but it better be fucking good."

I don't think you'll be too disappointed, I thought as he hung up.

The Dergvale Hotel in Gardiner Place is a small, clean, commercial hotel. That is to say, its dining room is used mostly for breakfast, and its bar doesn't come alive until after dinner. It was near enough to the paper so that Vincent could walk up there easily enough, but far enough away so that nobody else from the paper was likely to disturb us.

Margaret had gone down into Ranelagh earlier, to one of the photocopying places that are springing up all over the city, and had made good copies of everything I had written, and better copies of the documents than I had been able to make in Kilkenny. She had put the originals in an envelope, registered it, and posted it to me, care of Poste Restante, in the General Post Office in O'Connell Street. That way, when I needed the originals - and I didn't even want to see them until the edition of the paper in which they were to appear was ready to be set - they would be easily available, because the Post Office was fairly close to the paper's offices.

Vincent was waiting for me in the small bar at the back of the Dergvale. He was disgruntled, as he usually was when he was dragged out of the office. I often thought that he must have hated being a reporter - sitting at a desk suited him much better than the legwork that goes with my job.

Still, he had already ordered me a Paddy and water - my first in several days, I realised with a start.

It tasted good, and I sipped it slowly while he ripped open the envelope I had handed him. He read the first few paragraphs, and then looked at me. He had gone pale.

"Jesus, Jim," was all he said.

"Read on," I told him.

It took him a good twenty minutes to finish reading the story. Halfway through, I got up to refill the drinks, but he didn't touch his.

When he was finished, he put the paper down beside him. He seemed to be having difficulty figuring out what to say.

"Christ," he said eventually, "Christ Almighty."

"I know what you mean," I said. "That was my own reaction when I found the stuff."

"It doesn't say here where you did find it," he said. It was a question.

"I didn't put it in because I didn't think it was important," I said. I was already regretting using the word "found".

"Of course it's important," he said. "If this story is true, the only way the people who are implicated can help themselves is by trying to discredit you. If you did anything illegal ..."

"Of course I didn't!" I said (at least I was fairly sure that my actions hadn't broken any law, even if I had conned both O'Keeffe and old Mrs Barrington. By the time they discovered they'd been conned, it would be too late.) "Let's just say I got them from a source, and it's a source I have to protect."

He picked up the papers again, and looked at them.

"Jesus Jim," he said. "That's a hell of a story. It'll destroy Gibson, and Stafford, and it'll blow the whole election wide open. It might even destroy the Agreement, if Neil Kinnock decides he'd better put distance between himself and Gibson. And it'll certainly destroy us if it's not right."

"It's right," I said. "The notebook was McDonald's own - our legal people will be able to stand it up as genuine. There's a dozen places where it would be easy to find copies of McDonald's handwriting, no matter how long he's dead."

He sat there, biting his lip, saying nothing.

"As to the rest of it," I went on, "I've thought of all that. Of course there'll be repercussions when we publish, but now that we have the story, we don't have a choice. We can't stand by and let a murderer be elected Taoiseach."

That seemed to make up O'Byrne's mind.

"We have to move fast, Jim," he said. "This story will have to go to the legal people immediately, and management will have to see it. You'd better come down with me to the paper ..."

"I'm not sure about that," I said. "I tend to feel that I should stay out of the way until the story is ready to go."

He thought about it.

"O.K." he said. "I'll give you a ring later on."

"I'll ring you," I told him. "I'm staying with a friend, and I haven't got the number with me."

We left the hotel, he to go to the paper and me back to the flat. It was quite a while before I was able to piece together what happened after he left me.

THE EDITOR

Vincent O'Byrne's mind was in a turmoil as he walked back down to Abbey Street. He'd been a reporter for twenty years, and in all that time he'd never seen a story like this one. It was bigger than Watergate, bigger than Kennedy's assassination. It would make Flynn, himself, and the paper famous around the world.

And it would destroy a man who would never forgive him.

Vincent O'Byrne knew Andrew Gibson. Sixteen years earlier, when he had been a young, newly-married, and penniless parliamentary reporter, Andrew Gibson was the young politician who had befriended him. O'Byrne had built many a story, in those early days, out of tit-bits that Gibson had fed him from Parliamentary Party meetings and from behind various other closed doors. And of course, O'Byrne had seen to it that everything Gibson said and did was faithfully reported.

They were never friends, in the normal sense of the word. They simply had a mutual interest in cultivating each other. But Gibson never threw a party that Vincent wasn't invited to, and his parties were the best in Dublin. It was at one of them that he had met Finola Robinson, who was soon to become Andrew Gibson's wife. She had taken the young reporter under her wing, introducing him to all her girlfriends, and generally ensuring that he had a good time. For a young man, without the money to make his own entertainment, and with a heavily pregnant wife at home, it was a heady period. His lateness in coming home, even the smell of drink on his breath, could all be excused as being in the line of duty. Even the occasional nights when he didn't come home at all didn't cause too many rows. His wife Mary never found out about Jackie.

Jackie was a model, like Finola. Vincent's affair with her had started in the guest bedroom of Gibson's house, at one of Gibson's parties. As far as Jackie was concerned, it was all pretty casual. She knew Vincent was already married, and that an affair with him wouldn't last. He was a friend of Andrew's and Finola's, and that made him all right.

Until she got pregnant.

There was no question of her having the baby, of course. Her career was already beginning to blossom - she had landed a number of jobs which had taken her backwards and forwards to London, and the future looked too bright to allow a baby into the picture.

No, there was only one course open - Vincent would have to organise an abortion. But that was out of the question for O'Byrne. The cost, even in those days, was out of his reach. In his panic, he turned to Gibson, and the rich young politician took the matter in hand. Not only did he pay for the abortion, but Finola had travelled over to London to see Jackie through it, and Gibson gave Jackie a cheque for £1,000 when she got back, "to help her get over it".

Vincent and Jackie did not see each other again - Jackie went on to make quite a name for herself in London. And Gibson waved away all of O'Byrne's offers of thanks and repayment - so convincingly that even as money became easier, repaying that debt was something Vincent O'Byrne never got round to.

He saw less and less of Gibson as his own career prospered. Their intimacy - if it could be called that - had lasted only a few months, and it was years since Vincent had given it more than a passing thought. Not only had he never been asked to repay the money, but no journalistic favours had ever been hinted at. Gibson had always had a fair shake from the paper, naturally - Vincent did not need to be asked to know that he owed the man that much.

But however infrequently Vincent O'Byrne thought of the secret he shared with the Taoiseach, he never fooled himself about its significance. He knew that if it ever came out that his mistress had secured an abortion that had been paid for by a politician, both he and the politician would be ruined. He could not expect to hold his job - still less his marriage. And in Ireland the politician who financed an abortion, even if his motives were totally philanthropic, would disappear without trace. But there was no reason why the secret would ever come out - only four people knew it, and it was in none of their interests that it should ever be made public.

Until now.

Now, O'Byrne had been put in a position where he had it in his power to destroy the man with whom he shared his secret. And he knew that Andrew Gibson was not a man to go down alone. He didn't know how, or when, it would happen - but he knew that Gibson would bring him down with him.

He couldn't let it happen - he knew that. And that was why, as soon as he got back to his office in Abbey Street, he picked up the phone and dialled Tim Hanrahan's direct line.

"It's absurd, Vincent!" Hanrahan said. "It's crazy! The boss would never be involved in anything like this. And Stafford - I know he's a rough diamond, but he's bloody good at his job. He's no criminal!"

They were sitting in the lobby of the Burlington Hotel. It was the venue Hanrahan had suggested as soon as O'Byrne had told him he needed to see him urgently. He didn't know O'Byrne well, and certainly didn't know his background, but he knew that O'Byrne was the Editor of a major newspaper, and if so senior a journalist wanted to see him urgently, he wouldn't be doing his job if he kept him waiting.

He was appalled at what he had just read. He didn't believe a word of it. He knew Gibson better than almost anyone else, knew his hot temper especially, but he didn't believe his boss was capable of the things described here. Especially in relation to Maura Barrington. Hanrahan had known her slightly, just as he had known McDonald slightly.

He had been shocked when she had done away with herself, and he remembered what had always seemed to him to be Gibson's genuine grief at her death. It had been aggravated, of course, by the fact that he had had to resign over his wife's suicide, but he had always seemed to be sincerely upset by what had happened to Maura as well.

But even if it wasn't true, the damage it would do if it was published! Everything would be over, everything he and Gibson had worked for. They would never live down a story like this, even if they could prove that every word of it was a lie. The only comfort was that O'Byrne had already told him that he didn't want to publish the story, that he regarded it as something he was stuck with. It had been brought to him by one of his most senior reporters, Jim Flynn, a man with a solid reputation for getting his facts right. And in journalistic terms, the story stood up.

Hanrahan didn't know why, in that case, O'Byrne was reluctant to publish the story. He imagined most editors would be slavering over an item like this. But he didn't really care why O'Byrne was reluctant. He was just grateful that he was. He remembered bitterly that it was only a few days since they had entertained that bastard Flynn to dinner - in the Taoiseach's own house, of all places. I'll bet that prick was planning to screw us even then, he thought.

"Look, Vincent," he said, "I'll lay money that this whole story is a distortion of something perfectly innocent. What I'd like to do is to go to the Taoiseach immediately, and ask him about it. In the meantime, I'm asking you to hold off - not to publish anything."

"I can hold off for a couple of hours, Tim, no more than that. By four o'clock, at the latest, I have to take this up to the Chief Executive of the paper. I decide editorial content, and he'll abide by my decision - but only if I make a hell of a case to him."

Hanrahan said, "Vincent, if there is a case to be made, I'll see that you have it. And I'll see that you have it within two hours."

THE TAOISEACH

Hanrahan was usually prepared to wait in the ante-room outside the Taoiseach's office, to take his place in the queue just like everyone else. When he asked for the meeting to be interrupted - immediately - the staff of the private office knew that something was up. But they knew better than to ask what.

The Taoiseach, despite being interrupted, was in high good humour.

"You've heard the news, Tim," he exclaimed happily when his

adviser went in. "The Provos have announced their cease-fire. No conditions, no ultimatums, no time limits. They went even further than I thought they would."

"I hope it's enough to help you get over this," Hanrahan said sourly, handing Gibson the photocopy of Flynn's story. Gibson glanced at it, and stiffened.

"Where did you get this?" he demanded.

"I got it from a news editor who proposes to publish it in the next couple of hours," Hanrahan told him.

"Jesus Christ!" Gibson said. "Who is it? How do we stop it?"

"I think you'd better read it first," Hanrahan replied.

"Yes. Yes, all right," Gibson muttered.

He seemed to shrink into the giant chair. As he read, he almost appeared to stop breathing. Except, every now and then, he uttered an almost inaudible word or two. The word was usually an oath. As he watched him, Hanrahan found himself wondering, could it be true? When he was finished, he looked at Hanrahan for what seemed like an age before he said anything.

"There isn't a word of truth in this, Tim," he said at last. "McDonald went mad, you know. I think it was the cancer, and the pain. In those days there was very little they could do to help him. And he wouldn't stay in hospital. He discharged himself, and tried to ease his own pain with brandy. He was probably drunk when he wrote those notes. And Maura's mind had been gone for several years. I assume she did write those letters - she wrote some to me from that hospital as well, and they were along the same lines, but she was raving most of the time by then."

Hanrahan was relieved. He had known he wouldn't have the nerve to ask Gibson if the story was true or not, but Gibson's explanation was enough to satisfy him. But there still remained the question of what to do. Whether the story was true or not, most newspapers would believe there was enough to go on. And once it appeared in print, the questions that would be raised in the public mind would be devastating.

There was already a tough schedule of public appearances worked out for the remainder of the campaign, and Hanrahan had a vision of the Taoiseach having to deal with the rumours that would flow from the story at every stop.

"Who's in charge of the story?" Gibson asked again.

"Jim Flynn wrote it" - "that bastard!" his boss interrupted - "and Vincent O'Byrne is the man who came to me."

At the mention of O'Byrne's name, the Taoiseach smiled.

"I think you can leave him to me," he said.

The voice on the other end of the phone was warm and friendly, but O'Byrne was in no doubt about the unspoken threat.

The Taoiseach started the conversation by remarking how little they saw one another nowadays, "not like the good old days". He went on to enquire about Vincent's wife and family, and say how delighted he had been to watch Vincent's career progressing in leaps and bounds.

"If we can be serious for a moment, Vincent," the Taoiseach continued. "Tim Hanrahan has shown me the story that Jim Flynn brought you, and I have to say how shocked I was to read it. I'd always regarded Jim as a most responsible reporter, but I must say he hasn't exactly covered himself with glory with this one. The story is totally untrue, and those letters are the ravings of a man - a great and dear friend of mine - who was driven crazy with drink, and with the pain of a cancer that was eating him alive."

"You're denying the story then, Taoiseach?" asked O'Byrne.

"Vincent, I'm surprised you need to ask," said the Taoiseach, adding, for good measure, "after all we've been through together. I would hope that you would know me better than to think I could be responsible for the things I'm supposed to have done to my wife" - O'Byrne thought for a moment that he detected a catch in the Taoiseach's voice - "not to mention murdering a man I met only once. Of course I'm denying the story. The whole thing is a figment of a madman's imagination from start to finish."

"I see," said O'Byrne. He couldn't think of anything else to say. There was a silence, which the Taoiseach broke. He had obviously decided to be explicit.

"Vincent," said the Taoiseach, almost sternly, "that story must not appear. Not for my sake - I wouldn't want you to feel that you owed me anything personally - but for the sake of the country. Even though it is not true, it would cause a major scandal, one that would be impossible to cope with. The inevitable result would be immense pressure on the British Prime Minister to withdraw from our agreement before it can be ratified by Parliament here and in Britain. And that would be an immense tragedy for the nation. We've already seen the good the agreement can do," the Taoiseach concluded, "After all, who would have predicted even a couple of weeks ago that a cease-fire by the Provisional IRA would be possible?"

There was no doubt, O'Byrne told himself, that Gibson was making a good case. He knew that he was fooling himself when he decided to spike the story "in the national interest", and not out of any personal anxiety he might have had for his own future. But it made him feel a lot better.

And there was a certain sneaking satisfaction in being able to refuse the Taoiseach's request for the return of the letters, because all he had was photocopies and Flynn still had the originals.

It didn't occur to him that he was placing Flynn in terrible danger by giving the Taoiseach that piece of information.

CHAPTER 11

JULY 6th - THE ELEVENTH DAY

THE REPORTER

"You've what?"

I was almost screaming. All the previous night, O'Byrne had refused to come to the phone. Every time I rang, his secretary had a different excuse. He was with the Chief Executive; he was in a production meeting; there was a problem in the copy room and he'd gone down there.

I knew there was something wrong, but I couldn't figure out what. It never occurred to me for a moment that they would suppress the story. It was a good story - a great story - and it stood up to the most critical journalistic examination. OK, a defender in a court room might have been able to undermine the notebook, because of its use of initials, and Maura's letter - maybe even Annie Deane's testimony about Stafford's behaviour. Gibson might have got off on a technicality.

But journalists don't operate in a court room. It's our job to satisfy ourselves that there's a case to be answered before we publish anything, and to tell the truth to the best of our ability as we see it.

That often means giving people the benefit of the doubt. But it doesn't mean proving everything beyond a reasonable doubt. No responsible journalist will publish something destructive if he doesn't believe it to be true. If he does believe it, and if he believes the public ought to know, then he has an obligation to publish, no matter how destructive or hurtful the story is.

Reporters are human too. We all fall into the same traps that everyone else does. We're more inclined to believe damaging stories about people we don't like, and to discount the same stories about people we admire. We have to bend over backwards constantly, to make absolutely certain that we're not building up a story because it hurts someone we wouldn't mind hurting.

And I'd done that. Again and again, I'd examined the elements of my story, to be sure that I wasn't just relying on circumstantial evidence to bolster my own prejudice. It was all there, especially when you combined what was already known about Gibson with what I had discovered. His sudden wealth, based on Tom Deane's death; the scandal over his wife's death; the behaviour of Stafford when Annie Deane went to him; Stafford's subsequent rise to the top, hand in hand with Gibson himself; the funny business about the transfer of ownership of Leinster Resources; and the letters that McDonald had written, accompanied by large amounts of money.

Even if you discounted one or other part of the story, it hung together. There was much more than circumstantial evidence - there was a solid case. I had one source who was prepared to be named - that was Annie Deane - and I had another, who had written down everything he wanted to say, and signed it. I couldn't think of anything I'd left undone. I said as much to O'Byrne, when I finally cornered him in his office.

"That isn't it," O'Byrne said to me. "It's a good story, I'm not denying that. The reasons it can't be published are different."

He was ill at ease, almost shifty.

"I discussed it in considerable detail with the legal people," he said. "We decided it couldn't run without a reaction from Gibson."

I nodded. That was reasonable. I had intended to include a comment from Gibson in the story anyway. That's only fair, and besides, it minimises the prospect of a libel action later.

But you don't normally go for the comment from the subject of your story until everything is set to go.

"He denied it, I suppose," I said.

He didn't react to the sarcasm in my voice.

"Yes," he said. "He gave a very full, and persuasive, account of Christopher McDonald's state of mind, and that of his wife, when they wrote all that stuff - and he denied absolutely that any of it was true."

"And you believed him?" I said. "For fuck's sake, Vincent, what was he going to say? Did you expect the man to admit that he had finally been caught after all these years?"

"Look," O'Byrne said, "that wasn't the only consideration. We couldn't publish this story, unless we were absolutely certain of it, given the international repercussions that would flow from it. We're talking about an international agreement here, we're talking about historical developments ..."

"We're talking about a murderer who wants to be elected Taoiseach," I said. "For God's sake, can't you see what you're doing? We can't stand by and let that man get away with it. How can you do it?"

"I'm doing what I'm paid to do," O'Byrne said stiffly. "I'm paid to decide what goes into the paper and what doesn't. Just because you're hooked on a personal vendetta ..."

"Is that what you think it is?" I screamed at him. "You sent me out on this thing, I bring back the story of the century, and you tell me I'm on a vendetta. Who the fuck do you think you are?"

He started screaming too.

"I think I'm the editor of this paper - and I think you have a cheek to come in here and try to tell me how to do my job."

I got up and leaned over the desk at him.

"I don't know whose job you're doing," I said into his face, "but you're no editor. This story is going to be published, whether you like it or not."

Before I slammed the door of his small office behind me, he had time to shout that if my story appeared in any other newspaper, I was finished in my present job.

I contemplated going over O'Byrne's head. But I knew that would be useless. The Chief Executive of our paper is a businessman. His background is in advertising, and his interest is revenue. He has always let his editors get on with running their bits of the paper, and every day, at the meeting where he is supposed to take all the final decisions, he rubber-stamps theirs. He wouldn't over-rule O'Byrne.

I was going to have to take the story somewhere else. But where? I knew that O'Byrne, even if he didn't want to, would have to fire me if I gave a story to the competition. I could try to have it published without any by-line, but I couldn't see any newspaper in the country agreeing to that, given the sort of story it was. I could give it to a reporter from one of the other papers. But it was my story, and I'd want to be really desperate before I'd give it to anyone else.

In the meantime, I had to break the news to Margaret.

THE POLICEMAN

"It isn't going to be easy," Stafford said.

Gibson was tired. He had been flown to Donegal the evening before, to address a rapturous public meeting. The meetings had got bigger and bigger since the campaign started, and the crowds more and more enthusiastic. Last night he'd had to speak in the open air, because there wasn't a hall big enough in the whole county to accommodate the crowd.

But it was a great place to be on the night that the Provos announced their ceasefire. County Donegal, because of its proximity to the border, has a population which has seen much tangible evidence of the damage that Provo violence can do. More than a few are sympathetic to the Provos also. So everyone was pleased - both those that welcomed the prospect of an easing of violence, and those that thought, "the Provos are on our side now".

Because of the size and the enthusiasm of the crowd, the rally had run very late - too late for the Air Corps helicopter to bring Gibson back to Dublin. That was irritating enough in itself - the way Hanrahan had organised things, with the helicopter parked at the edge of the crowd, Gibson would have been able to make a tremendously dramatic exit, striding through the crowd to the chopper, and then circling over the cheering faces before flying into the setting sun. But it also meant that for several hours he had to suffer the attentions of hordes of local politicians, all of whom wanted to be seen in intimate conversation with the Leader.

Because he felt it imperative to see Stafford as early as possible the following day, he had to be up at first light, in order to take the bumpy helicopter ride back to Dublin. The reason he needed Stafford was simple. Gibson knew he hadn't killed Flynn's story, only stopped it temporarily. As long as Flynn had documents, the story was likely to surface somewhere else. And Gibson was determined to stop that happening.

"Unless he's a fool," Stafford continued, "he won't be carrying the papers around with him. That means we have to find him, and make him tell us where they are. And I've already run a check on his whereabouts. He's not at his own flat, and while I'm going to get a man to watch the newspaper, I don't think it would be wise to pick him up there, if that's where he turns up. I've also put out a call for his car, but it might take a couple of days to turn that up. We will get him. What do we do with him when we catch him?"

"Just get him," Gibson snapped. "We'll figure out what to do with him then."

Stafford had known the truth about Andrew Gibson for years, and it had never bothered him. That very first day, when he went to Gibson with the letter that Annie Deane had given him, they made a deal. And Gibson had kept his side of the bargain. Stafford had done whatever was necessary to prevent the story of Gibson's row with Tom Deane from surfacing, and Gibson had ensured that he had not gone unrewarded.

Now he was kicking himself. They had been lucky to get the letter that went to Annie Deane, and Gibson had always believed that the one to Mrs Barrington had been destroyed. It should have occurred to them both that McDonald was capable of keeping a notebook. Now Stafford would have to go through the whole process again.

Finding Flynn was only a matter of resources. But keeping him out of the way while they found the documents - that was a different proposition. It would mean holding him prisoner somewhere - and the more he thought about it, the surer he was that it would be unwise to involve P3 in that. He needed somebody else's help.

He called Gibson on the secure line to check that the Taoiseach had no objection to the course of action he was going to propose, then set up a meeting, using the same route that he had used the other day.

The meeting was with Padraig Norton. This time it was in an abandoned house off the Leopardstown Road, a considerable distance from the location of their first meeting. When he got there, two hours later, Stafford didn't beat about the bush.

"There is a man, Padraig," he said. "He's on the loose in this city, and he represents a grave threat to the future of your agreement with the Taoiseach. He must be stopped, before his actions place the present Government in jeopardy."

"Why can't you catch him yourself?" Norton asked. "You have far more resources than we have for that kind of work."

"Oh, we can catch him," Stafford replied. "But we need a way of holding him that can never be associated with us."

"Who is the guy?" Norton asked. "What kind of damage can he do?"

"I don't think we should go into that," Stafford said. "But believe me when I say that it's as much in your interests as ours that he is taken off the street as soon as possible, and kept in a very safe place."

Norton thought about it. The irony of the situation appealed to him. Here was the country's leading policeman asking him, of all people, for help. And from the sound of it, asking him for help to do something illegal. He knew that it wasn't really necessary for him to have too much background about the problem.

Norton appreciated security better than most people. He had stayed free, and had remained effective all these years, because he had built an extraordinary wall of security around himself. Even when he was running a major operation which involved the use of three or four of the Provos' cells, the cells rarely knew of each others' involvement.

And it was even rarer for anyone beside himself to have the overall detail of an operation. He had a keen sense of history, and knew that betrayal had been a frequent feature of the armed struggle against the British. What you don't know, you can't betray, he reasoned.

"O.K.," he said. "You find the guy, you let us know where he is, and we'll take it from there."

He scribbled a telephone number on a slip of paper, and handed it to Stafford. As Stafford got up to leave, Norton asked, "Do you want us to take ... er ... permanent care of this guy?"

"No," said Stafford. "At least, not yet.."

CHAPTER 12

JULY 7th - THE TWELFTH DAY

THE REPORTER

When she was angry, Margaret was something else again.

I told her the news that the paper was refusing to run the story as soon as I got back to the flat. She went white. When I explained that they were taking Gibson's denials seriously, she cursed, loudly and at some length. When I told her that they were quoting the national interest as a reason for killing the story, she exploded.

"The bastards!" she cried. "The lousy, rotten bastards! How could they do that? Don't they know what they're dealing with? The man killed my father, and he killed his own wife as sure as if he put a knife through her. How could they cover all that up?"

Tears were standing in her eyes as I looked at her. I wasn't in too good a condition myself. I had walked to and from the paper, deciding it was as easy to leave the car parked outside the flat as to try to find parking in the city centre. On the way back, I had been trying to rationalise the whole thing. No matter which way I tried to figure it out, there was only one explanation that made sense.

Gibson had got to them. That had to be the reason they would turn down a story like this. I didn't know who he had got to - O'Byrne, the Chief Executive, who - and I didn't know how. But the arguments that O'Byrne had used to me didn't stack up. There was just no way they were the real reasons.

If newspapers decided not to publish stories just because they were denied, most papers would carry a lot of blank pages. In all my years as a reporter, I've never confronted anyone with a story and heard him say, "you're right. I admit it. I'm guilty." Everyone always, but always, denies it. The quality of denial will vary, of course, from attempts to fudge your story, to barefaced, on the record, detailed, lies. And sometimes the denial will be persuasive enough to give you pause, to make you wonder if you've got it right, to make you check your facts and your sources again. But a denial will never make you kill your story. You know the libel laws, and you know the risk if you've got it wrong. So you do your best to get it right, and then you run it. If you didn't do that, there'd be an awful lot of stuff - all of it true - that the public would never know.

And as for this national interest crap - well, there have been times when I've been prepared to accept that particular stories could be damaging, and I've gone along, however reluctantly, with letting them be killed. But how could it be in the national interest to allow a murderer to be elected as Head of Government? O'Byrne knew as well as I did that no paper worth its salt would allow "the national interest" to be used to protect criminals, or to prevent the exposure of crime.

I was reluctant to believe that either of the people I suspected had been got at. I'd worked with O'Byrne for years, and he was good. Maybe we didn't get on as well as we should, but I had never had any reason to believe that he was bent. And the Chief Exective, even though I didn't know him, because he was remote from day to day operations, was too well-known and too much in the public eye to risk being corrupted by a politician. But one of them, or somebody else, had been got at - I was sure of it.

Margaret was less inhibited about my colleagues when I told her my suspicions.

"Of course!" she said. "He's bought them off, or he's blackmailing them. It's exactly how he would deal with the situation."

But she was equally firm when I told her what I had decided to do, on my walk back to the flat. In the end, I had no choice. I had to resign, and take my story to one of the other nationals.

"No!" she said. "No way! You're not going to lose your job because of the story that Mum and I told you. I won't allow it. Besides, Gibson's probably ahead of you already. If he can buy one newspaper, he can buy them all. There must be a better way of getting all this out in the open."

We argued about it for a long time. I had no idea how to get my story aired, other than to bring it to a newspaper. But Margaret had a suggestion. A couple of years ago, one of her colleagues in the hospital had gone out with a politician, Pat Crowley. She suggested that we should go to see him.

At first the idea struck me almost as funny. It's a peculiarly Irish failing - no other race on earth believes so firmly in asking their politicians to fix things. People who have problems with their plumbing, with their marriages, with their sex lives, with their neighbours - they all take the problems to their local politician. And now look at us!

On the other hand, Pat Crowley was no ordinary politician. He had been an able and effective Minister for Finance in his day, and was close to Charles Page, the Leader of the Opposition. He had never married, although I gathered from Margaret that he might have if her friend had been willing.

I knew Crowley fairly well myself, and had a certain amount of respect for him. He was a conservative, but even conservatives can be honourable. And it occurred to me that he might be a good way to get to Page. I could go to Page directly, but I wasn't one of the journalists with whom he had a particularly good relationship. Besides, he was almost certain to be out of town - there was an election campaign going on around the country, after all. If he had to be brought back to Dublin in a hurry, he'd be more likely to come for Crowley than for me.

Even though it was fairly late at night when I rang Crowley

at home, he was friendly. I said that I needed to see him urgently on a private basis. I could tell that he was immediately intrigued. He invited me to his house the following morning.

It was one of those big houses behind high gates on the Adelaide Road in Glenageary. I parked the car on the road outside, and walked up the short driveway to the front door. Crowley answered my ring himself and took me into a comfortable study where a pot of coffee was already waiting.

I hadn't brought a copy of my story with me, although I had the photocopies that Margaret had made in an inside pocket. I had decided that the best way to deal with Crowley was to tell him everything, and let him cross-examine me.

"I've come across a news story," I began, "and I believe that it's in the national interest that that news story be made public. My paper has told me, however, that they think the national interest demands that it be suppressed. So I've come to you, to ask you for your help in making it public."

His eyebrows came together as he looked at me. I wondered if he was suspecting a trick. Then he smiled. "I take it you'd allow me to know what this story is, and to form my own judgement about where the national interest lies," he said.

"Of course," I told him. "But I must have your assurance that you will respect my confidence in the matter. If you don't feel you can help, you must at least undertake to keep what I'm going to tell you to yourself."

Again the eyebrows met. This time he didn't smile.

"Look, Jim, this isn't some kind of a joke, is it?"

I had started off badly. I apologised.

"Would you mind," I said to him, "if I just told you a few things that I have discovered? Then you could decide if you want this conversation to continue."

He nodded. While he poured two cups of coffee, I began to talk. I told him that I had solid evidence that the Taoiseach was a murderer, and that he had effectively incarcerated his wife in a psychiatric hospital. I told him that when the evidence of the murder first came to light, it was stolen, for Gibson's benefit, by Deputy Commissioner Stafford. I gave him the dates and the names of all the people involved.

As I talked, his coffee went cold. He never interrupted me, and never took his eyes off me. In those eyes I saw, at first disbelief, then gradually, horror.

When I was finished, I emptied the cold coffee in my own cup in one swallow. He coughed, but even after clearing his throat, the voice that came out was hoarse.

"Can you prove any of this?"

"I found a notebook, written by Gibson's legal partner before he died in 1970," I said. "It amounts to a deathbed confession of his own role as an accessory, and to an accusation of what I regard as two murders against the Taoiseach. And then I got hold of letters that the same man had written to two relatives of the victims, and letters that Maura Barrington herself had written in hospital."

"Do you have all these documents?"

I took the copies out of my pocket, and handed them to him. His hands were trembling slightly as he took them. As he read them, I saw him shiver, just as I had done when I read them first.

He read them several times. Then he handed them back to me.

"I don't know what to say," he said. "I'm stunned."

He shook his head violently, and got up to walk around the room. I watched him, but I couldn't make him out.

"You shouldn't have come to me," he said. "You should have gone to the police. You should go to the police now."

Of all the answers he might have given me, this was the one I least expected. The police! With the Taoiseach and one of their own highest-ranking officers involved!

"Are you crazy?" I managed to say at last. "How could I take this to the police? The first person to know about it would be Stafford. It would be buried in minutes, just like he buried it before."

"No!" said Crowley. There was an urgency in his voice. "Not all Gardai are bent like Stafford. There are many decent men ... I could give you the name of one now, and he would make sure this matter would be fully investigated. It might take a little longer, but it would be the right way. Gibson would be caught in the end..."

"If you really believe that, you're a fool," I said. "Even if it was possible to get a proper investigation, which it isn't, the election would be well over before the investigation was completed. There'd be no charges, no publicity, nothing, until Gibson was safely installed in Government Buildings again. And you know as well as I do that once that happens, nothing would be done. The file would be closed - or more likely, it would just disappear."

He was wringing his hands.

"Don't you see?" he said. "I can't help you with this. Anything else, but not this. I can't attack Gibson. I can't let Charles Page attack him. We just wouldn't be believed. It would look like more of the personality politics that we've had to get away from. We're the last people who can attack him on those grounds. Ask someone else - anyone else ..."

"Are you in Gibson's pocket too?" I said.

Before I could move, Crowley had hit me, hard, across the face. I staggered backwards into an armchair, tears filling my eyes from the stinging slap, which had caught me full on the nose. Instantly, he reached out and grabbed my arm.

"I'm sorry, I'm sorry," he babbled. "I know how you must feel. I shouldn't have done that. But you must believe me - there is nothing I wouldn't give to see Gibson get what he deserves. I will help in any way I can to bring that about. But it wouldn't work if I were to do it, or if Charles Page were to do it. It just wouldn't work."

He was breathing hard. I was breathing through my mouth.

I wasn't sure, but I thought perhaps he had broken my nose. I felt it, gingerly. Jesus! It stung, but it seemed to be all there.

Crowley sat opposite me, his elbows resting on his knees, his head slumped forward. I said nothing - I was more interested in recovering my breath. After a while, he looked at me.

"You know," he said, with a half-smile, "the only thing you did wrong was you went to the wrong politician. You should have taken this story to Dan Horgan. He wouldn't be seen as having an axe to grind, and I'm fairly sure that if he believed your story, he'd be prepared to accuse Gibson publicly."

"I'll think about it," I said, "but I've had enough of politicians for one day."

"OK, OK," he said, "I guess I had that coming. But I mean it all the same. He is the Leader of the Labour Party, and even though they're very small, he's well respected. If he were to call in the press to tell your story, it would be covered all over the world."

I didn't shake hands with him when I left. And I didn't see the Toyota that pulled out behind me as I drove off.

As I drove back to the flat, I thought about Crowley. I suppose I should have figured it out before I went to see him. I knew that his Party had been badly damaged by Page's attack on Gibson's character at the start of the campaign. I could see how, in the normal course of events, they wouldn't want to make the same mistake twice.

But surely this wasn't the normal course of events. How could anyone stand by, knowing the story I had just told them, and do nothing? It meant that, at best, Crowley was calculating that the way for him to take the smallest risk was to do nothing. All he was concerned about was his own position and his Party's. The real truth of the thing was only slowly beginning to dawn on me. When you have a story like the one I was carrying around, you're on your own. I had finally come up with the story that every reporter dreams about, and I was discovering the meaning of the phrase "too hot to handle".

Maybe that was all there was to it. I wasn't offering people a story that they knew they ought to hear; all I was doing was offering people the chance to open a can of worms - and worms with vicious teeth at that.

The more I thought about it, the more certain I became that there was no point in going to another politician, although Dan Horgan was much more my kind of man. I had always voted Labour, and over the previous few years he had steered the Party in the right direction for me. When it seemed as if the swing to the right in the early eighties would destroy them, he had managed to keep them intact, and they were a respectable size in terms of the number of Dail seats they had. But I knew he would be under immense pressure at the moment, in the middle of an election campaign like this one. Especially since he was articulating the unpopular position of opposition to the Agreement, on the grounds that it undermined the country's sovereignty.

If Crowley's example was anything to go by, Horgan would welcome a visit from me like a hole in the head.

At least, I thought, I won't have to break more bad news to Margaret until later on, and by then I might have figured out what to do next. She was at work, and wouldn't be home until later in the afternoon. Even if she rang from the hospital, I could avoid answering the phone until I was ready.

As I negotiated the narrow back entrance to Mount Pleasant Square, I noticed that Margaret wasn't the only one at work. Even though it was a Saturday, there was only one other car in the Square, and it was parked outside the house where our flat was.

The two men sitting in the other car both got out while I was parking. One of them spoke to me as I locked my car.

"Mr Flynn?"

Although I realised immediately that something was wrong, it was too late. They had me, one by each arm, and they were both big men. The back door of their Toyota was open. One of them grabbed my car keys and pocketed them.

I could see that the other one was already holding something in his free hand, but I didn't know what it was until he hit me with it, in the stomach, to double me over and make me easier to get in the car.

I still don't know what it was. I just hope I'm never hit with anything that hard again.

The pain was an eruption. I've never felt anything like it. All I could see was the back seat of the car swimming in front of me. And all I could feel was a solid mass of screaming pain, which started in my stomach and spread, instantly, all over. In a way it was a relief when he hit me, again, on the back of the head, and I slumped forward on to the back seat. Although they moved fast, I was unconscious before they closed the door.

The last thing I remembered was the smell of my own vomit.

CHAPTER 13

JULY 8th - THE THIRTEENTH DAY

THE TAOISEACH

There'd never been an after-Mass meeting like it.

On the Sundays of an election campaign, the after-Mass meeting is a peculiarly Irish institution. Although it has largely died out in the larger urban areas, it's still one of the great pastimes of rural Ireland.

With a few exceptions, the Irish hate their politicians, but love their politics. In very few other countries in the world will people stay up until three in the morning, watching the results of an election on television, and spend all of the following day analysing swings and trends, who's up and who's down. Every pub in Ireland has its resident political expert. In the pubs of other countries, they'll talk about sex scandals, but the Irish politician who's been unfaithful to his wife has never been reported - even when, as in the case of a number of them, they voted against liberalisation of the law on divorce.

Double standards are an accepted feature of Irish life. When insider trading on the Stock Exchange was rocking the establishment in London and New York, it was acknowledged in Dublin that that sort of behaviour would be impossible to avoid in a town where everyone knew everyone else.

The same double standards have destroyed many an Irish politician, and rescued many another. The politician who seems to have something to say - particularly if he seems to be willing to hold up a mirror, in which people can see things that need to be changed - politicians like that prosper and are listened to in other societies. But Irish political graveyards are full of them.

On the other hand, the politician who represents his people faithfully will last for ever in Ireland. That doesn't just mean taking their messages. If he's to be really successful, his people must see a little bit of themselves in him. It might be that he has the education they always wanted, or the money they'd know how to spend. It might be that they can fantasise about his lifestyle, or about the scrapes he gets involved in. But as long as they're involved with him - as long as the mirror he's holding up shows them something that they recognise and like - he'll last. The most important quality an Irish politician can have is to be "one of our own". As long as he's that, nothing else matters a lot.

Andrew Gibson, of course, had this quality. Despite the grandeur of his home and the glamour of his wife, despite the impressive car and the important office he held, his people were proud of the fact that he was one of their own. Every one of them felt that he or she could have risen to that same office, and been driven in that same car - if Andy could make it, so could they. And Andy never stopped telling them that he could not have made it without them.

That was why, when there was an election on, and people knew that Gibson was going to be speaking after Mass in any part of the constituency, the local clergy could count on a packed Church and overflowing collection plates. People used to drive from all over the county, to go to Mass and mill around afterwards to rub shoulders with their hero.

But this particular Sunday, they hadn't just come from around the county - they seemed to have come from everywhere.

It was the second Sunday of the campaign, of course, the halfway point. Polling day was the Tuesday after next, and by now the experienced politicians knew how it was going to go. The door-to-door canvas that was essential was already giving a perceptible and accurate feed-back. And despite what the media reported, each Party was getting the same feed-back at this point. The Parties who were in trouble knew it, and the Parties who were ahead knew it too.

For those in trouble, this was the moment when panic began to set in. About now, Gibson was sure, Charles Page would be meeting his advisers, and they would be telling him that something had to be done to change the direction of the campaign. Because Gibson knew he was ahead. From all over the country, the members of the Government who had arrived in Kilkenny last night were able to report that they were running away with the campaign.

Barring accidents, there was no way they could be stopped. And Gibson knew that he had taken care of all of the possible accidents. What he needed to do now was to create a bandwagon that became irresistible. The best way to do that was to look and sound unbeatable.

That was why almost the entire Cabinet had come to an after-Mass meeting. They were all there except Kelly, who was on his way to America, and Scally, who had pleaded urgent constituency business of his own. At first, Gibson had been inclined to order Scally to come, but instinct told him that Scally was only damaging himself by not being there. He suggested to his own local people that if any of them were asked why Scally hadn't attended, they could suggest that Scally's seat was in danger, and that was why he was afraid to leave his own constituency.

The meeting was in Callan, about ten miles from Kilkenny City, outside the huge old church that dominated the town. In a good campaign, you could expect maybe three hundred people to gather after Mass to be harangued by the local politicians.

Today there were at least thirty thousand people present. Politicians from all of the opposition Parties had wisely stayed away. The crowd stretched as far as the eye could see. Only a tiny fraction of them had been able to squeeze into the Church for Mass, and Monsignor Hogan cursed himself for not having had the wit to send collection plates outside. God alone knew what he might have been able to do if he'd filled a few baskets from a crowd of that size - maybe even change his old car. It was the size of crowd he remembered from his schoolboy history - the size that was addressed by Daniel O'Connell himself at the height of his powers, or by Parnell before (he blessed himself at the thought) that O'Shea woman had dragged him down to disgrace.

One after another, the members of the Cabinet mounted the platform that had been erected outside the front door of the church the night before. The presence of three camera crews - one from RTE, the national television station, and two from Britain - drove them all to great heights of eloquence. Each in his turn mentioned the enormous contribution that the Taoiseach had made to a lasting and just solution of the age-old Irish question. Listening to them, Gibson reflected with amusement that now that it was safe to do so, more and more of them were themselves beginning to sound like Provos.

O'Flynn for instance, whom no one could remember ever having uttered a word in Cabinet about the North of Ireland, was now in full flight.

"For generations," he was shouting, "it has been the dream of every Irishman and Irishwoman that we would have a country that was not just Irish, but free as well; not just free, but Irish as well. That day we have all longed for is coming - that day when the foreigner would no longer occupy our soil. And when it comes - when that great day dawns - there will be one man to thank. The greatest Irish patriot in history, the man who'll be remembered for generations as the Taoiseach who united his country - *my Leader and yours, Andrew Gibson!*"

The Taoiseach's name was roared out in the manner of someone who was introducing the winner of a wrestling match. The speakers were responding to the crowd, and the crowd in turn was responding to them. It was a historic occasion, and the Agreement that Gibson had negotiated would put his name in the history books. Everyone outside that Church knew that they were part of something enormous that day. And that was why, when it was the Taoiseach's turn to climb on to the platform, a roar began to well up, almost as if from the centre of the crowd, growing and growing until it seemed that the old Church would shudder and fall under the weight of the noise.

Gibson stood in front of them. Even from the back of the crowd, he dominated the platform, well over six feet tall, with his broad shoulders and flowing hair. Gradually, the roar began to change. From somewhere in the middle, a chant of "Andy - Andy" had begun, and within seconds the whole crowd took it up. They began to sway, too; thousands of middle-aged men and women from the heart of rural Ireland, feeling and behaving like teenagers at a rock concert.

It seemed they would never stop. Again and again, the cameras panned backwards and forwards over the crowd. The ITN producer, who had filmed political rallies from Chicago to Manila, had never seen anything like it. Here was a small town in the middle of Ireland on a Sunday morning, and what was supposed to be a routine election rally, with maybe a couple of thousand people present because these people knew how to organise that sort of thing. And instead you had a totally spontaneous outpouring of affection for a politician who was certainly not the most charismatic he had ever seen. He'd been there while Pope John Paul worked a crowd, while Lech Walesa was inspiring the shipyard workers in Gdansk, and during the historic night when the Berlin Wall fell - but Gibson hadn't even started to speak yet, and the emotion was coming at them in waves.

"This guy could be President for life," he muttered to the cameraman beside him.

"My friends," the Taoiseach began, grinning down at them, "I think it's safe to call you all my friends ..."

Again the roar started. Again Gibson's trick of seeming to

communicate with individuals in the audience had worked. It took another couple of minutes to silence them again. Gibson noted the British TV crews with satisfaction; their film would do a lot to sell the Agreement - and him - in Britain.

"My friends," he began again, "our future is bright. This last week or so has been like the start of a great adventure for all of us. I can feel it - as I have travelled around the country I have been able to feel the excitement in the air. There is a new pride, a new sense of purpose, in being Irish. For the first time in generations we are being offered the right to determine our own future - together, as one nation!"

Again he had to stop. The roar from the crowd was like thunder. Only now was it dawning on Gibson that in approving the Agreement, he was unleashing some long pent-up emotion in the Irish people. At heart, he had never cared much about the tenets of nationalism himself. Nobody would ever know it from his public utterances, but to him the whole question of the partition of the country was just a matter of making the right ritualistic noises. But at meeting after meeting around the country in the last few days, when he wasn't too preoccupied to notice, the excitement over the Agreement had been building up. Now, he reflected, if this was Palm Sunday, and I was Jesus entering Jerusalem, I wouldn't be getting a better reception. At the thought, he shuddered involuntarily - not because of his unspoken blasphemy, but because, suddenly, it occurred to him that Palm Sunday was only five days away from Good Friday.

Nobody noticed, and in a moment the image was gone. When the crowd grew silent again he continued,

"You've heard speakers saying nice things about me this morning. Don't believe it. This is *your* Agreement! I could never have done anything in public life unless you had put me there. And it was with your help that all the obstacles were overcome. This isn't my moment of glory - it belongs to all the people of this country, and especially to you!"

To a man, the crowd was standing, roaring. As Gibson tried to climb down from the platform, a thousand hands prevented him, making sure that he remained where everyone could see him while wave after wave of applause broke over him. It was an awesome sight, so powerful that the scene was to be shown again and again on every television channel in the British Isles that night. Even ITN, who pride themselves on their ability to edit any item of news down to its essential thirty seconds, showed Gibson's speech, and the reaction he got, in full.

Only one person in the crowd wasn't cheering. She was a woman who looked older than her years, a woman who looked as if all hope had been taken away from her. Throughout Gibson's speech, she had stared up at the platform, her hatred for the man who was speaking clear for all to see.

But no one in that crowd had eyes for her.

It was true - all hope had been taken away from Annie Deane. Only that morning, Margaret had rung her to say that Jim Flynn had gone. In her own distress, Margaret had told her mother the full story: How she had thought Flynn was going to write a story - how he had got the proof that they needed - how, suddenly, he had just disappeared. Even then she hadn't believed that Flynn would betray her, until he had stuffed a note in the letterbox of her flat in the middle of the night. She had found it early that morning.

It said simply "Thanks for the couple of days. I'll be in touch sometime." And it was signed by the man she thought she'd fallen in love with.

THE ADVISER

While his Taoiseach was being mobbed in Kilkenny, Tim Hanrahan was enjoying a second iced vodka with his caviar.

He wasn't a good flyer - in fact, he hated aeroplanes - but travelling first class across the Atlantic was different. He had travelled in the rear of an Aer Lingus 747 in the past, and had needed valium before he could be persuaded that he wasn't going to die. From the moment he had come on board on this trip, when the hostess handed him a glass of champagne and orange juice, he had decided he might as well enjoy it. By now, he was relaxed. The caviar was a new experience, as was the neat, chilled vodka. And the steak Chateaubriand which was being carved on a small table beside his seat looked a great deal more inviting than the usual airline food.

If I didn't have to sit beside Sean Kelly, he thought, I could get quite used to this.

Foreign travel wasn't, as a rule, one of his perks, because the Taoiseach had a phobia about leaving the shop unattended. But it was the Taoiseach who had decided that he should go with Kelly on this trip. First, he knew that with Hanrahan along, Kelly would not be tempted into any of his usual extra-curricular activities. And second, Hanrahan's presence would not only infuriate the Foreign Affairs officials whom Gibson despised, but would be a signal to the domestic press that this was really Gibson's trip. As Gibson's man, Hanrahan would be seen as second in status only to the Foreign Minister, and his presence would be prominently reported at home.

The Foreign Affairs people had their own little ways of making their displeasure felt. The briefing book which was supposed to be available for each member of the party had only found its way to Hanrahan late last night, giving him no time to read it, so he was going to have to devote most of the trip to studying the details of protocol and personnel that were an essential feature of trips like this, which would ensure that he didn't get an opportunity to have any sleep on the flight. And his diplomatic passport hadn't been handed to him until he was boarding the plane, ensuring him a few moments of anxiety about whether or not his own passport was in order.

Hanrahan had decided that he wasn't going to let this bother him. If he hadn't been so busy with the campaign, he wouldn't have let Iveagh House get away with this kind of treatment. He knew, of course, that they guarded their privileges with an intensity unmatched anywhere else in the Civil Service, and took it as a personal affront that someone outside the diplomatic service was being allowed to accompany their Minister. For a start, it meant that the number of officials who were allowed to go was reduced from three to two. In this case, the Private Secretary to the Minister was being left behind. And that meant that the First Secretary in the Anglo-Irish Division, whose principle function on the trip would normally be briefing the Minister, would also have to look after such menial tasks as making sure they had no hassle at Immigration, and ensuring that all the bags were looked after. Fortunately for him, the amount of luggage involved was slight, since they would be coming back the day after tomorrow.

Hanrahan occupied himself during dinner (which was as good as it looked) by reading the briefing documents. Most of it was standard stuff - who would be attending the signing ceremony, what their various titles were and how they should be addressed (he noticed with amusement that he had been given the American title of Special Counsel to the Prime Minister). There was also a sheaf of clippings conveying an impression of American media coverage of the Agreement, which was universally favourable.

There was to be a lunch after the signing ceremony, hosted by the President of the USA, in the White House itself. The briefing book even contained a table plan for the occasion. Searching for his name, Hanrahan discovered that he had been put at a table well away from the top. When he discovered that the Secretary of the Department, who was the other official travelling in the party, was at the top table, he scribbled him a note, suggesting that the Special Counsel to the Prime Minister should sit beside the Special Counsel to the President (at the top table). Grinning, he passed it across the aisle to where the Secretary was sipping contentedly at Aer Lingus's best Burgundy.

That should help his digestion a bit, Hanrahan thought to himself.

Tim Hanrahan was not a particularly vindictive man - even though he did not like being messed around, and usually ensured that the same person did not do it twice. With Hanrahan there was seldom anything personal involved - he just believed that the system worked better for him if the people involved knew that he wasn't easy pickings. His years serving someone in high office had shown him that the Civil Service responded best to people who knew what their objectives were, and were deadly serious about attaining them.

The politician who was along for the ride had all of his objectives dictated for him by the people who were supposed to serve him. They told him first that he should concentrate on what was possible; then they told him that ninety per cent of what he might like to do wasn't possible. And they could produce six well-reasoned pages on any subject under the sun, provided the purpose of the pages was to ensure the maintenance of whatever they perceived to be the status quo.

Hanrahan could recognise bullshit when he saw it, and it was that gift that had made him respected - and thoroughly disliked - throughout the Service.

He also had a talent for insatiable hard work, which was the thing that had made him so invaluable to Gibson. No detail was ever too small, and the hour of the day was never too late, for Hanrahan to attend to whatever needed attention. Finally, of course, he was single. His obsession with politics had left him little time for anything else, and had over-ridden any interest he might have in the comforts of a private life. All in all, he was an asset to any politician. Gibson was lucky that Hanrahan had settled on him.

In a way, that had been an accident. Tim Hanrahan's seed, breed and generation had been involved in Gibson's Party since long before Gibson's time - right back to the founding of the Party, in fact. He had decided two things at an early age - one, that he had to be involved in politics; and two, that he wanted to work in a back-room capacity. He had an aversion to the side of a politician's life that involved appearing in public - when Gibson had appointed him to the Senate, for example, he never spoke in the Chamber, and appeared there as seldom as possible. Behind the scenes was where he worked best, and where he liked to be.

He had known from the first moment he met Andrew Gibson that the young politician would go far. At the time, there was an election on, and Hanrahan had volunteered to work for Gibson's campaign simply because he was living in the constituency. But it was clear that Gibson had the qualities to make it. Hanrahan had not lost faith in him after he had been forced to resign over his wife's death. He admired the absolute determination that Gibson had displayed at that time, even as it had turned into ruthlessness. Hanrahan believed in toughness. As far as he was concerned, there was only one way to get things done, and that was to get to the top.

That was why he despised men like Sean Kelly, who was sitting beside him now. He was a politician who had inherited a safe seat, and had office virtually handed to him on a plate. But his interest was only in the trappings - Hanrahan believed he probably spent more time choosing his suits than working out his policies.

And that was also why there was very little Hanrahan was not prepared to do to help his boss stay on top. At the time that Gibson had succeeded to the leadership, it was Hanrahan who had masterminded the campaign. The decision as to who should lead the Party was made by the Party's deputies, and Hanrahan had approached the task of converting many of them on an individual basis, studying the form of the person he was dealing with, and developing tactics that were different in almost every case.

Once, for instance, he had organised for the deputy concerned to be telephoned by his constituents constantly - three hundred calls in a week - to be told that the people he represented wanted Gibson in the top job. In another case, it had taken only one call, from

Gibson himself, offering the deputy concerned a place in the Cabinet in return for his support. Other deputies had been dealt with in a variety of ways ranging from extreme pressure to out-and-out flattery, and Hanrahan was satisfied, even though it was a secret ballot that had elected Gibson, that his tactics had been correct in every case. And where he had not succeeded, either the Taoiseach or his wife had sewn up the necessary votes.

Hanrahan knew that there were some cases where Andrew or Finola Gibson had some kind of a hold over members of the Party. It wasn't his way to enquire too deeply into the nature of such arrangements - he assumed they were necessary.

Only one of the deputies he had dealt with in that period had involved him in unpleasantness. He had been forced in that case, where a deputy was being particularly recalcitrant, to make the individual involved aware that he, Hanrahan, knew that the deputy was a practicing homosexual, whose frequent trips to London could become a matter of some speculation in the British gutter press. It had secured another vote for Gibson, and even though Hanrahan never felt comfortable about what he had had to do, he had made up for it (in his own mind, at least) by persuading the Taoiseach to give the man a spell as a Junior Minister.

Politics wasn't always a dirty business. A lot of Hanrahan's job was done as the buffer between Gibson and his own constituents, and he took a genuine pleasure in the opportunity to help people that his position gave him. Although in Ireland a great many people came to politicians for favours that they were entitled to anyway, there were other times when people in real trouble came to the office that Hanrahan attended once a week in Kilkenny. Over the years the people of the constituency got to know that seeing Hanrahan about their problems was the same as seeing the Taoiseach. Some still preferred to wait until Sunday to call to the Taoiseach's house, but in many cases they were content to leave their problems with Hanrahan, secure in the knowledge that he would bring it to the Taoiseach's personal attention. He seldom did, of course, but the constituents involved always got a letter from Gibson anyway. The letter always began "Tim Hanrahan has asked me to look into your problem ...". It was a formula they had perfected over the years.

Many of the problems that constituents brought involved writing standard letters to Government Departments, or to local agencies. They had a very high success rate. Part of the reason for that was because a letter from the Taoiseach's Office gets results, or at least attention, anyway. But a major part of the reason was that Hanrahan never wrote a letter that he didn't follow up with a phone call a week later. And he went to considerable trouble to assemble a list of the appropriate people to call. Where other politicians would ring the relevant Minister's office, and ask the Private Secretary to look into whatever matter they were following up, Hanrahan would ring the official most likely to be dealing with the matter directly. Over the years, officials who were passed a letter from the Taoiseach's office came to know that they would be hearing from Tim Hanrahan very soon. And usually, they didn't wait to hear from him twice.

When the problem was one of real need, Hanrahan would take a much more personal approach. Once, he was visited by a middle-aged woman, a cleaner in the local Health clinic, who was being victimised by the porter she worked with. She had suffered a slight stroke, and was partially disabled as a result. She could still work, but slowly, and it had become clear to the porter that if Elizabeth Shanahan could be got rid of, there would be an opening in the clinic which would suit his own wife admirably.

It was a nasty business. If Elizabeth went to the toilet, she would find on her return that the bucket of water she had been using had been spilled all over the just-finished hall. When she came in in the morning, ashtrays would be spilled all around the waiting room. Her cleaning materials kept disappearing, and the suggestion was made that someone - meaning herself - must be pilfering. If she was late coming in to work, the porter would be standing in the hall, looking at his watch and loudly bemoaning the dirt of the place.

Elizabeth Shanahan was a nice woman. As she told Hanrahan her story, tears rolled down her face. She couldn't prove that the porter was out to get her, but she knew it all the same. Hanrahan believed her, so he went to see the porter in the Health Clinic. He took him into the Dental Surgery, which was used only once a week, and introduced himself. He told the porter that Elizabeth Shanahan was a friend of his, and that he was particularly anxious that she be well treated. The porter's own job was at stake, he said. And it would be a terrible pity if the porter were to lose his job, because he understood that the porter's Social Welfare file was missing - or could be missing soon. If that were to happen, there would be no unemployment benefit if he lost his job. And he could guarantee that there would not be another job in a twenty-mile radius of Kilkenny.

A radiant Elizabeth Shanahan came back to him a month later, to tell him that things had never been better in the clinic. Not only had all the mischief stopped, but now, if she was having trouble getting everything finished before the end of the day, the porter would give her a hand. As a result, the clinic was gleaming. She didn't know how Mr Hanrahan had done it, but she wanted him to know that Mr Gibson had a vote for life.

That was as much reward as Hanrahan ever asked for. He had got involved with Elizabeth Shanahan because he was moved by her condition, and it gave him a considerable amount of satisfaction to be able to use his position to make her situation better. But he never lost sight of the fact that his job was to secure his boss's position. If Elizabeth Shanahan had not come back to him, he would have gone to her the next time a vote was needed, and reminded her that she owed him one.

There were those who regarded him as unscrupulous. That didn't bother him unduly - he reckoned that in his kind of job, you had to have enemies to be successful. Even the thought that if Gibson ever found himself deposed, none of the likely successors would want to see Hanrahan around, didn't disturb him. He knew that his reputation as Gibson's political hatchet man was well-deserved, but someone had to do it.

If he hadn't done it, and if he hadn't been good at it, Gibson wouldn't be where he was now, about to secure the reunification of the country. That in itself was a measure of achievement as far as Hanrahan was concerned - he'd done a lot of rough things along the way, but great things were being done as a result. That was the payoff.

In all the years that he had worked with Gibson, the Taoiseach had never asked him to do anything illegal. He was glad of that, at least partly because he didn't know how he would react. He half-suspected that the habit of serving his master, of doing whatever needed to be done, would overcome his respect for the law of the land. And yet he wasn't sure - it made no sense to him that a man as powerful as Gibson would ever need to resort to breaking the law.

Bending it maybe - they'd all done a bit of that, especially if a friend or an important constituent was in trouble. But to his knowledge, neither he nor the Taoiseach had ever wittingly committed what any ordinary person would regard as a crime.

That was one of the reasons why he'd been so shocked when he had read Jim Flynn's story, and why he had refused to believe it. He'd heard of Annie Deane, of course, although she had never come to see him. But he knew that she was eccentric, maybe even mad, and that she had hated the Taoiseach for years. She wasn't the only mad constituent they had, and there'd never been any reason to take her seriously. And the Taoiseach's denial had been very emphatic.

Still, the more he thought about that story afterwards, the more anxious he became. He kept remembering that the Taoiseach had had no interest in reading it - his immediate reaction, the moment he had seen it, was to ask how it could be suppressed. He kept remembering the look on the Taoiseach's face as he read the story, a look almost of terror.

And he kept remembering the scene in Gibson's office when he had almost strangled Sean Kelly. In all the years he had known the Taoiseach, he had seen him lose his temper many a time, but he had never seen violence like that. He kept telling himself that it was the pressure of the campaign, but he couldn't shake off the thought of Gibson taking pleasure in his plan to send the tape of Kelly making a fool of himself to Kelly's wife. Kelly deserved to be fired, that was sure; but Hanrahan didn't believe anyone deserved what the Taoiseach had in mind - and Kelly's wife certainly didn't.

But then, Kelly's wife didn't deserve Kelly either. Hanrahan noticed that the Foreign Minister had been hitting the sauce since the plane took off. He had ignored his food and gone straight for a bottle of Hennessy brandy. If I don't get him off this stuff, Hanrahan thought, we'll have to carry him off the plane in Kennedy Airport. That'll make a great start to the trip.

"Sean," he said, not too gently, "don't you think you ought to eat something?"

"No," the Foreign Minister replied. "I'm not hungry."

His speech was already thick, and his complexion, usually a high pink, was already on the way to being purple. Hanrahan decided to be more direct. He leaned across Kelly, and shoved the cork back into the brandy bottle. Then he called the hostess, and asked her to take it away. Finally, he took the brandy glass from Kelly's hand, and poured its contents into the dregs of his own coffee cup. For a moment, Kelly was too stunned to react. Then he spluttered.

"Just who the fuck do you think you are?" he said, in a stage whisper that was so hoarse and so loud that Hanrahan was sure it could be heard in the cockpit. "That was my fucking brandy; what right have you to tell me I can't drink it?"

Hanrahan took him by the arm. Again he wasn't too gentle.

"Upstairs!" he hissed, motioning to the spiral staircase that led to the first class lounge. At first he thought Kelly might resist him, but after a second the other man wavered. He shook Hanrahan's hand free, and led the way upstairs.

The first class lounge had been reserved for them, to make briefing easier. Kelly slumped in one of the swivel chairs next to the window, and sat staring at the Atlantic six miles below. Neither man spoke for a while. When Kelly turned around to face Hanrahan, the Foreign Minister's eyes were full of tears.

"I'm finished Tim, aren't I?" he said. "He's going to get rid of me after the election is over, isn't he?"

Hanrahan didn't know what to say. He knew Kelly's career was almost over, and he would have fired him himself the other day if he had had the authority. But he had to get him through the next thirty-six hours in one piece. The Taoiseach wouldn't thank him if the Foreign Minister had a nervous breakdown on the Rose Lawn of the White House. He decided to try to humour him, even though his stomach was turning at the sight of him.

"C'mon, Sean," he said. "There's no need for that ..."

Suddenly Kelly was on his knees in front of him, tugging at his trouser leg. Hanrahan was appalled.

"Please, Tim!" The Foreign Minister was babbling now. "You can speak for me. You have influence with the Taoiseach. You're the only one who has. Please, Tim! You can't let him just dump me - how would I explain it? How could I explain it to Ruth?"

Hanrahan was horrified. Suppose any of the crew, or the Iveagh House officials, came up to the lounge? The sight of the country's Foreign Minister on the floor, crying like a baby, would be all over the plane in an instant. He thought of hitting him, as Gibson had done, but couldn't bring himself to do it. Instead he spoke as sharply as he could, using the same words he remembered the Taoiseach using.

"Cut that out!"

It had some effect. Kelly let go of his leg, and pulled himself into an upright position onto the couch beside Hanrahan. Despite his reservations that Kelly had already had too much to drink, Hanrahan went to the bar in the corner of the lounge and poured a stiff brandy for the Foreign Minister. Then, after a moment's thought, he poured another for himself.

When Kelly had taken a drink, Hanrahan began talking as fast as possible.

"Look, Sean," he said. "You know and I know that you really fucked up in Brussels - you almost blew the whole election campaign. I don't know whether the Taoiseach intends to fire you or not - frankly I wouldn't be too surprised if he did. But you have a great chance now to buy yourself some insurance. How can he fire the man who signed the Treaty in the White House? If you carry off the next couple of days with dignity, you could end up Foreign Minister for life!"

His words were having the desired effect. Although he still sniffled occasionally, Kelly had stopped crying. Again they sat in silence for a while. Hanrahan sipped at his brandy, remembering suddenly that there were ten reporters in the economy section of the plane, all of them accompanying the trip to Washington. Christ! he thought. What if any of them had come looking for the Foreign Minister?

"He's a bastard, Tim," Kelly said suddenly. "A vicious cruel bastard. I don't know how you can work so close to him."

"You voted for him," Hanrahan said shortly. He remembered it well. At the time Kelly was regarded as someone who might be a potential Leader himself, and his public declaration of support for Gibson's leadership had been important in securing the job.

"Yeah, I did," Kelly replied shortly. "And if I hadn't he would have destroyed my marriage then - or his bitch of a wife would. You probably know that already."

"I don't know what you're talking about," Hanrahan said.

Hanrahan looked at him for a moment before saying anything.

"Well, maybe you don't at that," he said. "I always assumed you were involved."

"I told you - I don't know what you're talking about," Hanrahan repeated.

So Kelly told him. The affair in Brussels wasn't the only time he'd been caught with his pants down. The only difference was that on the previous occasion, Gibson had organised it - or so Kelly had always believed. Kelly had thought he was seducing Gibson's mistress. In reality she had seduced him. After a couple of glorious nights, she had come to him in great distress one day, to say that Gibson had got hold of a film of them making love. How could there possibly be a film? She said it turned her on to be filmed making love. She didn't know how Gibson could possibly have got his hands on it. But he had, and he was coming for Kelly. She had never seen him so angry.

But when Gibson had come, he had been all charm. He never mentioned the film. Instead he said he had been meaning to talk to Kelly about the imminent retirement of the Leader. He was going to make a challenge, he said, and he was going to win. He felt sure he could count on Kelly's support - it would be in both their interests, he said - and he wondered if Kelly would consider, when the time was right, declaring publicly for him.

Kelly swallowed hard, and agreed. And that was it. To this day he couldn't be sure whether there was a film, or whether Finola Gibson had made the whole thing up, or whether she and Andrew had planned it all. But he had always believed that he had been set up.

"You probably never will know," Hanrahan told him.

But in his heart he knew that if there was a film, Kelly would find out eventually.

Most visitors to America make their acquaintance with the dreadful pap that's shown on late-night American television as a result of jet lag. Hanrahan was wide awake, but he didn't feel like watching television. He woke up sweating, and it was several minutes before he realised that he had been having a dream.

He had been lying naked in a field, and Gibson was standing over him, with a fence post in his hand. Again and again Gibson raised the fence post, and again and again it seemed to go right through him, to hit the ground on which he was lying. Standing to one side, beside an over-turned tractor, was Finola Gibson, blood dripping from her mouth as she screamed with laughter at each blow. Suddenly Gibson stopped, and stared over to the edge of the field.

Hanrahan, lying there on the ground, turned his head. Someone was crawling towards him, trying with an upraised hand to stop the beating that Hanrahan was getting. At first, Hanrahan couldn't recognise him. But as he got closer, it began to look more and more like Christopher McDonald.

But what had happened to him? Pieces of flesh were hanging from his face, his hands were the hands of a skeleton. Steam was rising from his body. His face was set in a terrible grin, and he never uttered a word. He simply crawled, horribly slowly, closer and closer to them.

Suddenly Hanrahan knew. McDonald was dead, and his body had somehow escaped from the grave to rescue him. Then he knew that he couldn't be saved. If there was nothing to rescue him but this rotting, decomposing corpse, then he was done for.

He turned his head again, to look up at Gibson. The fence post was being raised again, for one final, mighty blow. This time Hanrahan knew that the blow was meant for him, and not for the ground. He opened his mouth, to plead for his life, but nothing happened.

Higher and higher the fence post went, then it paused, and began to descend.

He staggered to the shower, and stood under the streaming water for five minutes before the image of his dream faded. Then, wrapped in a towel, he ate some of the fruit that had been left on his bedside table, to take the awful taste from his mouth. Finally he poured a glass of duty-free whiskey, and drank it in one gulp.

He looked at his watch. It was four in the morning. That meant it was ten o'clock on Monday morning in Kilkenny. Gibson would still be at home, since he was campaigning in his own constituency. Hanrahan felt the need to check in with his boss, to make a connection with reality. He picked up the bedside phone and dialled Gibson's number.

"Tim!" Gibson was jovial. "How's it going? Is everything all right?"

"Yes, fine, fine," Hanrahan replied. "We're flying down to Washington in the morning for the ceremonies. How are things back there? How did the rally in Callan go? I was hoping for a good turn out."

"You surpassed yourself, Tim," Gibson told him. "There was an enormous crowd, thousands of them. And we got a great reception. They played it on all the television channels last night. I reckon it was the sort of television that makes us unstoppable. I don't know how you organised that size of a crowd."

Hanrahan was pleased. He had put a lot of work into making sure there was a good crowd present, and he had guaranteed the TV crews they would get good footage. He was glad it had worked out.

"What about that story, Andy?" he asked. "I presume it hasn't appeared anywhere?"

"Of course not," Gibson told him. "I spoke to the Editor, you know that. He killed the story. There's no danger of it appearing anywhere now."

"But what about Flynn?" Hanrahan asked. "Have you spoken to him? He could take his story to someone else."

"Don't worry about him," Gibson chuckled. "Joe Stafford has taken care of him."

That was when Tim Hanrahan finally knew that Flynn's story was true.

CHAPTER 14

JULY 9th - THE FOURTEENTH DAY

THE REPORTER

The first thing I noticed was the smell. Someone had obviously been sick all over the place. It took me a while to realise that it had been me.

The next thing I realised was that I was hanging upside down, and swinging gently backwards and forwards. Even that was hard to figure out. I was in pitch darkness, and unable to move hand or foot.

Although I was desperate to remember what had happened, and how I had got here, my recollection was patchy. I remembered being hit on the head, and being bundled into the back of a car - a Toyota, with grey upholstery. Then nothing, until I was sitting on a kitchen chair, in a room with only a naked bulb for light - the sort of interrogation room I had always imagined from cheap American thrillers.

There were two other men in the room - two very big men.

They wanted to know who I was staying with. I wouldn't tell them. That is, I wouldn't tell them until one of them tied a rag around my face and chin. Not too tight, but close enough so I could feel the wetness, and smell the petrol in which it had been soaked. Then he sat about four feet away from me, and flicked lighted matches at me while he repeated the question. When one of the matches struck my cheek just before it went out, I told them

I had been staying with a girlfriend for a couple of days. That seemed enough for them to go on with.

"Are you expected back there for dinner?" was the next question.

In other circumstances it would have struck me as funny. The way in which they asked me made it seem almost as if they were anxious to invite me out to dinner. But I decided that maybe I could alarm them a little. So I told them that not only was I expected, but I was fairly sure my girlfriend would ring the police if I went missing.

That had no effect, except that they decided it would be a good idea if I sent her a note telling her not to expect me. They had to untie my hands while I wrote what they dictated. For a moment I thought I might get a chance to make a run for it. But almost as if he was reading my mind, one of them took a small but evil-looking gun from a back pocket. It was pointed at my head all the time I wrote the note.

The sight of the gun increased the uncontrollable trembling in the pit of my stomach. But even though I have never felt so frightened, the main thought going through my mind was the hurt that Margaret would feel when she got the note.

They didn't want to ask me any more questions, so I asked for the rag to be taken from around my neck.

"Sure," the bigger of the two men grinned, and stepped behind my back to undo the knot.

Suddenly, instead of loosening it, he began to pull it tighter and tighter. I felt the air leaving my body, and my eyes filled up with water, so that the room began to blur. I was going to die right here, and I didn't even know why it was being done.

"Jesus, he's after puking again," I remember the man in front of me saying, his voice heavy with disgust. And then the lights went out for the second time.

When I came to again I was in the back of a van. I was bound hand and foot - completely trussed up, in fact, like a large smelly parcel. We were obviously travelling fast.

Every time we hit a bump I bounced against the floor or the walls of the van. The pain in my head and throat was already overwhelming - my throat, especially, felt as if it had been through a furnace, and the fear was like nothing I have ever experienced.

Fortunately perhaps, I didn't stay awake too long. Despite the pain, which was being added to by every bump, the overall effect of the beating I was taking was an incredible drowsiness. The motion of the van, which was going somewhere in a hurry, put me to sleep again. And the next time I woke up I was hit once more, this time by one of two men who were manhandling me out of the back of the van. All I can remember about that is that it was the middle of the night - at least, I'm fairly sure the stars I saw were in the sky.

Now I appeared to have arrived - but where, and why? The room I was in was almost totally dark, so dark that at first I thought I was blindfolded. Gradually I began to see chinks of light. So I was in a room that had been blacked out. Even though I could see nothing, little by little I could tell it was not a prepossessing place.

The smell, for instance. I was contributing a good deal of it myself, but as my head began to clear, other smells began to come through, in particular a strong smell of oil, such as you get in a garage. And there was something else, something I couldn't define.

And it certainly wasn't comfortable. I appeared to be lying on my back, with my legs in the air. My legs were tied at the feet, so that the bones in my ankles were sticking into each other. And the rope tying my feet together was itself tied to some kind of beam, keeping me more or less suspended from the bottom up. Whatever my back was resting on was equally painful and seemed to consist of a collection of ropes which were cutting into my back.

I tried to move my feet, and would have shrieked only for the heavy tape across my mouth. The ropes cut into them viciously, and I immediately abandoned the effort.

Where the hell was I? It seemed to be the garage of somebody's house, yet why was it swaying like that? And what was that other smell, that I couldn't identify?

Suddenly it dawned on me. I was on a boat! The smell I had difficulty recognising was fish. No wonder the bastards had plenty of rope! They had me tied up in the hold of a fishing trawler.

I listened. There was almost no sound, except that now that I knew where I was I was able to discern the lapping of water against the sides. It seemed to be a long way away. I was as sure as I could be of two things - first, that this boat was not going anywhere, and second, that I had it all to myself.

But that information wasn't going to do me any good. It appeared that I was to be left here, like a trussed chicken, to starve to death. Try as I might, I couldn't even move my hands or arms. I decided that they had used a strait-jacket, or something that gave the same effect.

In all the circumstances, I've never been able to blame myself for what I did next. I started to cry.

In fact, I cried myself to sleep again. I didn't sleep well - in the cheap novel that I felt I belonged in now, I would have tossed and turned, but that was out of the question. And the chinks of light were still visible when I woke up. I assumed it was the same day.

I say woke up. Actually, I was woken up, by the simple yet effective expedient of having a bucket of ice-cold water thrown over me. This time, despite the tape over my mouth, I managed a small scream.

I could only see the silhouette of the man who had thrown the water over me, as he was standing with his back to a hatch through which bright sunlight was flooding. The light was almost as painful as the water, especially when I couldn't shield my eyes.

I could see enough to tell me that this man was as big as the others. He wasn't one of them, though. Neither of the others had had a Northern accent.

"Christ, you stink!" was his opening remark. He was right. But I didn't consider it my fault. He grinned as I wriggled at his feet like a big angry worm.

He had a long, vicious-looking knife in a belt around his waist. He used it to cut the rope that was tying me to one of the crossbeams across the roof of the hold. Without any way of preventing myself from falling, I rolled off the coil of ropes which had been supporting my back, and into a pool of dirty water on the floor. I lay there, unable to move, and feeling very sorry for myself.

He knelt over me, and pressed the sharp point of the knife into the back of my neck.

"I'll tell you what," he said. "I've been told to look after you, and make sure you behave yourself. I don't know who you are, and I couldn't care less. As long as you're a good boy, we won't have any trouble between us. If you get out of hand, I won't have any time for politeness. Is that understood?"

At the word "politeness" the point of the knife went a little deeper. I tried to speak, but all that came through the tape was a sort of high-pitched squeak. He reached under my face and ripped off the tape, and with it most of the two days or so of stubble that I had grown. I squeaked again.

He laughed, satisfied that he had made his point. Then he began systematically untying the ropes that had made me totally immobile. It took him a few minutes, and when he was finished he told me that I could come up on deck.

I tried to stand, but the circulation that was beginning to find its way back into my hands and feet made the effort impossible for a while. When eventually I was able to stumble up the ladder that led out of the hold I found I was standing on the deck of a small trawler. To judge by the amount of rust it was a craft that had seen better days.

We were at anchor. We seemed to be in the middle of a small, rocky harbour, about fifty yards away from the pier. Although there were a couple of yachts tied up to the pier, there was no sign of life - no-one to shout to. A narrow road led from the end of the pier up a hill. Halfway up I could see a pub, with some people sitting outside it. A group of children was playing with a skipping rope. But they were at least half a mile away - the noise they were making only carried very faintly.

My jailor saw me looking longingly up the hill, and grinned.

"You could use a bath, my friend," he said.

With that he suddenly grabbed me by the arm, and swung me over the side of the boat. I hit the water sideways on, and went down for what seemed like an age. When I resurfaced, I was gasping. Although I was a reasonable swimmer, I knew that I couldn't cope in this water, wearing a suit and with my shoes still on. The most I could do was tread water, and that's what my guard let me do for a few minutes. Then he leaned over the side and threw me out a length of rope. When I had grabbed it after a few attempts, he pulled me in and hauled me on board.

I stood there, shivering, like a dog who's just been bold and knows he's in disgrace.

"At least you smell a bit better now," the man said. Then he told me to go to the cabin under the wheel-house in the stern, and find myself some fresh clothes.

Oddly enough, by the time I had dressed myself in the blue sweater and jeans that I found in his cabin, I began to feel a bit better. Even though they were several sizes too big for me, they were clean and warm. The other thing that helped me to feel a bit human again was the sound and the smell of frying sausages from the wheel-house over my head.

When I want upstairs, he pushed a huge plate of fried food towards me.

"Eat that," he said, "and you'll feel a bit better."

"What is it?" I asked him, "breakfast, lunch or dinner?"

"Think of it as a late lunch," he said, laughing. "It's four o'clock in the afternoon."

"In that case," I said, "I suppose you haven't any whiskey?"

He had, and my God, it never tasted better. It also made me realise how hungry I was, and I wolfed the food he had given me, and followed that with half a loaf of white bread. When I was sipping a mug of steaming tea, I asked him,

"Who are you? Why are you holding me prisoner like this?"

He put down his own cup, and looked at me.

"I'll only tell you this once more," he said. "I don't know anything about you, and I don't give a shit. I've been told to keep you out of harm's way for a while, that's all. I could have done without it - I have a job to do, and I can't afford you getting in the way. But there's no reason why we shouldn't get on, as long as you behave yourself. If you don't, my orders are to fuck you over the side - and to make sure you sink. And that's all right by me too. So you see," he concluded, "it's really up to you, isn't it?"

I stared at him. Just what the fuck was going on here? Who was this guy? From the moment I had been hit on the head - was that really only two days ago? - I had been in a state of deadly fear. These people could talk to me any way they liked, and I had lost whatever capacity I had to stand up for myself because of that fear. And only now was I beginning to be even curious about why all this was happening. I assumed it had something to do with the story I had written - but how could Gibson or anyone else organise for me to be kidnapped like this? What kind of resources did the guy have?

It was probably the food and the whiskey and the clean clothes, but the fear in me was beginning to fade, and to be replaced by anger. I had rights, dammit! I was a reporter in a democratic country where the freedom of the press to tell the truth is supposed to be cherished. And somebody was prepared to go to incredible lengths to stop me from telling the truth. Even to the lengths of having me killed if necessary. Well, they weren't going to get away with it. Fuck them, I thought, I've been in tighter spots than this one.

That thought brought me up short. What was I talking about? I'd never been in a spot remotely as tight as this one. The closest I'd ever been to danger before was when the paper's accountant had nearly had apoplexy over the state of my expenses. How was I going to get out of a mess like this?

The more I thought about it, the more clear it became that I was up against resources that were way beyond anything I had at my disposal. These people had found me in the first place - and I had been congratulating myself on how well hidden I was. And wherever we were now, it was a long way from Dublin. I couldn't count on finding any friends or colleagues to come to my rescue here. After the screaming match I had had with O'Byrne, I couldn't expect him to discover I was even missing for at least a week.

My newfound anger, it occurred to me, wasn't going to do me any more good than the fear had.

I would have to keep my wits about me if I was going to get away from here. I wasn't under any illusion that they were going to let me go -how could they? The story I could publish now was much more dramatic even than the story I could have published before I was abducted. I presumed that they just hadn't got around to making the decision about when and how I should be killed.

"You needn't worry about me," I told my companion, who was peeling an apple with his enormous knife. "I'm not in any condition to cause you any trouble."

"Then," he grinned at me, "we should get on fine."

I had assumed I was going to have to spend the rest of the day back in the stinking hold, but in fact he locked me in the cabin. It was the only one on board, a small, bare room, with a bunk slung on each wall. There was a line of three tiny portholes running the length of each wall, but since they weren't much bigger than the size of my fist, there was no chance of escape through them. Otherwise there was little or nothing - a few blankets, some old clothes, and a couple of mattresses. There was nothing that could be used as a weapon.

I lay down on one of the bunks to assess my situation.

I had crossed a powerful man. I had done so without realising how powerful he was, or how he was prepared to use his power. There was no doubt in my mind that Gibson had ordered that I be found and abducted. But in order to find me, he would have to use the resources of the Gardai. They would need to believe that I had done something wrong before they would look for me – and I didn't believe that they would abduct me in this fashion.

Unless Joe Stafford was involved? That made sense. He wouldn't need any persuading, and he had the resources. He could easily have found my car from its registration number, and he had the men and equipment to hold me indefinitely.

I would just disappear, and if called upon, Stafford would lead the search for me himself. That made it more certain that I was in mortal danger. Letting me go, in addition to all the other secrets that would come out, would blow the lid off Stafford as well as Gibson. And Stafford would never allow that.

What was clear was that whatever ambition I had to end the career of Andrew Gibson, it was much more likely that he would end mine first. There was no way I could get off this boat, and it was surely only a matter of time before the man who was holding me prisoner got instructions to kill me. Then, no doubt, I would be taken out to sea and that would be the last that would ever be seen of me or my story.

That was when I made the resolution that I would go down fighting. The anger that I was feeling was probably no more rational than the fear which preceded it, but I decided that there'd be no whimpering when the time came, and that I wouldn't make it easy for them to make me disappear.

I lay there as the light faded outside the porthole windows, waiting for something to happen. But nothing did. I could hear occasional movements on the deck above my head, and once or twice the sound of the two-way radio in the wheel-house, although I couldn't make out the words being used. It seemed that my captor was having a day off.

Shortly after dark, things began to change. For a start, the footsteps above my head became more frequent. And then I heard voices, at least two voices in addition to the one I was already familiar with. All three were gathered in the wheel-house.

After they had been on board about an hour, there was a sudden flurry of activity on the deck. And then, so suddenly that I was startled, the engines, directly underneath me, came to life.

We were going to sea.

THE CELL

There were three of them, two men and a woman. One of the men was the detonator, the other two were his communication link. They had all been in position for over a month.

The main difficulty they had had was in renting a house. From the beginning of the tourist season, it is almost impossible to find a house, or even a hotel room, within a ten mile radius of Blackpool. In the end, they had succeeded in finding one just outside Poulton, about a quarter of an hour away from the piers and promenades of England's premier seaside resort. There, they had filled in their time much as other holiday-makers do. They'd spent a day at Pleasure Beach, and at the other sea-side attractions. They'd gone to some of the shows that drew huge crowds to see second-rate comedians every night.

And everything they had seen convinced them that the English had no sense of history or culture. The basic contempt that they had each shared for Britain's working classes had been deepened by the month they had spent in close contact with them.

Today was the day that it was all going to prove worthwhile. It had been a long time since a foreign Head of State had expressed a wish to see Blackpool. But today the President of Greece was coming, at his own request, and accompanied by a senior British Minister, to see the town, meet the people, and take the elevator to the top of the famous Blackpool Tower.

That was where they were going to blow him up.

At least, originally they had planned to blow the elevator out of the Tower itself. IRA intelligence had let them know that there would be cameras trained on the tower as the President was rising to the top. It would have made spectacular television if they could have done it.

But after they had made a number of reconnaissance trips, both together and separately, they had come to the conclusion that there was no way they could position the plastic explosive without the risk of discovery. There was security on the tower every day, and it was odds on that security would be tightened as the Presidential visit drew closer. Even though the plastic would escape detection by sniffer dogs - it was Czechoslovakian, and had been driven into England through Weymouth from Cherbourg - it was too risky to hope that the four pounds they would need to use would remain hidden in or around the elevator.

That was why they had settled on hiding the plastic just inside the door of the amusement arcade which was itself right at the entrance to the tower. It would be just as effective, although the television pictures would not be nearly so dramatic. The only other problem was that it involved split-second timing. To be absolutely sure of eliminating the target, the bomb had to go off as the President was passing the door of the arcade.

The detonator had positioned the bomb over a week previously. He had spent an hour playing the slot machines in the arcade, the plastic nestling under the armpit of his jacket, until he was certain that he could slide it under the machine without anyone seeing. It would sit there until it was discovered or until he sent the high-frequency signal that would send it, and the heavy metal machine, sky-high, scattering shrapnel in a huge arc.

He was ready now, waiting. The girl had volunteered to take the real risk. She was standing at the crush barriers outside the tower, almost invisible in the crowd of onlookers, a tiny walky-talky concealed in her hand. Ten seconds after the President walked past her, she would give the signal. Both the President and the British Home Secretary would be inside the tower then. They had chuckled at the irony that the Foreign Secretary, who would normally be accompanying such an important foreign visitor, would probably be saved by the fact that he was in America to sign the Irish Agreement.

After the girl gave the signal she would have a further ten seconds to get to the back of the crowd. With any luck, she would survive the blast. But she had known that there was a certain risk when she had volunteered for the mission.

The detonator was three blocks away, sitting in a MacDonalds restaurant behind the tower. Although it was a cool day, he was sweating slightly. The earphones he was wearing made him look as if he was enjoying listening to his Walkman while he ate french fries.

Even though he was listening intently, he could still hear the sirens that meant that the motorcade was coming down the pier. He was even close enough to hear the applause as the President alighted from his car at the tower, together with the Home Secretary, to be greeted by the Mayor of Blackpool.

Despite his experience, he was startled when his earphone crackled into life. It was just one word, whispered at him.

"*Now!*"

Silently, he began to count, his hand reaching into his inside pocket. He was already standing, moving out of the restaurant, as he pressed the button. The driver had seen him standing, and the car was at his side almost as soon as he reached the pavement.

The mass of the buildings between them and the tower meant that they were fully protected from the shock waves from the blast. All they had to go on was the sound of the explosion. For just an instant after the button had been pressed, the detonator wondered if something had gone wrong. The delay that always occurred if you were depending on the sound to know if a bomb had gone off was something he had never quite got used to. But everything went so smoothly that they were already on their way back to the house in Poulton before the first ambulance arrived. Now all they had to do was wait for the girl to make her way back to them.

But she never made it. As the President stepped out of the car, he had turned to wave at the crowd. In response, the crowd had surged slightly forward, knocking her off balance. On the ground, and unable to see the target, she had taken the chance that he had already passed, and had given the signal.

By the time she had struggled to her feet, she was able to see her mistake. Instead of entering the tower, the President had walked over to the crowd, and was shaking hands. She saw him being thrown to the ground by the force of the blast, but she never knew whether or not he survived. Pieces of the building showered down on the crowd, and many of those who died were subsequently found to have been killed by vicious shards of glass.

That's what killed the girl. She was one of the first taken to hospital, but the glass had entered her eye, like the stabbing of a knife. Even if she had lived, she would never have seen anything again.

CHAPTER 15

JULY 10th - THE FIFTEENTH DAY

THE REPORTER

By my reckoning, we sailed until about midnight.

I'm not a good sailor. Not that I've had that much experience - the once or twice I've been on a boat would not qualify me to sail around the Horn. But the going seemed to be easy tonight. After we had come out of the little harbour in which we were anchored, the water never seemed to get more than choppy. Even so, the smell of oil and the gentle rolling of the room in which I was locked, together with the steady chugging of the engines, began to make me feel decidedly queasy.

I was determined not to be sick again. Every time these men came near me, I threw up. And since I was sure the next time I saw them would be the last time, I decided that there would be none of that. So I lay on my bunk, keeping as still as possible, with my eyes closed, until the feeling wore off.

But they never came for me. Instead, they laughed and chatted in the wheel-house. I could hear the occasional sound of bottles clinking, and the two-way radio crackled now and again.

Eventually we stopped, and the engines were cut off. To judge by the steady swell, we were fairly far out from land. I could see no moon through the portholes, but it was a cloudless, starry sky. We drifted gently in the water, obviously waiting. I had no idea what we were expecting, but I didn't have long to wait.

In the stillness of the night, I heard a sound, very faint at first, then getting louder as it got closer. We were being joined by another boat, somewhere out in the middle of the Irish Sea, or the Atlantic, or wherever we were.

I could see from its silhouette as it came alongside that it was substantially bigger than ours. There was a good ten minutes of throwing of ropes backwards and forwards to tie the two boats together before someone from the other one stepped onto ours.

I began to think that they had forgotten I was below. In any event, there was no effort to conduct a conversation in hushed tones - instead it was loud and boisterous, with a lot of back-slapping and more clinking of glasses. The only trouble was, although I could make out that they were talking Spanish, I couldn't understand a word of it. In spite of everything, I chuckled at the thought that I was feeling like a reporter again - I would have given anything to know what was happening on deck.

The other thought that occurred to me was that maybe the point of this rendezvous was to put me on board the Spanish boat. But nobody came down to the cabin. Instead they began loading something from the coaster on to our boat. Whatever it was, it was heavy. There was a great deal of grunting and groaning, as our new cargo was piled piece by piece on to the deck of the trawler. It went on for about an hour - I counted about twenty heavy pieces of cargo - before another bout of drinking and back-slapping. Then the ropes were untied, and the coaster pushed off. In less than ten minutes the sound of its engines was no longer audible.

There was silence on deck, then a hushed conversation. Either they had remembered they had me on board, or they were deciding what to do with me. I stood up, with my back pressed against the bunk. I was convinced that the moment had come.

But when the door above me opened, I knew that resistance would be useless. The man who lowered himself into the room was carrying a short, ugly-looking machine gun.

And he was carrying it loosely in one hand, with the confidence of someone who knew exactly how to use it. Before his feet had touched the floor of the cabin, the gun was braced against his underarm and pointed directly at my head.

"You!" he said. "Lie down on that bunk, with your face against the pillow."

I did as I was told. The anger that had been building inside me had dissipated in an instant at the sight of that machine gun. It was replaced by the same cold, sweaty fear that I knew so well by now.

He reached under the bunk and took out a length of rope. Then, quickly and expertly, he tied my two hands together at the wrists, told me to bend my knees and looped the rope tightly around my ankles. In about five seconds he had tied my hands and feet together in such a way that I was completely unable to move.

"That'll keep you out of mischief," he said with a grunt as he tied the last knot. Then he shouted to his companions on deck,

"OK! You can start bringing the stuff down now."

There were two others, including the one who had given me the bath. Between them they lowered a wooden crate, about four feet long and three feet square, down into the cabin.

When it was stacked neatly against the wall, they brought down another one. Then another, and another, until all twenty were piled up in the cabin. It didn't leave much room for anything else.

The new man, the one with the machine gun, was evidently the leader of the group. He had supervised the loading operation, and now, while the other two rested, panting and sweating, he went up on deck and came down with a crowbar, with which he wrested the top off one of the crates.

The crate was full of guns, just like the machine gun he had slung around his own shoulder. He took the top one out, and threw it to one of the others.

"Well, Mick," he said, in the same soft Northern accent, "not a bad night's work?"

The other man hefted the gun, expertly. He evidently liked the feel of it.

"These should make a hell of a difference, Padraig," he said.

Padraig! I knew his face was familiar. I had never seen him in the flesh, but Padraig Norton's photograph was on the wall of every newsroom in Ireland. But what the hell was he doing here? I had assumed that I had been taken prisoner by Stafford's men - what possible interest could the Provisional IRA have in me?

Mick saw me eyeing the machine gun, and grinned at me.

"You needn't worry your head about these, mate," he said to me. "They're absolutely harmless without the firing pins, and we won't be leaving any pins down here with you."

They all found that funny. With a single flick of his knife, Mick, my jailor, cut the rope that tied my wrists and feet together. I sat up on the bunk, rubbing my arms.

"The rules are the same," Norton said to me. "We're supposed to make sure you don't cause any trouble. Provided you stay quiet, there's no reason anything should happen to you."

I didn't believe him. There was no way, I knew, that they were going to let me go in the end. But I figured the end would come a lot quicker if Norton realised that I had recognised him. So I said nothing, just watched as all three went back up the steps out of the cabin.

The way Norton had expressed himself planted a thought in my mind. Could it be that they were looking after me on Gibson's behalf? It seemed absolutely outlandish, and yet he had spoken as if they were operating under some kind of instructions. If that were true, then it probably meant that the Provos' ceasefire was part of a deal between Norton and Gibson. I wondered if I was part of the same deal. If I was going to be killed, wouldn't it be much more convenient all round if I were killed by the Provos?

Within a few minutes, we were under way again. Dawn was breaking before we anchored. To judge by the view from the porthole, we were back where we started. The door of the cabin opened, and Mick came down with a plate of food for my breakfast.

"Another couple of hours," he said, "and you and I will be back on our own again."

In fact three or four hours more elapsed before Norton and his companion left the boat. In that time we had travelled from the little harbour from which we had started the night before to another, bigger harbour. From the window of the cabin I could see a sign on the quay side. It said: "Day trips to Cape Clear. 2.00 pm from Schull, 2.30 pm from Baltimore".

That was the first inkling I had of where we were. Both Baltimore and Schull were in West Cork, about two hundred miles from Dublin.

Obviously it was still early in the day. The quayside was quiet. I could see a number of yachts bobbing about in the harbour, but there was no sign of life anywhere. No point in shouting for help - and anyway, Padraig Norton was not the sort of man to flinch at the thought of what might happen to any innocent passersby.

There was a short, hushed conversation on deck before they left. We weren't tied up directly alongside the quay, and I could see their legs as they clambered over the boats that were between us and the jetty. Then Mick and I were alone. But we couldn't be alone for long. Those guns had to be unloaded soon, probably before the local people began to converge on the harbour.

I could hear him moving about on deck, shifting things from place to place - no doubt trying to look like a busy fisherman. I looked around the cabin again. It was ridiculous - the place was full of guns, and yet there was nothing I could use as a weapon. The only way I could use one of them was as a club.

That was better than nothing. Taking one out of the open crate, I crouched behind the steps into the cabin, hoping that he would pay me another visit before anyone else came back.

It seemed like a long time before he did, but in fact it wasn't more than fifteen minutes or so. What brought him down to the cabin I never found out, because everything went with the smoothness you only get in dreams. He came down the steps without even looking around. I stepped out from behind him and hit him as hard as I could on the back of the head. I'd never hit anyone like that before, but the effect was gratifyingly the same as you see on television. His legs buckled at the knees, and he hit the floor face first. The sight made up for a lot, although I was hardly able to believe it. I grabbed some of the rope that I had been tied with, and tied his hands behind his back as tightly as I could. Then I got off the boat in a hurry.

There was a warehouse on the pier, with a big sign outside advertising the Schull Fishing Co-operative. All I knew about the place was that it was a long way from Dublin. It's a fishing village in West Cork, and at this time of year it ought to be full of visitors - yachtsmen and their families, tourists from Cork City and from further afield. As well as all those, I figured there was probably an influx of Provos, the reception committee for all those guns in the cabin. That meant that they would discover I was missing before long, and there was no doubt in my mind that they would come after me. The problem was how to get out of Schull as fast as possible.

I walked up the road from the harbour, and within a minute I was in the village. I got a double shock there. In a shop window in the main street, a clock told me it was still only half-seven in the morning. If I knew rural Ireland, that meant that at least another hour would pass before there would be any sign of life, and I had been developing a theory that I'd be safer if the streets were busier. The same shop window also showed me my reflection - and Jesus, did I look a mess!

In fact, I looked so bad that if I'd been a policeman, I'd have arrested me on sight. The clothes I had been given to wear were about two sizes too big for me - a blue woollen jumper, a pair of old denim jeans, and canvas shoes that had bits hanging off them. My hair looked as if it had been tortured, I was sprouting several days of scruffy beard, and although I was no longer stinking, I was far from clean. If a man looking like me said to a policeman "there's a boat in the harbour with twenty crates of guns for the Provos on board", they'd assume he was either drunk or mad. And besides, there were all the signs of collusion between the Provos and the Gardai - how else did I end up a prisoner on the boat in the first place?

I was tempted to go to the Gardai. I didn't know how to get away otherwise - I had no money and no means of identification. But if my suspicions were correct, one phone call from them to Dublin would result in my being a prisoner again.

I thought of stealing a car, but in my line of work that's not something in which you acquire a great deal of experience. And besides, what better excuse could the Gardai wish for if they wanted to pick me up? In a funny sort of way, I felt that the only thing I had going for me was the fact that I hadn't done anything wrong. All I'd done was to get myself kidnapped, beaten up a few times, and held prisoner on a boat.

The boat! There'd be money there for sure. And even if the Provos discovered it had been stolen, they were hardly going to report it to the Guards. But could I go back, and get away again? The very thought of it made my palms wet.

By the time I had decided that I had no alternative but to try the boat again, another ten minutes had passed. The absence of people, and particularly the absence of noise, gave me some confidence. I knew that when the Provos came back, they would have to be in a lorry of some kind, so there was a good chance I'd hear them coming.

I climbed back over the yachts that were tied to the jetty, and on to the boat, as quietly as possible. There was no sound from below. I wondered if I should go and check - what if I had killed Mick?

What if he had got free, and was waiting down there for me? With a start, I realised that I was still as afraid as I had been when I was convinced they were on the point of killing me. I shook myself. Fuck them, I thought. And fuck you too, Flynn - get on with doing your job. That made me feel a little better. So did the realisation that there was no need for me to go below - I had already searched the cabin, and there was hardly likely to be any money in the stinking hold where I had started my journey.

The wheelhouse was in a bit of a mess, with plenty of evidence of the previous night's eating and drinking still lying around. Otherwise all that was in it, apart from the radio, a radar, and other bits of nautical equipment that meant nothing to me, were two small lockers. The first was full of food and cooking utensils. The pots and pans were none too clean, even though I could still remember how good the food they had provided had tasted a couple of days ago.

The other one was stuffed with sea charts, which all fell out when I opened it. Behind them was a small tin money box.

The reputation that the Provos have for accumulating large sums of money is well earned. A lot of it comes from bank robberies and other crimes, in addition to the money they gather from voluntary subscriptions. So I wasn't surprised to discover a roll of ten pound notes and some loose change, at least a couple of hundred pounds in all. The only other thing in the box was a couple of cassette tapes.

They looked perfectly ordinary - the sort of thing, I assumed, that any fisherman would have on his boat to while away the hours when there was nothing on the radio. To say that I was in a hurry would be an understatement, and I had no interest at all in Mick's musical taste, so what made me glance at the neatly typed labels on the cassettes God only knows. One said "Gibson 1", the other "Gibson 2".

At that moment, startling me, there was a loud moan from the cabin below. I had almost forgotten Mick. Quickly, I stuffed the money and the tapes into the pockets of my jeans, and climbed off the boat and back onto the jetty. I was half-way up the hill back into the village before I looked back to be sure I wasn't being chased.

There was no sign of anyone. The trawler was lying quietly on the water, tied up to several other boats, all of which were also quite still. I stopped dead in my tracks, though, when for the first time I noticed the name of the boat on which I had been held prisoner. It was painted high on the prow, in letters which had begun to fade into the rust - "Margaret".

My heart lurched. What could she have gone through since I was abducted? At least I knew where I was, but all she knew was that someone she had befriended - had fallen in love with, I hoped - had disappeared without a word. Even though it was only a couple of days since I had been with her, it seemed an awful lot longer. And how much longer must it seem for her, wondering why I had left, and probably believing by now that I had been bought off like all the others.

My immediate instinct was to ring her, to reassure her that I hadn't done a bunk. But I knew that was crazy. If Joe Stafford was involved in all of this, and I was certain that he was, it would be an elementary precaution for him to put a tap on her phone. He could even have taken her off somewhere, for all I knew.

So I decided to concentrate on getting back to Dublin as quickly as possible. That's when I had my first bit of luck in quite a while. I was hiding in the doorway of a shop, uncertain of which way to move, and sure that Norton would be back at any moment, when I heard a tractor coming up the main street. Watching him approach, I was able to make certain that it was neither of the two men who had been on the boat. I thumbed him down and asked him for a lift.

He was hauling milk to the creamery in Skibbereen, and was glad of company at that hour of the morning. I told him that I was having a problem with the engine of my yacht - I even motioned to one of the yachts in the bay to convey the impression that I was really a well-to-do sailor - and that I was anxious to get in to one of the garages in Skibbereen as early as possible for some spare parts.

He seemed to consider this an adequate explanation for my appearance, and we chatted for the rest of the journey about crops and milk, and about how the good summer, though it might be a blessing for tourists like me, was a curse for the farmers. You needed a bit of rain for the grass to grow, and besides, in this hot weather, the cattle needed watering twice a day. In the course of the next fifteen miles, I learned a lot more about farmers' problems than I felt I needed to know.

Although it was only fifteen miles, I was glad when it was over. There is no room for passengers on a tractor, and I had to stand all the way, bracing myself against the side of the cab. My adventures of the last couple of days were beginning to take their toll, and as the adrenalin of my escape subsided, I became more and more weary.

He dropped me off outside a hotel at the edge of the town. Despite my anxiety to be on my way, I went in and ordered the biggest breakfast I have ever eaten. The only newspaper available at that hour, the *Cork Examiner*, provided no cheering news. It was full of a terrorist explosion in Blackpool the previous day, apparently aimed at the President of Greece. He had survived, but more than twenty bystanders had been killed. The newspapers were speculating that the attack had all the hallmarks of the Provos, even though they had not admitted any liability.

The obvious question that was being asked was whether there were any implications in the explosion for the ceasefire announced only a few days previously. On balance the expectation appeared to be that "Gibson's ceasefire" would hold.

The other main story was the latest national opinion poll, which gave Gibson's Party sixty-two per cent of the vote with only a week to go to polling day. That would be enough to make him a virtual dictator - and there was no doubt in my mind that that was what he would become.

There was already, before the election was even over, open speculation that Charles Page was on the point of resignation from the leadership of his party. He was reported to be in a state of deep depression over the indifference his campaign was receiving. If the Leader of the Opposition were to resign before polling day, the few people left who wanted to vote against Gibson wouldn't know who to vote for, and extra seats would fall like ninepins into Gibson's lap. For this reason, the paper's political correspondent wrote, Page's closest advisers, including Pat Crowley, were urging him to stay and make a fight of it.

I snorted when I read this. I had given Crowley the chance to stop Gibson once and for all, and he had refused it. If and when Gibson won the massive majority that the polls were now predicting, Pat Crowley would be one of the people to blame.

Skibbereen is much bigger than Schull, and was already, at that hour of the morning, bustling. The numbers of people on the streets made me feel safer. Like most country towns in Ireland, it had several of those shops where you can buy anything, and in one of them I bought a new summer shirt, jeans, underwear, and canvas shoes. I was able to change in a cubicle at the back of the shop.

Then I had a shave and haircut in one of those old-fashioned barbers that are hard to find nowadays in Dublin. Finally, both refreshed and respectable again, I hired a car. I was worried that the girl in the small rent-a-car place would want my driver's licence, but she was more interested in the ten-pound notes I waved around.

I explained that I was on a boating holiday - not the sort of holiday where you normally carry your driver's licence - and that I had been called back to Dublin in a hurry because of an illness in the family. And I signed the form Andrew Hanrahan.

Even though I paid cash for everything, I still had over a hundred pounds of Provo money in my pocket as I set out on the six-hour journey to Dublin.

It was the middle of the afternoon when I got back to the outskirts of Dublin. I abandoned the car there, took a bus into the city centre, and another one to Ranelagh.

Mount Pleasant Square, where the flat is, is bounded on three sides by houses. The main road through Ranelagh itself is the fourth side of the square. In the middle of the square there's a small park. Although it has a couple of tennis courts, the park consists mostly of trees and shrubs. There are high railings all around it, to prevent the kids from the working-class houses nearby from having any access to the tennis courts.

I walked up and down the railings by the main road until I found a gap big enough to squeeze through. Once I was in the park, it was easy enough to find some bushes on the far side that would give me a good vantage point. I had decided that I wouldn't take any chances this time; I wanted to make certain that nobody else was watching the flat.

Because it was a basement flat, its natural light was limited. That meant that if Margaret was home, the light in the front room would almost certainly be on. I was fairly sure that she wasn't at home.

I was right. It was six o'clock when her little car drove in to the square, and she went into the flat. At first I wanted to go in after her immediately, but some instinct kept telling me to wait - to be certain that nobody else was waiting and watching. So I crouched there, until the midsummer light began to fade. The street lights came on, the flow of traffic in the square eased off, and still there was no sign of anyone.

As the evening drew in, the temperature dropped, and I found myself shivering in the thin shirt I had bought earlier that morning. I'm still not sure why I waited so long that night - maybe it was the memory of the beating I had taken outside that door a couple of days previously. Or maybe I didn't want to see the look on Margaret's face when I rang her door-bell.

In the end, it was nearly ten o'clock when I screwed up the courage to climb the railings and cross the street to her door. If I was expecting to be hit over the head, I was disappointed. There was nobody waiting in the street for me. But the expression on Margaret's face when she opened the door was like being hit. It was neither hatred nor contempt - the look was one almost of distaste, as if a bad smell had come into the room.

"What have you come for now?" she asked.

I was more or less expecting the question, and the look on her face. I had a fair idea what she had been through since I had left. I could still remember how casual the note I had been forced to write had sounded, and I knew that if I had been in her position I would have come to the worst possible conclusions. But I had been through a lot as well, and when I heard her ask the question, all I could think of was how bloody unfair it was of her.

"Let me in," I said shortly, "and I'll tell you."

My tone took her aback. I could see that she wanted to refuse, to close the door in my face, but something stopped her, and she just stared at me for a moment. Then she stood to one side, to let me through the door.

"Come in Jim," she said, and this time there was a different trace in her voice, a trace of the beginning of understanding. She knew already, before I had said anything, that she had come to the wrong conclusions. It was almost enough to unman me. I slumped into a chair at her kitchen table, trying to regain my composure, while she closed the door of the flat. She waited to be told what had happened to me.

While she waited, I was trying to forgive her for thinking badly of me, and trying not to resent her because I felt guilty. I still can't explain the feelings that went through me just then - I remember thinking Jesus Christ! What gives her the right to be so understanding? Here we are - I've just had the shit kicked out of me for two or three days, and she's forgiving me for letting her down!

"Since I saw you last," I said, "I've been beaten up several times, tied upside down in my own puke, and been held prisoner on a fishing boat. I've also been interrogated, threatened, and thrown into the sea. I almost killed a man this morning - he might even be dead by now, for all I know - and I've stolen several hundred pounds to get back to your welcoming arms."

She winced as if I'd struck her. The sight cleared my head of all the shitty thoughts that had been going through it. I needed her then like I had never needed anyone before or since. I held out my arms to her, almost in despair.

"Oh, Margaret," I said, "forgive me ..."

She came to me at once, cradling me, rocking me backwards and forwards. She knew I was reacting, that the tension and fear and pain of the last few days was boiling over. She held me to her, as a mother holds a weeping child, so close that I could hear her heart. Then she lifted my face to hers, and kissed me. Again and again and again, with a passion that was overwhelming.

CHAPTER 16

JULY 11th - THE SIXTEENTH DAY

THE REPORTER

Sometimes it's only when you try to wake up that you realise how long and how tough the previous day was. It was eleven o'clock on Thursday morning before I awoke. I lay there for quite a while, feeling stiff and bruised all over.

But the tapes that I had taken with me from the boat soon woke me up. They were a recording of a meeting between the Taoiseach of the country and the Chief of Staff of the Provisional IRA, a meeting that had never been publicised, and no doubt would be denied if it were ever reported. But it couldn't be denied now, now that I had a complete record of it. It was all on the tapes: Gibson asking them for a ceasefire, Norton specifying his terms for agreeing. Among the things that Gibson agreed to was to pay them a million pounds in cash. That was obviously something that couldn't be done legally, but I had no doubt that there were ways of describing money like that which would make it impossible to discover.

And another of the things that Gibson had agreed to was to turn a blind eye to what was obviously a major arms shipment. And I had been there when that shipment had been delivered!

Most staggering of all was the knowledge that Gibson had made himself an accessory to some major crime that the Provos were about to commit in Britain itself. I remembered the *Cork*

Examiner headlines that I had read the previous day about the bombing in England - the tape that I had just listened to tied the Taoiseach irrevocably to that atrocity.

Clearly, even apart from the attempted assassination of the President of Greece on English soil, the Provos weren't serious about laying down their arms. If they were, why were they going to such lengths to get fresh guns into the country? I knew that they had brought in enough weapons to equip a small army. Gibson knew - it was obvious - that the whole thing was a manoeuvre to allow the Provos to refresh themselves, and to emerge stronger than they had ever been. I don't know what calculation he had made - possibly he had reasoned that when the six months was up they wouldn't have the stomach or the support, in the new situation that would exist, to come out fighting again. But it seemed to me that it was more likely that he just didn't care. A Provo ceasefire would be a huge feather in his cap, and it would copperfasten support for his Party, especially if it appeared that the ceasefire was a direct response to the Agreement. I figured Gibson would have been prepared to pay even more than he had for an arrangement like that.

The Head of the Government might be within his rights, for all I knew, in agreeing to an amnesty, but there was no doubt in my mind that the discussion about the boat that had been unloaded in my presence was a conspiracy to assist the Provos to commit a crime. Of course, no guns had been mentioned. But there wasn't a court in the country that would believe Gibson if he alleged that he hadn't known what would be on the boat.

The load of dynamite I was carrying had become even more lethal to Gibson than it was before - and my duty to use it even more urgent. For whom should I play those tapes? Certainly to no one at my own paper - I was certain by now that O'Byrne had been got at by Gibson.

That left Crowley. After the experience I had had with him, I didn't have much confidence that he'd be willing to help. But

I was fairly sure he was honest, unlike O'Byrne. I had tried to puzzle out his reaction on the day I had gone to see him, and the only conclusion I could reach was that he was scared. Not scared of Gibson, as such, but scared that if he accused him, it might just be seen as prejudice.

He would have to act, though, if he heard the tapes. Charles Page led a law and order Party, and Crowley himself was known for his hatred of the Provos. I knew that he would regard what Gibson had done as a gross betrayal.

The excitement was returning. I could already see myself sitting in the front row of the Press Conference, savouring the moment as Crowley read out a list of accusations to a stunned collection of reporters. Of course, I'd have my story written before the Conference started, and I had no intention of leaving anyone under any illusions about who had really broken the story. I wanted to see O'Byrne try to kill it now!

Margaret could see all the possibilities too. We had listened to the tapes together, and there was no need for me to explain the implications of the agreement Gibson and Norton had made. She urged me to ring Crowley.

He answered the phone himself, and recognised my voice immediately.

"Jim," he said, "where have you been? I've been scouring the country looking for you, but nobody's seen you for days."

"That doesn't matter at present," I said shortly. "Why were you looking for me?"

He didn't beat about the bush. "I behaved shamefully when you came to see me, Jim," he said. "Since then I've realised that what you know must be said publicly. What's more, I've discussed the whole thing with Charles Page, and he agrees. He wants to meet you as soon as possible."

We were in business!

"Where and when?" I asked him.

"My house, in about three hours," he said. "Is that OK?"

I looked at Margaret, who nodded furiously. I told Crowley that I'd be there.

"That's great, Jim," he said. "And don't forget to bring the papers."

I was glad of the three hours, because I had nothing to wear apart from the clothes I had bought yesterday. I still had some of the Provo cash, and Margaret went out with it to buy me some clothes.

Her taste turned out to be a little different from mine. I hardly recognised myself when I had put on the shirt, jacket and slacks she had bought.

This time, Margaret insisted, she was coming with me. I protested, but secretly I was very glad that she'd be there. If anything happened this time, the one thing I wanted to be sure of was that Margaret would know - that she would never again believe that I could deliberately let her down.

Charles Page was already in Crowley's study when we arrived. I knew him reasonably well, of course, although I hadn't met him since the campaign started. We could see that the strain of the election was telling on him. He looked older, and very tired. Still, he stood as we came into the room, and shook hands warmly with both of us. The famous charm was still intact.

"It was good of you both to come," he said after I had introduced Margaret, and explained that she knew everything I knew. "Especially good of you," he said to me, "after the short shrift you got on your last visit."

I shot a glance at Crowley, who had the grace to look embarrassed.

"Now," Page said, "perhaps you wouldn't mind telling me the whole story."

I told him everything I had told Crowley, giving him the photocopies of the McDonald papers at the appropriate point. Even though Crowley had evidently told him already, it was easy to see that he was completely shocked by what I had to say.

"And since I was here the other day," I added, "I've discovered rather more."

"It's hard to imagine what more there could be," Page said softly.

"Would you be surprised to discover that the Provisional ceasefire is as a result of an agreement between Gibson and them?" I asked him. "And that Gibson has paid for the deal with a million pounds of cash, an amnesty of some of the most vicious criminals around, and a large supply of weapons? And that Gibson knew that the Provos were planning to assassinate someone in Britain - probably the Blackpool bombing - and did nothing about it?"

Page was sitting bolt upright in his chair.

"That's crazy!" he said. "Even Gibson wouldn't dare to do something like that. If he were ever found out, there's no way he could defend it. He'd be destroyed instantly."

"Well, he's done it," I told him, "and what's more, the Provos taped the meeting."

I took the cassettes from my pocket. "These are the tapes of the meeting," I said. "They'll prove that everything I told you is true."

Page was staring at me in amazement. "How did you find all this out?" he asked.

So I told him that too. He shook his head, almost in disbelief.

"This is the most incredible story," he said. "If what you're saying is true, then the Taoiseach conspired with the Provisional IRA to have you kidnapped, and perhaps killed."

I bridled. I had been through it after all - I knew what was true.

"The tapes I have will prove it," I said shortly. "But if you're not prepared to believe me, I don't see the point ..."

He held up a hand. "I believe you Jim," he said. "I believe you implicitly. But you have to admit that this story is amazing, to say the least."

"Listen to the tapes," I told him. "You can have them - on one condition."

"What's that?"

"That you act on them - and that you do it before the election."

"You have my word," he said. "I will expose Gibson's crimes and his treachery within the next twenty-four hours."

He paused. "I need a couple of things," he said. "First, I need the originals of all the documents - I'm not going to take any chances of having Gibson say they're forgeries. Second, I want you to help me to write the statement I will have to make. You're so familiar with all the facts, there's much less chance of you getting anything wrong."

I agreed. At last the story was going to see the light of day, and I would be more than happy to write it. The only problem was that I'd have to get the originals out of the General Post Office. I looked at my watch. It was nearly four o'clock.

"If I hurry," I said, "I can get the letters and be back here in an hour."

"That's fine," Page told me. "In the meantime, I'll set the arrangements for a Press Conference in train. I think it's better if we don't give anyone a clue about our intentions. There's an opinion poll out in the morning, and it's bound to show Gibson way ahead. So I'll let it be known that I'm holding a Press Conference to react to that. The press will probably think I'm going to throw in the towel - they won't want to miss that!"

I stood up, and put the cassettes back in my pocket.

"If you don't mind," I said, "I'd like to be here when you listen to these."

"Sure," he grinned, "I can wait for an hour."

The General Post Office in Dublin is right in the heart of the city, in O'Connell Street. Because it was the location of the famous Easter Rebellion of 1916, its façade has been preserved, and its fine doric columns dominate the capital city's main street. Inside it's like any grubby post office anywhere in the world. Why is it that post offices and bus stations are always the dirtiest public buildings? In the middle of the floor there is a bronze statue of Cuchulainn, a mythical Irish warrior, which commemorates the heroic deeds performed in the building more than seventy years ago. Nowadays the only heroes are the cleaners, who have to grapple every day with cigarette butts and mountains of waste paper and sweet wrappings.

I had taken a chance, for the sake of speed, and had parked the car directly outside in O'Connell Street, even though it was a no-parking zone. Margaret was waiting at the wheel to drive around the corner if any traffic wardens threatened us.

When you're in a hurry, you're guaranteed a queue. I was ten minutes waiting at the Poste Restante counter before they handed me the letter I had addressed to myself a few days previously, with McDonald's notebook and the letters inside. And the heat and noise of the place was beginning to make me sweat.

I tucked the letter into an inside pocket, and turned to go. That's when I noticed the man leaning against the bronze statue. It was only afterwards that I realised why he looked out of place. It was the middle of July, a sweltering day, and even hotter in the fuss of the GPO. Yet he was wearing a raincoat, with one hand in his pocket.

That's why something odd registered, but it didn't register quickly enough. As I walked past him, he put out his free hand and stopped me.

"You have to come with me," he said.

I was too startled to react immediately. Even so, the thought of running must have shown on my face. Very quickly, he opened his raincoat and closed it again. There was just time for me to see the gun he was holding inside the coat.

If I had thought quickly, I would have run anyway. There was simply no way he could afford to open fire in that crowded place. But it's only in the movies that people think that quickly. I just stood there, while he took a grip on my arm.

"Where's your car?" he asked me.

At first I thought he would have to let me go in order to go through the revolving doors. But we both squeezed through together, and he never lessened his grip on my arm. Margaret was still sitting there, waiting. He opened the front passenger door, and thrust me in. Then, before either of us could do anything, he was sitting in the back, his gun pressed to my ear so that Margaret could see it.

"Drive," he said.

THE TAOISEACH

Stafford was exultant. "Everything is on course," he said.

The tone in the Taoiseach's voice changed his humour immediately.

"Get over here immediately," Gibson told him, before slamming down the phone.

"Where's Norton?" the Taoiseach demanded as soon as Stafford was shown into his office. "I'm taking terrible heat. The Brits know that it was the Provos that tried to blow up the Blackpool Tower yesterday. One of them was killed, and they've identified her as a Provo."

"Yes, I know all that," Stafford told him. "My own sources

have been feeding me stuff during the morning, and I would have been in a position to brief you ... "

"You don't understand!" the Taoiseach barked. Stafford had never seen him so agitated. "What if they ever find out I knew about this in advance? The British Prime Minister has been on to me twice already, and he is absolutely furious. He's already as much as accused me of misleading him about the ceasefire. He seems to think the whole thing was a plot to lull them into a false sense of security. Now he's saying that if the perpetrators aren't caught, and soon, he's going to rethink his entire attitude to the Agreement."

"But we know it was just a one-off ..." Stafford began.

"I know that, you fool," Gibson almost snarled at him. "But how can I tell him that? Norton has to help us now."

"I know where he is," Stafford said. "He's back in Dublin, and I can get to him easily enough."

"Tell him I have to see him - now," Gibson told him.

"I have something for you," the Taoiseach said. He pushed a slip of paper across the table. Norton glanced at it. Six digits were written on the paper. He looked at Gibson, his eyebrows coming together.

"It's a bank account number," Gibson explained. "One million pounds was lodged in that account this morning from -" he paused and grinned at the Provisional Chief of Staff - "the Military Intelligence Budget."

Norton shrugged. "It's not a lot of use to me without the name of the Bank being written on it."

"There's a reason I haven't given you that, Padraig," the Taoiseach said. "This whole agreement we have is in danger of unravelling, if I can't secure the arrest of whoever tried to assassinate the British Home Secretary and the President of Greece."

"Come on," Norton said. "You knew there was a danger this would happen. You can't renege now - you're playing for stakes that are too high."

"We're both playing for very high stakes," Gibson told him. "I've promised you an amnesty - when I deliver on that, you'll be in a position of strength. I've already delivered on your arms shipment - but I know where they are, right now. And I can deliver on the money. But only if you give me the bombers."

There was silence.

"We can blow it, or we can make everything all right." The Taoiseach spoke into the silence. "There's no point in either of us pulling back now."

Norton looked at him. He had never betrayed one of his own. But he knew Gibson was right - they had gone too far to pull back now. He scribbled down some words on a sheet of paper, and almost threw it at Gibson.

"No more killing," he said. "I want them arrested only."

"You have my word on that," the Taoiseach told him.

CHAPTER 17
JULY 12th - THE SEVENTEENTH DAY

THE TAOISEACH

The opinion poll that day was very good. In fact, considering how close they were to the end of the campaign, it was quite remarkable.

Not only had the Opposition failed to make any impression on Gibson, but he had drawn further ahead. His Party now stood at just under seventy per cent of the vote, with Charles Page reduced to nineteen per cent, and the smaller parties sharing the balance between them. It was clear that a landslide was inevitable.

Gibson still refused to take anything for granted. When he was asked to comment on the poll, all he would say was that the only poll that counted was the one next Monday. "If we are going to win this election," his statement added, "it's our responsibility to get every vote out on the day."

Privately, he was elated, so much so that he didn't notice how taciturn Hanrahan was when he brought the papers that morning. But then, he was bound to be suffering a bit from jet-lag. The trip to Washington had been another publicity boost, and Gibson was confident that it would consolidate their lead still further.

It had not happened in time to be reflected in this morning's poll, and Gibson had no doubt that it would add further to the atmosphere of triumph that the Agreement had generated. The commentators in the morning's papers had agreed. Unanimously, they all expressed the view that the Agreement had caught the public's imagination.

But there were other factors too. The Taoiseach's masterful handling of the transport strike; the declaration of a cease-fire by the Provisional IRA; the general outpouring of affection for the Taoiseach himself; and the lack-lustre campaigns run by the Opposition, were all regarded as reasons for Gibson's extraordinary performance in the polls.

The press had been told that Stafford would be briefing the Taoiseach this morning, but naturally, they hadn't been given the real reason. As far as they were concerned, the Taoiseach was being briefed on the security precautions that had been taken to prevent any spill-over of violence from the Orange parades that were due to take place later in the day.

The 12th of July is always the day on which the rituals of triumphant Unionism are given free rein in the North. They had an added significance now that Unionism was no longer triumphant. In fact, there had been a great deal of media speculation that this would be the day on which Unionist opposition to the Agreement, which had so far been expressed in a lot of huffing and puffing, could erupt. The Unionist leaders had been calling for hundreds of thousands of their followers to take to the streets today, to demonstrate that they would never be sold out.

In fact, all of the intelligence reports available suggested that the show of opposition would fizzle out. The Agreement, and especially those elements of it which guaranteed Unionists a place at the Cabinet table in the governing of the whole island, was proving attractive to some of the leadership, and most of the huffing and puffing was seen as ritual. None of the leaders wanted to be the first to indicate acceptance of the Agreement, for fear of being outflanked by any of their noisier colleagues.

But the Protestant people as a whole were war-weary, and there had been an audible sigh of relief across the North at the Provos' announcement of a cease-fire. That announcement in itself had seemed to knock the stuffing out of the Unionists, even more than years of killing had done.

So this morning's briefing about the security situation was hardly necessary. But it served another of Gibson's purposes. Throughout the campaign he had been careful always to look and sound like the Taoiseach in charge of the country. For that reason, he had avoided stumping around the country too much, and had been photographed far more at his desk in Government Buildings than out on the hustings. And the campaign events in which he had taken part had all been carefully planned and prepared, so that he never had the experience of speaking to a small crowd, or of turning up at any venue that hadn't been adequately warmed up in advance.

A briefing this morning, followed by a soothing statement re-emphasising the message that he was on top of any situation that might arise, would consolidate this effect. That's why the photographers were allowed in to the Taoiseach's office, to picture him in conference with his security chief. Hanrahan had ushered them in, and he left with them.

"I have a little bonus for you, Taoiseach," said Stafford as soon as they were alone.

He produced two cassettes from his pocket. "They're the tapes of your meeting with Norton," he said.

"How on earth did you get hold of them so soon?" Gibson asked him. He was obviously delighted.

"To be honest," Stafford said, "they fell into my lap. Flynn had them on him when we picked him up. They must have been keeping them on the boat with him."

"So your plan worked out even better than you had hoped," Gibson said.

"Yes," said Stafford. "It worked - except in one respect."

Quickly, he outlined what had happened. The Provos had let Flynn escape, after Stafford had made contact with the boat by two-way radio. One of his people had even given Flynn a lift into Skibbereen. When he had hired a car, they hadn't had to follow it very long. When Flynn had stopped for a cup of coffee in Cork City, one of Stafford's people had planted a bug on the car, which enabled them to keep tabs on Flynn's movements for the rest of the day.

The purpose of the plan was simple. Flynn had to think he had escaped, or he wouldn't go looking for the originals of his documents. And they had failed to find them any other way. They had found photocopies easily enough in Margaret's flat - so easily that she hadn't realised her flat had been broken into while she was at work. And they had traced photocopies waiting for Flynn in his office, and in an envelope addressed to him on the mantelpiece of his brother's house. But even though they had turned Flynn's own flat upside down, they had drawn a blank in their search for the originals. In the end, the General Post Office was an obvious place for them to have looked - so obvious that it hadn't occurred to them. Stafford had cursed himself when the report had come in that Flynn was heading for the GPO. If he had thought of it in time, they could have intercepted Flynn before he went to see Charles Page in Crowley's house.

That had given them some anxious moments. Stafford had bugs everywhere - in Margaret's flat, in the houses of most of the members of the Opposition front bench, including Pat Crowley. They had never been a more useful tool than they were in this exercise. The fact that they knew everything that was going on enabled Stafford to make quick decisions. His first reaction, when he realised that Flynn was going to go to see Page, was to stop him, especially as there had been no time to consult the Taoiseach.

But if he stopped him now, he mightn't get hold of the originals. They had watched Flynn very carefully, and Stafford was certain he wasn't in a position to give them to Page. So he had let the meeting go ahead, and now he had to tell the Taoiseach that Page knew everything, but could prove nothing.

That was when Hanrahan came back into the room, to tell them that the Leader of the Opposition, whom they had just been discussing, was demanding to see the Taoiseach immediately and in private.

Gibson looked at Stafford. "At least we know what he wants to see me about," he said.

"What?" asked Hanrahan.

"It's this Christopher McDonald business," Gibson told him. "Apparently Page thinks he knows something about it."

"And does he?" Hanrahan asked. He looked at both of them expectantly.

"Whatever he knows," Stafford said with a smirk, "he can't prove anything."

Hanrahan started to say something, then stopped. Instead, he shrugged.

"What do you think, Tim?" the Taoiseach asked him. "Should I see him?"

"That's up to you," Hanrahan replied shortly. "Personally, if the Leader of the Opposition had something on me, I'd want to see him."

"I think you're right," Gibson said, ignoring the other man's tone. "Tell him I'll see him in an hour."

When Hanrahan had left the room, Stafford asked, "What's eating him?"

"He doesn't know as much about this business as you do," Gibson told him. "And besides, I think the strain of this whole election is beginning to get to him. I think it's best if he's humoured until the whole thing is over."

"Now," he continued, "let's get back to business. Are you absolutely certain that Page has nothing to go on except Flynn's word?"

"Yes," Stafford told him. "I listened to the whole meeting. Page was particularly upset about the deal you did with the Provos, but he didn't have time to listen to the tape himself before Flynn went to get the letters. We got lucky there - if Flynn had trusted him enough to leave the tapes behind, Page would have something solid to use."

"So what I have to do is to discredit Flynn in Page's eyes," the Taoiseach said. "Where is Flynn now?"

"I have him and the girl under lock and key, up in the Phoenix Park," Stafford said. "I'm not too happy about it. I prefer to get someone else to look after this kind of thing. But I haven't had time to organise any alternative arrangements yet."

"You're going to have to hold on to them yourself for the time being," Gibson said.

Stafford looked at him.

"You know what I mean, Joe," the Taoiseach continued. "This time they're going to have to disappear for good."

When Page was shown into the office, Gibson could see immediately that he was uncomfortable. Before he had arrived, Hanrahan had told the Taoiseach that Page had called a Press Conference for two in the afternoon.

Even though their relations had never been good, Gibson felt that it was best to be gracious. He ushered Page to one of the armchairs, and took the other one himself, so that there was nothing between them. He knew that had he invited Page to sit in front of his desk, the other man, who had used that desk himself in his time, would be offended.

"What can I do for you, Deputy?" Gibson asked him, formally but politely. He had decided that it would be going too far to call Page by his first name, and had settled on the title that any member of Dail Eireann is entitled to use.

"I'm afraid I have to tell you, Taoiseach," Page answered gravely, "that I have come into possession of a most extraordinary set of facts. I believe I have a duty to make those facts public, and I would consider it less than honourable if I did not tell you in advance of my intentions."

Pompous ass! Gibson thought to himself. Out loud he said, "I'm afraid I haven't the faintest idea what you're talking about."

"I have been told about the circumstances in which you came to buy the land which subsequently became the Leinster Mine," Page said, and paused, studying Gibson's face for any sign of a reaction. There was one, but it was not what Page was expecting. To his amazement, the Taoiseach suddenly began to laugh.

After a moment, Gibson said, "You're not going to tell me, I hope, that Jim Flynn has been to see you!"

Page was startled. What was going on here?

"Indeed he has," he said. "And he has brought me documentary evidence of appalling wrongdoing on your part."

Now it was Gibson's turn to be startled. Stafford had assured him that there was no evidence left. He decided to try a shot in the dark.

"Do you mean the photocopies?" he asked. "Has he been showing you bad photocopies of letters and notebooks, and telling you they prove I killed someone? And I suppose he's been telling you about my efforts to murder my wife as well?"

Page looked at him suspiciously. "What do you know about all this?" he asked.

"I'm going to be frank with you," Gibson told him. "In the circumstances, I feel I should tell you everything I know. Jim Flynn came to see me about a month ago. He said he had evidence, in the form of letters written by my former legal partner, that I had killed someone in order to be able to buy their land. And that I had incarcerated my first wife in a mental hospital even though there was nothing wrong with her. I asked him if I could see these letters, and he showed me some rather grubby photocopies."

"What did you do?" Page asked him. Despite himself, he was intrigued.

"Well, obviously I was concerned," the Taoiseach told him, warming to the story. "There wasn't a word of truth in any of it, but Flynn is a journalist with a certain amount of credibility, and those letters, even though they were untrue, could have done a great deal of damage. Not just to me, but to the negotiations I was involved in at the time. But what really shocked me was when he told me he did not intend to publish them at all - provided I was willing to cough up twenty thousands pounds."

Page was aghast. "I don't believe you!" he blurted.

Gibson shrugged.

"I'm sorry," he said. "But that's what happened. He made me a very firm, very direct offer - pay up or else. What he was interested in was blackmail - not journalism."

Page didn't know what to believe. This was the man he despised above all others. He knew in his own heart that the reason Flynn's story had seemed entirely credible was because he knew that Gibson was capable of doing the things that Flynn described. But where had Flynn gone? And what kind of a fool would he look if he turned up at a Press Conference, to make accusations of which he had no proof, after being told Gibson's side of the story? He had no choice, he decided, but to press on, to see what else he could winkle out of Gibson.

"Did you pay Flynn?" he asked.

Gibson paused, as if considering what he should say.

"To be honest," he said, "I thought about it. And maybe if I had decided that that would be the end of it, I would have paid him. But in the end I decided that the very act of giving him money would have been an admission that I had conspired in my wife's death. And I wasn't prepared to do it. I told him to publish and be damned. I've been half expecting to see those letters and notes appearing somewhere ever since."

"He told us that his own paper had refused to publish the story," Page said.

"I'm not too surprised at that," Gibson replied. "It is a responsible paper, after all. But I expected at least one of the magazines to run with it. Some of them have no instinct for what's fair."

"What about the Provos?" Page asked suddenly. "Did you do a deal with them?"

Gibson hoped that the expression of outrage on his face looked genuine. "What deal?" he asked. "What are you talking about?"

Page faltered. "There were tapes," he began. "Tapes of a meeting between you and Padraig Norton ..."

"Where are these tapes?" Gibson asked him sharply. "Can I hear them? What rubbish is this?"

It was Page's turn to look deeply uncomfortable. He was sorry he had raised the subject, especially as he had never heard the tapes.

"I've seen them ..." he tried.

"Well, can I see them?" Gibson demanded. "Better still, can I hear them? If I'm going to be accused of doing deals with people I've never met, the least I'm entitled to, surely, is to hear the evidence against me."

Page had heard enough. He knew he couldn't allow this to continue. He didn't know what to believe himself now. From what he knew of Jim Flynn, the news that he was a blackmailer was hard to believe. But where was Flynn? All their efforts to locate either him or Margaret Deane last night had failed. He couldn't understand it, but he knew that without Flynn he couldn't take this any further. He would end up looking a fool, or worse. He stood up.

"Taoiseach," he said, "I'm sorry for troubling you. Clearly, I've been led on a wild goose chase. I felt that it was important that I came to see you before I took the matter any further, and I'm glad I did."

He stopped at the door of the office, and grinned ruefully. "I have to figure out what to tell a Press Conference now," he said.

THE ADVISER

Tim Hanrahan was in agony.

Ever since he had come back from the States, he had spent as little time in his boss's company as possible. He couldn't face him until he had screwed up the courage to tell him the one thing that had to be said. He had to tell him that he, Tim Hanrahan, Andrew Gibson's loyal and unscrupulous servant, knew that his boss was a murderer, and that he planned to murder again.

He'd had time to think on the way back from America. And the conclusion he had come to was that there was nothing he could do about the past.

Yes - what Gibson had done, on his way to wealth and power, was horrible. Tim Hanrahan knew - at least he thought he knew - that if Gibson had asked him to be his accomplice in the crimes that had been committed, he would have refused. But it had happened, it was over, and Gibson's accession to power had been worthwhile. The Agreement they all believed in had only come about because Gibson was there.

And besides, Hanrahan had told himself, who am I to be making judgments about Andrew Gibson? I've done a few things that were fairly shady myself - nothing like that of course, but still a few things I wouldn't like to be found out. And what good would it do to destroy Gibson now? What difference would it make? Who in the Party could take over and do half as good a job? Probably Sean Kelly, now that Hanrahan had helped him to become an international media star!

Hanrahan thought bitterly to himself - I could bring Gibson down, only to have him replaced by an absolute clown. And the first thing that Kelly would do would be to ensure that I have to look for another job. The more Hanrahan thought about it, the more clear it was to him that there was really nothing he could do. And the more clear that was, the more shame he felt. He wasn't going to lift a finger, and he despised himself for it.

And he began to hate the man who had put him in this position. That was why he had left the door to Gibson's office open.

Until the early 1980s the Taoiseach's office had been in the front of Government Buildings, overlooking Merrion Square. Then the Government had taken over part of the buildings which had belonged to the College of Science in University College. These buildings were between the Taoiseach's Department, and Leinster House, where the Dail sat, and their purchase had enabled the Department and the Dail to be linked.

One corridor in the new, linking, building had been reserved for Ministers' offices. They only used these offices when the Dail was actually in session, but it meant that if the Taoiseach needed them then, he had immediate access to them. The Taoiseach's own office had been transferred to the end of this corridor, half in Government Buildings and half in the Dail.

Beyond the Taoiseach's room was another room where his Private Secretary sat. The two rooms were linked by a small and totally private corridor, with a door at each end. One of those doors led into the Taoiseach's room. If you left it ajar, and stood in the corridor outside, nobody would see you, but you could hear everything that the Taoiseach said, to whoever was in the room with him. Hanrahan had stood in that corridor to hear Gibson and Stafford talking.

And he had heard the Taoiseach tell Stafford that Flynn and somebody else would have to be killed.

What was he to do? Whatever he felt about what Gibson had done already, how could he allow Gibson to do this? And how could he stop him? He knew now that Gibson was not going to let anyone stand in his way. If Gibson knew that he knew, he would cease to be any use to the Taoiseach. If Gibson could so casually order the killing of two perfectly innocent people, how could Hanrahan hope to escape, knowing all he knew?

And now Gibson wanted him in the office. Was he going to confide in him? Had the time come when his boss needed him to get involved in the crimes he had in mind? How was he going to look Gibson in the face?

He stood again in the corridor outside the Taoiseach's room, trying to compose himself. His hands were sweating. He took a deep breath, and walked in.

Gibson was standing at one of the tall windows, looking down into the College of Science car park below. He turned as Hanrahan came in. To Hanrahan's surprise, the Taoiseach was grinning broadly.

"I want a final rally, Tim," he said. "The biggest ever seen. And I want it right in the middle of O'Connell Street. On Sunday afternoon, the day before polling day."

Hanrahan avoided catching the Taoiseach's eye.

"Ok," he said. "But it'll take a bit of organising. That's only three days away."

"I know that, Tim," the Taoiseach said impatiently. "But you can do it. All it takes is phone calls. The Dublin constituencies will get the people out, and if we hype it up a bit in advance even non-Party people will come."

He looked closely at Hanrahan. "Are you all right Tim?" he asked. "Is there something on your mind?"

"No!" Hanrahan said quickly. He wanted to scream, but the words he needed wouldn't come. But he had to say something. He couldn't let Gibson grow suspicious.

"No," he repeated. "It's just that - well, a rally in the middle of Dublin just before polling day. It's a bit old hat, isn't it? That sort of thing hasn't really been done since the thirties - and we've already done so well with television and so on."

"But that's just the point, don't you see," Gibson said eagerly.

"I want to remind people of the old days - I want to make the link with the heroes they had then. Whenever O'Connell Street was full, people had a sense of history. That's the feeling I want to get across."

Despite the growing revulsion he was feeling for Gibson, Hanrahan could see that his boss had a point. It would certainly be a lot more impressive than anything the other Parties would be able to muster. And it would be possible to use some more modern techniques as well - laser lighting would look very impressive, for instance.

"I'll get on it straight away," he told Gibson. "You'll have the most memorable final rally I can organise."

CHAPTER 18

JULY 13th - THE EIGHTEENTH DAY

THE REPORTER

We were being held in a small dark room, not uncomfortable, but with no natural light, and a big oak door that was kept locked at all times. Its most astonishing feature was that it was in the Garda Depot in the Phoenix Park. The man who had kidnapped us was a policeman! He had directed Margaret to drive straight to the Depot, and when we had arrived at the gate, he had flashed an identity card which had us admitted immediately.

Our room opened out onto a courtyard, which looked as if it had once housed stables. For all I knew, Margaret's car was still parked directly outside, because we had been told to stop there, and then ushered into this room which had been locked immediately behind us.

It was like a small makeshift bed-sitting room, with two divan beds, two chairs, a table, and some bookshelves. There was even a transistor radio. A door in the wall led to a small clean toilet, with a wash-hand basin, soap and towels.

It made no sense. What was a place like this doing in a Garda depot? As far as I knew, the facilities that had been retained in the Phoenix Park, apart from a few offices, consisted mostly of garages and car-parking space for Garda cars, including the fleet of cars in which Ministers were transported. I couldn't conceive of any reason why there would be rooms like this here.

And still less could I imagine what we were doing there, being held prisoner by the Irish police, but not charged with any crime, and with no-one showing any interest in bringing us before a Court.

How had they found us, and why had we been brought here?

We didn't have long to wait to find out, and such time as we had we occupied by banging on the oak door. But our noise was met with a deafening silence. I had noticed on the way in that the courtyard was in a remote corner of the Depot, and it had evidently been well-chosen. Either nobody heard us, or nobody was interested.

About an hour after we arrived, we had a visitor. It was Joe Stafford, and he was accompanied by the same plain-clothes detective who had ordered us to drive here. This time, instead of a revolver, he was cradling an Uzi submachine gun, which dangled from a strap across his shoulder.

Stafford looked pleased with himself as he motioned us to sit at the table, but he spoke briskly.

"I don't have much time," he said. "Empty out all of your pockets on the table."

It was Margaret who answered. Although she hadn't spoken on the journey to the Park, she had been getting angrier and angrier all the time we had been locked in.

"Fuck off!" she told him.

He turned and stared at her. I didn't like the glint in his eyes.

"If you want to be held down and strip-searched, I'd quite enjoy obliging you," he said quietly.

She stared at him for a few minutes, then suddenly shrugged and threw the shoulder bag she was carrying on the table. He turned it upside down, and rummaged through the contents on the table until he was satisfied that there was nothing of interest. Then he turned to me.

I handed him the envelope I had picked up at the GPO. He

ripped it open, and smiled with satisfaction as he read the contents. Then he held out his hand again.

"Your tapes," he said.

How could he have known about them? Unless he had agreed to give them back to the Provos. I was beginning to wonder if Gibson even knew whose side this bastard was on. I gave him the tapes. He glanced at them, grinned triumphantly, and stood up.

There was something I had to ask him, even though I didn't think he'd tell me the answer. "How did you find us?"

He told me. I suppose he couldn't resist it. "I arranged for you to escape from the boat. Then I had you followed all the way back here. I knew you'd go straight for these papers. The tapes were just the kind of bonus you get from good police work!"

"But you knew about the tapes before I gave them to you," I said.

He was standing at the door, grinning. "One of the miracles of modern technology," he smiled.

When he had gone, I looked at Margaret. There were tears glittering in her eyes.

"The bastard!" she said. "The dirty rotten bastard!"

I moved over to where she was sitting, and put my arm around her. There wasn't really an awful lot to say. The thought that was on my mind was that there was no way Joe Stafford was going to let us out of here. I still found it incredible that we were likely to be the victims of a conscious act of murder, carried out by one of the country's top policemen, at the behest of the country's leading politician. If I had read about it in the paper, it would have been on the foreign news pages - maybe on the wire service from Latin America. And yet we were prisoners, and the same policeman had as good as told us that the way he had found out about the tapes was by bugging the home of a leader of the opposition. He wouldn't have told us that - or even come to us himself - if he had the slightest intention of letting us walk the streets again.

We sat there in silence for a long time. I glanced at my watch, to see that it was nearly ten o'clock at night. I switched on the radio to hear the late news. But if I was hoping to hear Charles Page denouncing the Taoiseach, I was disappointed. I knew it wasn't going to happen now anyway. He wasn't scheduled to have his Press Conference until the following day, but I knew - we both knew - that it wouldn't happen as long as we were locked up here.

We slept together, in one of the single beds, huddled together like children. We both felt the same - a sort of quiet depression. Somehow, the whole thing felt futile now. Who were we to believe that we could unseat someone as powerful and as ruthless as Gibson? It had been three lousy weeks, leading nowhere.

Just before I fell asleep, I felt the wetness of Margaret's tears on my arm. But when I tried to twist around to her, she turned away. I knew how she felt.

THE TAOISEACH

There had been so little time to relax. Andrew Gibson lay naked on the bed, face downwards, luxuriating in the thought of the power that would soon be his.

He was not in his own house. Whenever he saw her, he came to her apartment, just off Baggot Street. Obviously, they had to be careful. She was one of the country's best-known libel lawyers, and it wouldn't do for him to be seen slipping into her flat. The fact that it was a mews at the back of one of the large old houses that graced the street made it easier. Usually, like today, he was dropped at the apartment in an unmarked Special Branch car, which returned only when he called the detectives on the car phone. They didn't have far to come, since his office was less than two minutes away.

Every obstacle and every potential obstacle had been cleared out of the way, and nothing could stop him now. That fool Page had fallen for his story hook, line and sinker. He could search for Flynn until he was blue in the face, but Gibson knew that he would never find him. Soon, no one would ever find him.

Only another couple of days now, and he would be undisputed Taoiseach of the whole island. He smiled grimly at the thought of how surprised - even shocked - the press were going to be when he started to make changes.

In personnel, for one thing. There was hardly a single member of the Cabinet who was going to be kept on. He would take a particular pleasure in calling Scally to his room, to tell him that he was finished. The tradition was that if you were called to the Taoiseach's room after the Dail met, you were in. If you were out, you were normally told before the procession in and out of the Taoiseach's office started. He would let it be known that Scally was being called, so that everyone - especially Scally himself - could assume that he was going to be in the Cabinet. That would add to the sense of humiliation.

There were others whom he wouldn't even bother to tell. They could find out for themselves, from the media or from their own colleagues. None of them had the balls to complain about being dumped that way.

He thought about the people he would have to deal with after his re-election. And he thought about others, people who had gone before. And as he did, his anger grew. His stupid bitch of a mother, who had let his father beat him day after day, and told him it would be good for him. His mad business partner, who had tried to destroy him because he couldn't live with the things that needed to be done. The old Leader, who wouldn't stand by him.

Above all, the people who voted for him, who idolised him, who expected him always to deliver. Faces in a crowd, moronic, ignorant faces, the faces of people who knew nothing about power. About how much he had had to do to get it and to hold it, about how much he was willing to do. If only you knew how much I despise you, he thought.

Whenever the anger built, he knew he had to come here. She was the only one who understood it, who was ready for him in his rage. Even Finola, who was prepared for so much else, could not handle this. But she, lying on the couch near the window, she wasn't just ready for his anger - she welcomed it.

She was dressed all in white, in a transparent negligée that clung to her, hiding nothing of her full, even obese, figure. Turning his head to her, he could see the thick mat of black hair between her legs. Because she was lying on her back, her huge breasts were flat on her. He knew that when she knelt on all fours, they almost brushed against the carpet.

He towered over her when he stood up. Looking down, he could see the pleasure on her face already. You stupid bitch, he thought. I despise nobody more than you for the things you let me do to you. I'm going to hurt you, and you're going to love it. What a perfect representative of the Irish people you are! The thought made him laugh out loud. But she saw no smile on his mouth or in his eyes. His eyes were full of hatred, and his mouth was twisted in a snarl.

"Are you going to hurt me, Andy?" she asked him. Her voice was like that of a pleading little girl. She knew that would enrage him further.

"Get up!" he snarled.

As she began to stand, he seemed to change his mind, and shoved her violently back on to the couch. With one violent movement he caught hold of the negligée at the neck, and pulled it from her.

"I want you naked, you bitch," he said. "I want you naked, and crawling. That's where you belong!"

She almost tumbled off the couch, and began to crawl towards him. He sat for a while on the edge of the bed, while she tried to nuzzle into his lap. But all of her licking and sucking did nothing for him. He knew he had to hurt her, to humiliate her. Reaching down, he took a handful of her thick black hair, and almost threw her across the room. He picked up one of the paint brushes from her easel in the corner, a long thin black-handled brush. In two strides, he was standing over her.

"You're only getting what you deserve," he said, swinging the brush high, and watching as it cut into her flesh. Again and again, until her thighs were covered with vicious red marks. At first she whimpered, then she begged for mercy. But there were no tears, and she never screamed.

He was panting by now, and his erection had grown.

"I'll do anything, Andy!" she whispered, urgently. "Anything! Only don't mark me anymore."

"On your knees, bitch!" he snarled.

Instantly, she was on her hands and knees, looking over her shoulder as he positioned himself behind her.

"In there," she said. "Go in all the way, in the back. Don't be afraid - go hard."

The only time she screamed was when he drove in to her with all his force.

Later, after he had gone, she lay there, feeling the pain, knowing she would have to get up soon to go to the Four Courts. She hoped she wouldn't limp. She felt humiliated, degraded. And pathetically grateful.

THE CELL

Kendal, the closest town of any size to Lake Windermere, is a tourist centre. In the winter, it's a sleepy little place. Early in the morning, before the passing trade begins, it retains some of that atmosphere of old. It's certainly not the sort of place you'd go to find a terrorist.

But the two who had survived had made it here, following a long-established plan. They were two holiday-makers. The little house on the outskirts of the town had been rented for two weeks, and a deposit paid over three months ago. The idea was that they would rest here after the operation, all three of them. Kendal is only an hour and a half's drive from Blackpool itself: an improbable hide-out for that very reason.

The fact that there were now only two of them caused no problem. The booking had been made through an agent, and they only met him once, when they went to pick up the keys. Of course, the girl's death had hit them hard - Sean more than the detonator, because he had worked with her before. But they couldn't let it get in the way. They all knew these operations were risky. And the biggest risk came in the aftermath - if you didn't keep your head while the security operation was going on, you wouldn't last very long.

By and large, the mission had been a success. They hadn't hit any of the bigshots, but everything had happened on camera. There were fantastic TV pictures, and there was no doubt they were being shown all over the world. All the planning, and the tedium of waiting and setting the operation up, paid off when the TV propaganda was that good. It kept the Cause on the front pages.

The only thing that had given them pause was the ceasefire that the leadership had announced. They knew they weren't supposed to make any contact with Army HQ when they were on a long-term operation, and they knew that no one would be able to make contact with them until the operation was over and they were safely hidden in Kendal.

In the end they had taken the decision themselves, democratically in the group. The operation had been too long in the planning - they were the ones who had decided that it wasn't intended to be covered by any ceasefire.

Now, according to the radio, it had all worked out perfectly. The police and the army were mounting a huge operation at the ports and airports, but apart from that, most of the security was concentrated south of Blackpool. It was being assumed already that the bombers would have headed for Liverpool or Birmingham, enormous cities where they would have a much better chance of going underground.

It was all too smooth. That was what had led them to make their mistake. Normally, they would have picked up the signs of a security operation anywhere in their vicinity. But they relaxed too soon. It meant that they were surrounded in the cottage before they had a chance to move.

It was an SAS Captain who ordered them to surrender, and to come out of the cottage with their hands held high. They were shocked. How could they have been traced here so quickly? Could the girl have talked before she died? But no - she had been in Castlereagh in some of the worst times. Whatever the circumstances, she was no talker.

What were they to do? They had weapons, and enough ammunition to take a few SAS men with them. But not enough to blast their way free. They both knew the choice - surrender or die.

They decided to live. But that wasn't their decision to make any longer.

They both died within seconds of opening the front door of the cottage. There was no marksmanship involved. A dozen machine-guns started firing as soon as the door was ajar, and by the time the gunfire stopped, there was hardly a splinter of wood hanging from the hinges. It was all mixed up with the blood and intestines and slivers of bone that were spread over the hallway.

It was nobody's fault, really. The soldiers were only following orders. The Captain was only following orders. And the two men died knowing in their hearts that whoever might have betrayed them, it would never be Padraig Norton.

CHAPTER 19

JULY 14th - THE NINETEENTH DAY

THE POLICEMAN

It was like a dream come true.

For as long as he had worked in the Phoenix Park, Joe Stafford had wanted to use it to hunt. Every animal in the Park was protected, but still Stafford had dreamed of hunting them down. He knew he had the skill to bring down a deer, even in full flight.

And how much easier it would be to bring down two people, especially as they had been weakened by three days of close confinement. He had seen to it that they were fed, of course, but after the time they had spent in that little room, they would be disoriented by the huge empty spaces of the Park. And Stafford knew the Park intimately. He had walked every acre of it again and again over the years, and he knew that there was no one who could escape from him there.

It wasn't his first instinct to kill them himself. It was never a first instinct with him to do something himself if he could lay it off. But this was a job that would be almost impossible to lay off at short notice, and besides, as the idea had begun to form that he could do it any way he liked, it became so attractive that he wouldn't have let anyone else do it. He had known from the start that it would have to be done, sooner or later - it hadn't been necessary for the Taoiseach to issue the instructions, even though Stafford was happy that he had. It meant Gibson was involved too.

It would work - he knew it would. They would be found, but maybe not for a couple of days. And it would be another few days before they could be identified. He'd see to that, and he would arrange things so that the police came to believe that they had shot each other. He might even take charge of the investigation himself, especially if it was going too well!

But he had never been a man to make assumptions. In Stafford's life, things went well because they were well planned, and because nothing was ever left to chance. He had got to his present position that way, and he would never change. That's why, although he had destroyed the originals of the McDonald papers, he still had copies. And that was why he had had the Provo tapes duplicated on a tape-to-tape recorder before he handed them over to Gibson. He had a lot of that kind of stuff in the safe in his office.

Because he was a careful man, he took a long time to choose the weapon he wanted to use. Obviously he couldn't use anything from his own extensive collection, but that wasn't a major problem. What he needed was a rifle, one that was fairly easily accessible (it had to be the sort of gun that Jim Flynn could get hold of if he needed one). And it had to be a good one - even though the Park was going to be deserted, he knew he wouldn't want to risk too many shots.

There was no part of the Phoenix Park depot to which he didn't have easy access. At seven o'clock last night, he had used his security key to let himself in to the gun store.

It's no ordinary store-room. At short notice, unarmed detectives can be issued with standard Uzi machine guns from here, or with revolvers if they can't afford to be too noticeable. But the store also houses nearly every gun captured by the Gardai in the course of their work. They are all neatly catalogued in an elaborate card index system, and each one is the subject of a detailed ballistics report, which outlines both the suspected crimes in which the gun was used, and its properties and characteristics.

Stafford walked around the shelves slowly, picking up a gun

here and there, feeling it for weight and balance, and noting the card index numbers of any that he liked. When he had jotted down about eight numbers, he went to the file drawers and pulled the relevant index cards.

It didn't take long to narrow the choice down to one. It was perfect. A U.S. Rifle Calibre .30 MID sniper, it had been the property of a certain American tourist. This tourist had been hired some years previously, by one of Dublin's up-and-coming drug barons, to eliminate some of his less well-organised competition.

Stafford's people had spotted him coming into the country, with the gun ready to assemble in a specially-made briefcase. They had let him take care of one or two of his client's targets - people that they had had difficulty catching red-handed. It had been very convenient, as it was next to impossible to get a conviction in the Central Criminal Court for drug-dealing unless you caught the dealer with his customers and his produce. They had organised a few convictions, of course, by picking up some of the dealers and stuffing quantities of heroin or crack into their pockets on the way to the Garda station. Their protestations of innocence, when the heroin was discovered by the uniformed Garda searching them, usually cut little ice.

But that was a messy way of doing it, and they had enjoyed watching the American take out three dealers. After three, Stafford ordered the American to be taken - that way he got the kudos for capturing a wanted killer, as well as a reasonable reduction in the number of dealers. The man was a professional, and was very surprised to have been cornered in what he had thought was a hick town. He had made a living in his trade in Philadelphia, after all, and they had never caught him there. And he was twice as surprised to discover that Stafford's men could shoot as well as he could himself. Stafford had been on the scene when the shoot-out happened. It would have put the icing on the cake if the American had confessed to the identity of the dealer who had hired him.

But all the American had said before he died - and Stafford had always taken it as a genuine compliment - was, "I gotta hand it to you guys"!

The gun he had left behind was a beauty. Although it had a long barrel - over two feet long - it was very light. And there was a night sight in the briefcase. Its rubber eyepiece fitted against Stafford's cheek as if it was made for him. There were more than enough cartridges in the briefcase to do the job Stafford wanted.

Even though he had already pretty well decided this was the gun for him, the glowing ballistics report made up his mind. It was a superb piece of equipment, semi-automatic and accurate at half a mile. He smiled to himself, thinking of the damage it would do at twenty or thirty yards.

The next thing to do was to make the gun disappear. Since all the index cards were numbered, he had to invent a new card. A missing index card would be discovered far more quickly than a missing gun. He opened another of the drawers, and took out one of the cards at random. Then, laboriously, he copied the details onto a blank card on the manual typewriter in the corner, changing only the gun's serial numbers. He put back the second card he had pulled, and the new one he had made up, in their proper places. That way, although there was now a card in the file for a gun that didn't exist, there were no missing cards, and there were none out of place. Bureaucracy was served.

There were two other things he had to do to make sure the gun was untraceable. He took it back to his office, and spent an hour carefully filing off all identification marks. He decided that when he was finished with it, he would keep the sight, and leave the gun beside the bodies. It was a bit more elaborate than the sort of gun that could easily be acquired, but so hard to trace that the Gardai would have to conclude that it belonged to one of them.

The following morning, Saturday, he went over to the Harcourt Street headquarters. Because it was a Saturday, it was quieter than it would normally have been.

Those manning the computer room were used to seeing Stafford at odd hours, and it didn't occur to anybody that this was a strange time for him to be here.

He was one of the few people with sufficient access to the computer to be able to alter material. And that was essential, because the catalogue in the gun room was automatically stored and updated in the central computer. It was the work of a few minutes to punch in the card number of his gun, and alter the details to correspond with the fake card he had left behind the previous night. His gun had now disappeared, and the computer would be unable to provide the Gardai with any clue that it had been used before in any way.

Stafford could hardly wait for nightfall. He chafed at the thought that it wouldn't be really dark until eleven o'clock, and the Park would not be deserted enough until one in the morning. He was surprised at his own impatience - normally, he knew how to wait quietly until the moment was right. As darkness fell, he sat in his office, watching lights go out all over the depot. Soon, only the security men would be left. There was nothing he could do about them, but they were used to his comings and goings. It shouldn't be a problem.

He sat until he figured it was safe to start getting ready. Then, for the sake of the discipline, he waited for another hour. While he was waiting, he assembled the gun and broke it down a couple of times. He wanted to be sure that he was as comfortable with it as possible. Then he changed. He took off the suit that he was wearing - he almost never wore uniform - and put on a tight-fitting woollen sweater, comfortable trousers, and canvas runners. All the clothes were dark; he wanted to be sure that he could see his targets, but that they would have difficulty seeing him. When he was finished, he surveyed the overall effect in the mirror in the private bathroom that he had had built on to his office. He smiled at his reflection.

He was ready.

THE REPORTER

We had nothing left to say to each other. For three days, we had tried to figure the whole thing out, tried mainly to convince ourselves that it was all a dream, that this couldn't be happening.

But all our efforts led in one direction. There was no way out. I had spent a good deal of the first full day, when we weren't listening to the news on the radio, trying to find a way out of the room. But there was none. Every few hours the door would open, and the same policeman would be there, machine gun in one hand, a tray of food in the other. He would put the tray on the floor, and leave without saying a word. He never even took the dirty trays away - we just piled them up in the little toilet.

There was a window in the toilet, but it was in the ceiling, and only large enough to provide ventilation. Even if we could reach it, neither of us could fit through.

As the days passed, and the immediate fear began to subside, we settled into a kind of routine. No spare batteries for the transistor radio had been supplied, so we turned it on only for the news headlines. The news we wanted to hear never materialised, but that didn't surprise either of us unduly.

What was most depressing was the constant stream of news about Andrew Gibson, about opinion poll predictions of a landslide of historic proportions, and about the enormous crowds that were expected in Dublin for his final rally on Sunday afternoon. Nobody commented about the megalomania inherent in holding a rally in the middle of the capital city's main street, something that hadn't been done since before the age of mass communications.

When the radio wasn't on, we talked. We talked as if we were trying to pack a lifetime's relationship into a couple of days - which I suppose we were. Sometimes we talked like an old married couple, sometimes like teenagers, but always like people who were running out of time.

Once, I can't remember which night, I woke up. At first I didn't recognise the sound. It was Margaret, and she was being violently sick in the toilet. I ran in, to see her kneeling on the floor, retching into the bowl. With one arm I held her head, with the other I pulled her as tight to me as I could.

"I'm so scared, Jim," she kept saying. "I'm so scared."

All I could do was cradle her in my arms, and rock her backwards and forwards, there on the toilet floor. There was nothing I could say that would take away the fear.

But when Stafford came for us on Saturday night, Margaret showed no fear. She looked almost proud when he came into the room - it was my hands that were shaking. He was carrying a rifle - we had got so used to the sight of the machine gun that it looked odd. But to our surprise, he was smiling.

"Come on," he said, "I'm getting you out of here."

For a moment, my heart leaped. But I realised almost immediately that the smile wasn't genuine. For one thing, his eyes never left us, and the gun was never lowered. This was some kind of a trick. There was a glitter in his eyes - almost, I thought, the look of a madman.

He saw that we weren't fooled, and the smile vanished. His face now looked definitely insane. He produced a pair of handcuffs, and threw them to Margaret. "You!" he snapped. "Put them on him!"

Margaret looked at me. I nodded - there was nothing else to do - and she started to put them on my wrists.

"Behind his back!" Stafford snarled. I looked at him. His eyes were manic now, and he was breathing hard, almost panting, and licking his lips continuously. For some reason, the sight of him calmed me. I turned my back to Margaret, and heard the handcuffs clicking into place. She had positioned them as loosely as possible.

"Now you!" Stafford said to her. I turned just in time to see him expertly handcuffing Margaret with one hand. The rifle in his other hand never wavered away from my chest.

"Outside!" was his next command. When we stepped into the courtyard, he ordered us into the back of a car that was parked just in front of our door. There was no-one else around, but he still made us lie down, me on the floor and Margaret on the back seat. He threw a rug over both of us.

He stopped at the gate to exchange a few words with somebody - I supposed the security guard. Despite myself, I marvelled at his nerve. What if either of us had called out? But he must have known us better than that. Neither of us made a sound; in fact I was conscious that I was trying not to breathe.

When we were out of the depot we went straight on for a minute. That meant we were heading for the main road through the park. Then we turned right. We were leaving the city centre behind us, and driving towards Castleknock. A few miles beyond that would be open country. Where was he taking us?

After less than a mile, when we turned left, I realised that we weren't leaving the Park at all. Instead we left the last of the street lights behind us, and drove in pitch darkness for about two minutes. If the sudden bumps were anything to go by, Stafford had pulled off the road and was driving on grass. Suddenly he stopped. The engine and the lights were turned off. We waited in silence while the sound of traffic on the road faded away.

Stafford got out of the car. Then we were ordered to get out too. We were standing on the grass.

"You're free to go," Stafford told us.

What was he playing at? I couldn't believe he was just going to let us go, especially with our hands tied behind our backs.

"What about these handcuffs?" I asked him.

He licked his lips, and then smiled, suddenly. Standing there in the half-moon I saw exactly what he had in mind. It was all written in that crazy smile. He was going to hunt us down!

Margaret must have seen it too. I felt her shudder beside me. That made up my mind.

"Run!" I shouted at her, and at the same time I lunged towards Stafford, hoping to catch him with my shoulder in the stomach. But he was too quick for me. As he stepped smartly to one side, he brought up the butt of the rifle, and hit me squarely on the shoulder. There was a crack, and a terrible stab of pain went through my arm.

And Margaret hadn't moved. She stood there, glaring at Stafford. He reached over to me and, hand hooked under my arm-pit, pulled me to my feet.

"I was going to give you a minute's head start," he said. "Now it's down to a half-minute. You'd better get going."

I was already out of breath with pain. I knew we wouldn't get very far. But perhaps there was some chance that Margaret could get away. I turned my back on Stafford.

"Come on!" I said to Margaret, and we began, half-running, half-stumbling, towards the dense wall of trees. As we ran, I looked back at Stafford. He was leaning nonchalantly against his car, the rifle butt resting on his hip, watching us.

"When we reach the trees," I panted, "you turn left, I'll turn right. He has to catch me first - you head back towards the main road."

But there was no way. "We're sticking together, Jim," she said. "Whatever happens, I love you, and I'm not leaving you here."

I wanted to hold her hand as we ran, but it was impossible. We reached the trees, and stopped. Stafford's car was still visible, but he was gone. Suddenly, a branch seemed to tear itself off a tree three inches from my head. Almost simultaneously, we heard the shot. He was in the trees with us, but all we could see were shadows. Just beside Margaret's head, another tree lost one of its branches.

"That way!" I gasped, and we began stumbling in what I hoped was the direction of the main road. On both sides of us, branches lashed at our clothes and faces. And still, every now and again, Stafford would shoot. He was taking his time, the bastard. Every shot was close enough to terrify us - we both knew that he was missing deliberately, and could hit us when it pleased him.

The other thing that was becoming clear was that we were not getting any closer to the road. The trees were getting thicker. We ran as fast as possible, but we were getting nowhere. I desperately wanted to stop and think, but that would just make us sitting ducks.

Suddenly we broke free of the trees. But there was no sign of a road. We were standing at the edge of a large open space, in the middle of which some animals were lying down. At the far side was another large clump of trees. In the moonlight it looked a good deal denser than the copse we had just left.

What were we to do? If we tried to make it across the open space, we would be very visible targets. On the other hand, if we could reach the far side before Stafford, it might be possible to lose him. For all we knew, he might be within three paces of us.

I tried to listen. But I could hear nothing through the very loud beating of my heart, and the rasping of my breath. I glanced at Margaret. She was bent over, trying to get her own breath back.

"What do you think?" I panted.

She shrugged. "You lead, I'll follow," she gasped.

There seemed to be nothing else for it. I pointed in the direction of the woods on the far side, braced myself, and ran, Margaret at my shoulder. Nothing happened behind us. As we ran towards the animals, they began to get to their feet. Then they were running too, a great deal faster than us. In the moonlight I realised what they were. It was a herd of deer!

Suddenly one of them stumbled and fell. Then another. Shots rang out from over on our right. The crazy bastard had decided to shoot a few deer before he finished us off!

The fact that he was distracted probably saved us. He got three of the deer, after firing about eight times, before they crashed into the woods about a hundred yards ahead of us.

To judge by the silence from Stafford's direction, he had to reload. That gave us time to make the relative safety of the trees. I knew I couldn't go much further. My shoulder was in agony, and I was having great difficulty in catching my breath. I leaned against a tree, listening to the noise of the deer receding further into the woods, and trying to summon up another effort.

Margaret wasn't in much better shape. She was slumped on the ground, her back against another tree.

"I can't go any further," I said. It came out in a moan.

Suddenly she was kneeling up, shaking me.

"Yes you can!" she snapped at me. "We're not going to let that bastard get us that easily. Now get hold of yourself! Come on!"

It helped. We both struggled to our feet, and began careering through the trees again. We were running blind now. I had totally lost any sense of where the road might be. For all I knew we could be running towards Stafford's rifle.

Without any warning, I stumbled and fell. And kept on falling. We had fallen into a hollow, about six feet deep, in the middle of the wood. I landed on my shoulder, and screamed with the pain that shot through it. I screamed again when Margaret landed on top of me. I tried to struggle up the side of the hollow, but with my hands still behind my back, and pain stabbing at my shoulder, it was impossible.

And then it was pointless. He stood there on top of the hollow, leering down at us, the rifle held easily in one hand. "You were pathetic," he said. "I could have shot you both at will. The deer were a lot more fun."

Slowly the rifle came around. As I looked up, I felt I could almost see down the barrel. I was glad that at the end the fear was gone.

Suddenly his gun twisted upwards. Although he had fired, the shot went harmlessly into the sky. As we watched him, his knees began to buckle, and he sagged forward into the hollow to land at our feet. As he passed me, the blood spurting from the back of his head drenched my jacket. He lay at our feet, his eyes staring skyward, seeing nothing.

As we looked at him, a heavy stone trickled down the bank and finished at my feet. I stared at it in total incomprehension. Then I looked at Margaret. She was looking upward, at another man who was crouching at the top of the hollow, panting and trying to catch his breath like us. It wasn't until he lifted his head that I recognised him in the moonlight.

It was Tim Hanrahan.

CHAPTER 20

JULY 15th - THE TWENTIETH DAY

THE REPORTER

"You were lucky I caught up with you," Hanrahan said.

We were in Hanrahan's flat, on Wellington Road, and he had just cooked us an early breakfast. Only now, when we were as comfortable as possible, were we going to get an explanation.

There had been no time earlier. Hanrahan had vomited all over the woods in the Park when he realised that Stafford was dead. He hadn't meant to kill him, just to knock him down. And he had only hit him once, with the nearest thing to hand.

Before we left, we drove Stafford's car in under the trees. There was very little doubt that it, and he, would be found soon, especially when the three dead deer were discovered. But taking his car off the road gave us some kind of a head start.

Hanrahan drove us back into town in silence. It was almost an hour anyway before I stopped trembling and was able to talk. Margaret sat beside me in the back of the car. After feeling my shoulder, she assured me that there was nothing broken. It didn't feel that way.

There was nowhere else to go except Hanrahan's flat. The first thing Margaret insisted on, when we got inside, was the loan of one of his bedsheets. To judge from his expression when she began to tear it up, he didn't have too many to spare. While Margaret strapped my shoulder, Hanrahan fried eggs.

After eggs and strong coffee, he began to explain what had happened.

"I discovered by accident that Gibson intended to have you killed," he said. Catching sight of the look on my face, he added, "You mightn't believe it, but I have had no involvement in any of your business with Gibson. I've only been finding out about it little by little.

"I didn't know what to do," he went on. "To be honest, there was a while when I thought there was really nothing I could do. But that decision led to a pretty sleepless night" he grinned sheepishly at us - "and last night I decided that I would go to Stafford myself. But when I got to his house he wasn't home. I waited outside for a while, and then I decided to see if he was still in his office in the Phoenix Park. He was on his way out as I arrived, but he turned up into the Park rather than heading for home. That's what made me decide to follow him."

"I'm glad you did," Margaret interrupted. He smiled at her.

"I lost you in the trees," he continued. "I could hear Stafford shooting every now and then, but I couldn't see a thing. And then I saw him, clear as day, trying to shoot the deer in that clearing. That's when I saw you two again, heading for the wood at the other side. He was actually at that hollow before you fell into it, you know. Even then, I think I didn't really believe that he was going to shoot you. It was only when I saw him actually aiming down into the hollow that I decided to hit him."

He took his head in his hands. I could tell that he was both exhilarated and horrified by what he had done. I reached over and patted him on the arm with my good hand. He looked up at me.

"In case you're worried," I said, "nobody's ever going to find out what happened to Stafford from us." He shook his head, and grinned.

"You've a lot more to worry about than I have," he said. "What are you going to do now? You may still be dangerous witnesses, but you haven't a shred of evidence. Gibson got it all, and he has convinced Charles Page that you were trying on a little blackmail with the help of forged letters. You have nothing left to go on."

"We have you," I said.

He looked startled. "What do you mean?" he asked.

"I mean you knew that Gibson wanted us killed. You saw Stafford trying to do it."

"What I saw was a policemen who'd gone berserk, killing deer and trying to shoot you," he said. "And have you forgotten I killed Stafford - my fingerprints must be all over that place, and all over his car, and on the rock that killed him."

Suddenly he was shaking. "Jesus Christ!" he said. "If I come forward as a witness, I'll end up as the murderer!"

I could see there was no point in pursuing the conversation. Hanrahan was right - every road was a blind alley. All we had to be thankful for was the fact that we were alive.

THE WINDOW SHOPPER

At four o'clock on a Sunday morning, O'Connell Street is as quiet as it ever gets. Maybe every twenty minutes, a passing car or two breaks the silence, but otherwise there is little sign of life. Around the corner at the back of Abbey Street, the rear entrance of Independent Newspapers is a hive of activity, with bundles of the country edition of the *Sunday Independent* being piled up ready for collection. In an hour's time, the newspaper vendor who does a roaring trade at that time every Sunday from the city's insomniacs will be setting up his stall where the Street meets the river Liffey. But just now, everything is quiet.

This particular Sunday was no exception. Work had gone on late outside the GPO, making sure that the platform was ready for the Taoiseach's rally that afternoon. They had done a fine job. Normally, the platform for a political rally was a make-shift affair.

As often as not, the back of a lorry sufficed. But this was more like an altar, draped in the national colours of green, white, and gold, and with a raised dais in the centre. The last of the workmen had left at around one, pleased with a job well done.

By four o'clock, there was only one person in the Street. He looked like an American student tourist, with a rucksack on his back, and a tightly-rolled sleeping-bag slung over his shoulder. In the middle of the night, in the city's deserted main thoroughfare, he was window shopping.

To be exact, he was studying the windows of Clery's department store, directly across the road from the GPO. It's an old store, Dublin's answer to Macy's of New York. By day its windows are brightly lit, but at this hour they are in total darkness. That didn't prevent the window shopper from staring steadily into them for several minutes.

He seemed to be satisfied with whatever he saw. After a few minutes he slipped around the corner, down the narrow lane that leads to Marlborough Street. Off that lane there is a small alleyway, one side of which is bounded by the great sliding steel doors that lead to the loading and unloading bays at the back of Clery's. There are three such doors, and each of them is held shut by a padlocked chain. The padlocks are big and heavy, their steel tempered to resist wire cutters.

So he ignored them, and cut one of the chains. He slid the door open carefully, and stood looking at one of the back doors that led into the shop. As he had thought, the doors would be easy to open - they only had Yale locks - but any attempt to do so would set off the very obvious alarm system.

Instead, he picked up a heavy metal dustbin that lay inside the sliding door, and carried it around to O'Connell Street. Then, after checking that there was still nobody in the street, he lifted the dustbin high above his head, swung it around once or twice, and hurled it through one of the plate glass windows, shattering it into hundreds of pieces.

Immediately, a loud bell began to ring insistently. He knew that another one would be ringing in Store Street police station, just a couple of hundred yards away. He ran around to the back, sliding the steel door shut behind him. It was the work of a minute to lever the Yale lock with a plastic credit card, and he was inside the shop. Opening the door did not set off the alarm now, since it was already making an unholy racket.

He moved smoothly and quickly through the store, to the very top floor. The door to the roof was locked only with a sliding bolt. He opened it, and was peeping over the parapet by the time the Guards arrived.

The first car screamed to a halt in front of the shop.

"Bloody vandals!" he heard one of the guards say as they surveyed the shattered window. "Just look at what the little bastards have done!"

For a while after that they were busy with their radios. Someone was obviously being summoned to turn off the alarm, but it never occurred to them to check any of the back entrances to the shop. He had known it wouldn't. From his perch on the roof, he could see everything that went on below.

In due course, an irritable manager arrived. The staff entrance at the side of the shop was opened, and shortly, peace descended on the street again as the alarm system was turned off. When the manager left, the patrol car stayed. It would have to remain there at least until first light, when someone could be found to cover the broken window with plywood. But it would be Monday before anyone would come into the store again.

The window shopper was happy now. He unrolled the sleeping bag and stretched out on it. Then he rummaged in the rucksack, to produce an apple. He grinned. There was time for a few hours' sleep. And he'd still have a great view of the Taoiseach's rally.

THE TAOISEACH

Andrew Gibson had written this speech himself. And he had decided that he would deliver it without script or autocue. It was going to be his finest hour, and he would do himself full justice. He had decided last night that there would be just two other speakers at the rally - the Lord Mayor of Dublin, and the Chairman of the Party's NEC, Senator Mulrooney. Both were tub-thumping speakers, and both would concentrate on extolling his virtues. He himself would adopt a statesmanlike tone, building steadily to a rousing crescendo. Hanrahan had told him that there would be a passage cordoned off, right down through the middle of O'Connell Street. They would come from the north end, past the Parnell monument on which was inscribed the words he proposed to open with: "No man has the right to set a limit to the march of a nation". The motorcade would stop briefly there, and there would be a camera crew strategically positioned to film him against the background of the monument.

His speech would also encompass the three other monuments in O'Connell Street. He would refer to the statue of Daniel O'Connell, "the Liberator", who had brought Catholic Emancipation; to Jim Larkin, whose statue was directly opposite the GPO, and who had raised the working people of Dublin from their knees; and to the GPO itself, which had been the focus of the 1916 Rising. By the time he had finished, the people who had come to see would be in no doubt that they were participating in history being made. And there would be no doubt either that the man they were watching was on a par with all the great figures who would feature in his speech.

The early morning news bulletins were already reporting huge crowds on their way to the city centre, normally deserted on a Sunday. The news reader was estimating that perhaps 100,000 people would be there. No traffic was being permitted into the city centre, and people were being advised to leave their cars at home. Extra buses and trains were being laid on. Already, the only comparison possible was with the Papal visit to Dublin in 1979.

Gibson smiled to himself when he heard this. His car would be here to pick him up shortly. He checked his reflection in the mirror. Everything was perfect.

THE REPORTER

We awoke around noon in Hanrahan's apartment. He was gone, but he had left a note. The note said:

I don't know what I'm going to do with you, but I reckon you'll be safe enough if you stay in my place - there's no reason why anyone should look for you there! In the meantime, I've got a rally to organise. If I don't turn up, it will create a lot of suspicion. I'll see you later.

P.S. As of 8.30 this morning, nobody had found Stafford.

I was angry. Not with Hanrahan, but with the futility of the whole thing. He was the only ally we had left, and he had to organise the ultimate triumph for Gibson. The Taoiseach had won everything. He had all the evidence, and he had us out of the way.

We talked over breakfast, Margaret and I.

"What are we going to do, Jim?" Margaret said. "When Gibson is re-elected, he can hunt us down just like Stafford did. We'll never get anyone to publish your story, and sooner or later he'll get us."

I looked at her helplessly. "I know," I said. "As of now, we're two fugitives. I don't know what to do."

She reached across the table and took my hand.

"Mum and I got you into this," she said. "If it hadn't been for us ..."

"Hey," I said, "don't forget I'm a reporter. I went looking for you, remember? And I got a great story. The only pity is I lost it."

Margaret had grown thoughtful. "Whatever we do now, or wherever we go, we'll have to include Mum. Won't they go after her as well?"

I agreed. What cheered me up was the realisation that Margaret was thinking in threes. Whatever happened, she was taking it for granted that she and I would be together. I thought about suggesting to her that I was at the greatest risk, and that there would be some safety for her in severing all connection with me. But I assured myself that she wouldn't hear of it, and I didn't raise the subject.

She was pacing the room. Suddenly she stopped.

"Jesus!" she said, so violently that I was startled. "Why should we be the ones who have to run? It's so unfair. We've done nothing wrong!"

"Yes," I said, "but ..."

"No, Jim, no buts," she interrupted me. "My mother was widowed by this man, and for years she did the only thing she could. And that's what I'm going to do."

"I don't understand," I said.

"I'm going to confront him," she said. "I'm going to go to his bloody rally, and I'm going to throw it in his face. If he wants to do anything about it, he can do it in the middle of O'Connell Street."

It was my turn to swear. She was right. Even if we couldn't bring him down, it would make it harder for him to come after us if we were out in the open. Shouting abuse at him might be a poor substitute for the story I had wanted to write, but the fact that I was well-known in newspaper circles would guarantee a bit of publicity. And if we became public figures, even public cranks, Gibson would have to think long and hard about putting us away.

By the time I had put on one of Hanrahan's suits, I looked every inch a crank. It was at least two sizes too small, but my own clothes were heavily spattered with Joe Stafford's blood. We stuffed them into the metal dustbin outside Hanrahan's back door, before we set off to walk the mile or so into town.

It was obvious that we weren't the only people heading for the rally. I've never seen so many people going in one direction. There were couples, and whole families, many of them carrying picnics. As we went down through Stephens Green, we were greeted by the sight of thousands of people, young and old, eating on the grass. There was a carnival atmosphere.

In College Green, in the small courtyard in front of the Bank of Ireland, a giant video screen had been erected to relay the activities from O'Connell Street. It occurred to me that it would have seemed like crazy optimism at the start of Gibson's campaign to imagine that a rally in O'Connell Street would overflow down this far. But it had happened. There was already a huge throng of people in College Green, and Westmoreland Street and on up to O'Connell Street itself was packed.

Suddenly there was a huge roar. The people watching the video screen had seen Gibson's car turning into O'Connell Street from the far end. It was making its way slowly through the crowds up that end of the Street. Gibson was standing, the upper half of his body visible through the sun roof of the car. And he was waving imperiously to the throng on either side, who were waving thousands of little tricolour flags.

THE TAOISEACH

Gibson was exhilarated. He had never seen anything like this. Despite the cordon, it had taken them more than half an hour to come from the Garden of Remembrance at the top of Parnell Square, where the motorcade had started, down to the Parnell Monument. And it was a distance of no more than about eighty yards!

All along the route, for as far ahead as Gibson could see, people were lined on both sides of the road, ten deep in some parts. They had all been equipped with little tricoloured flags (a nice touch by Hanrahan), which they were waving furiously. In front of the car, a brass band made up of three of the city's bands was marching in slow time, playing lively patriotic airs.

As he waved, first to his left, then to his right, Gibson found himself murmuring, "My people, my people". It didn't seem in the least incongruous to him. There was no doubt, he thought to himself, I can do anything I like with this crowd. He hadn't even reached the GPO yet, and already they were whipped up into a fervour the like of which had never been seen.

On the balcony of the Gresham Hotel, an RTE camera crew was filming his progress. As the car began to come abreast of the hotel, he reached down into the car and pulled Finola up beside him. She had come up to Dublin the night before last, especially for the occasion. They looked a fine couple, waving to the crowds, and the crowd responded with even more passion.

On the balcony of the Gresham, the RTE floor manager muttered into his mouthpiece, "Christ! Did you ever see such timing!" Gibson's gracious gesture of including his wife in the crowd's adoration was perfectly captured on tape.

Down in the car, Finola Gibson reached over and whispered in her husband's ear, "I've never experienced anything like this. My panties are wet from excitement!"

The Taoiseach smiled, and raised his wife's arm above her head in a champion's salute.

As they inched their way towards the GPO, the crowd became more excited. Now they were throwing things up at the car - hats, scarves, hankies, flowers. It was becoming like a ticker-tape parade. Even uniformed Gardai lining the route were applauding. Ahead, Gibson could see that the platform in front of the GPO was full of people. They too were all on their feet, eyes towards the approaching car, hands clapping furiously, each of them trying to outdo the others in sycophancy. This time, even Scally had turned up, the bastard, and there wasn't one member of the Cabinet missing. Everyone who was anyone, or wanted to be anyone, was there. That was when Gibson's Garda driver told him that the radio had just reported that Charles Page was addressing a final rally of about three hundred people in Cork, at that very moment. Gibson smiled. How could anything be more perfect?

THE REPORTER

We were having a great deal of trouble getting close to the platform. I was glad that Gibson was taking his time coming down from O'Connell Street, because we could only move forward in inches. By the time we got to the Larkin statue, further progress seemed impossible. Crowd control barriers had been erected in a semi-circle around the front of the GPO, to prevent people getting right up close to the platform. A green carpet had been laid across the open space formed by the barriers, leading presumably to the point where Gibson's car would stop. But the crowd was packed tight, and there was simply no way through.

Once again, I calculated without Margaret's determination.

"I'm going to faint, Jim," she whispered in my ear. "They'll have to let us move forward towards the barriers. There's no way of moving backwards."

Without another word she slumped forward on to the man in front of her. I grabbed her immediately, trying to ignore the shooting pain in my arm as I did so.

"Let me through please," I gasped. "Let me through. I've got a sick woman here."

The crowd parted, reluctantly. People were staring at us as I dragged Margaret towards the barrier. Grudgingly, one or two people began to give me a hand. I glanced down at Margaret's face. She opened her eyes for an instant, and winked at me. The gesture gave me new strength, and in another couple of minutes I had her at the barrier.

There was a group of Red Cross volunteers at the foot of the platform. One of them saw us coming, and hurried over to the barrier.

"Just some water," I said to him. "She'll be all right if she gets a drink of water." He produced a flask, and I dabbed some water on her cheeks. She revived slowly - a bit theatrically, if the truth were told - and took a drink from the flask. Then she wiped her forehead, assured the Red Cross man that she'd be all right, and turned and grinned at me.

We were as close to the platform as we could get, and only just in time. Gibson was arriving at the other side of the semi-circle, and making a stately way across the carpet with his wife. Then he was on the platform, and the crowd was going mad. It was ten solid minutes of cheering and shouting before any of the speeches could begin.

And all the while Gibson stood in the centre of the platform, on the raised dais that had been put there especially to exaggerate his height. Both arms raised in the air, he acknowledged the ovation of the crowd again and again. It was thund-erous. At both ends of the street the noise was echoing backwards and forwards. All around me, women - and men - were weeping in uncontrolled emotion.

As he finally took his seat, and the Lord Mayor began his speech, a uniformed Garda officer - a Superintendent - discreetly approached Gibson, and bending low, began to whisper in his ear.

And suddenly I was back at that meeting in Kilkenny, nearly three weeks ago, where the whole thing had started. The same hunted, fearful look was on the Taoiseach's face that I had seen that night. He glanced wildly around, then suddenly, furiously, waved the policeman away. They must have found Stafford. And Gibson must have decided to carry on with the rally. But now he knew that we were still somewhere out there.

THE TAOISEACH

What the fuck was going on? How could Stafford be dead? What had three dead deer in the Phoenix Park got to do with anything? And if Stafford was dead, where was that bollocks Flynn?

The Taoiseach's mind was in a turmoil. The Garda Superintendent who had brought him the news of the apparent murder of the Deputy Commissioner had been taken aback when Gibson's immediate reaction was to ask if any other bodies had been found, and surprised by the look of panic on the Taoiseach's face when he had told him that Stafford was alone. Wondering if that was what the Taoiseach had on his mind, Superintendent Deasy had added in the information that three deer had been shot not far from where Stafford had been found. But as Deasy told some of his colleagues later, "when I told him that he looked at me as if I was mad!".

He needed to get away, to think, to find out what had happened.

The palms of his hands were suddenly wet with fear. What could an investigation lead to? What if they began to dig into some of the files that Stafford kept? What if Flynn and his girlfriend were still locked up in the Park?

But now they were calling for him. Dimly, he became aware that the Chairman of the Party had finished his speech, and had called on him. The crowd was roaring his name, again and again. "Andy! Andy!" It was coming in waves. The whole platform party was standing and roaring too. He got up and went to the dais, trying to compose himself. When he held out his hands to silence the crowd, he saw that they were shaking.

Then he saw Hanrahan, standing at the foot of the steps. Alone among the crowd that he could see, Hanrahan wasn't clapping. Instead he was watching Gibson intently, with a look akin to loathing on his face. So he knows, Gibson thought. Well, fuck him! Fuck them all! he said to himself, and began to speak.

"My friends," he began, "on my way to this spot today, I passed a monument, a monument to a great Irishman, not a hundred yards from here. He was an Irishman who was both praised and vilified in his time. Despite the vilification, despite the fact that erstwhile friends turned against him, he was a man who never betrayed the ideals that he believed in. I too" - he paused, searching for words - "no matter what might be said about me, now or in the future - no matter what lies might be told - I too have never betrayed those same ideals."

Gibson could imagine the curious looks being exchanged on the platform behind him. He didn't care. The process of identification with the great Irish heroes was complete in his mind.

"On that man's monument these words are written," he continued. " "Let no man put a boundary to the march of a nation." That is the sentiment that has motivated me throughout my political life, and it is a sentiment that I know all of you share."

The tremendous roar that greeted this last sentence gave him heart. His confidence was growing now, his hands were back under control. Fuck them, fuck them, fuck them, he was thinking.

"And on the other end of this Street there is another statue, to another great Irishman, Daniel O'Connell, who shared many of the same ideals. Like Parnell, he was a man who had many admirers when he was alive, and many detractors after he was gone. But he never allowed himself to be swayed by those who accused him, or who muttered under their breaths. I too will never be swayed by any false accusations against me."

His voice was rising, almost breaking. The crowd was silent now. Many looked puzzled.

"And in front of me," the Taoiseach cried, "stands another hero, Jim Larkin, who was accused of every crime in the book in his time. But they could never make him bend the knee. And here in this very building, great men fought and died so that the people of Ireland could be free. They were spat on and abused when they came here to take up the fight, but they were not deterred."

His voice dropped dramatically. There was hardly a sound, and the crowd was now still, expectant.

"Great men are never deterred from their struggle, from reaching for their goals, by abuse or slander. I have never been, and I will never be, no matter what is said or done to me. Because my goal is your goal - my freedom is your freedom - my independence is your independence. And it is coming - our freedom is coming! Everything I have done, I have done to secure that goal. And freedom is now at hand! "

There were many in the crowd who had begun to wonder where this speech was leading, many even who had begun to feel embarrassed. But now he seemed to be getting back on track, and the ecstasy in the crowd expressed itself in an ear-splitting roar of approval.

That was when Gibson saw Flynn.

The reporter was standing, crushed against the crowd barrier, his hands cupped around his mouth, shouting. The Taoiseach knew that when the applause died down, Flynn's shouts would be heard. What if they believed him? What could he do? How could he stop it?

His hands were sweating again. His voice almost broke as he grabbed his microphone with one hand, pointing at Flynn with the other.

"Stop!" he was shrieking now. His eyes were searching the platform party, looking for Superintendent Deasy.

"Stop!" he shouted again. "That's him! That's him! That's the man who killed Joe Stafford. Down there at the front. That's him! Stop!"

Suddenly he stopped shouting himself. There was something strange. Above the noise and confusion of the crowd, he had heard something else. A loud, sharp crack. And this terrible pain in his chest. He looked down, and was amazed to see the spreading red stain across the front of his shirt.

No! It was almost within his grasp, and now somebody was trying to take it away from him. He wouldn't let them. He wouldn't.

He looked out again at the crowd, who were now suddenly silent, bewildered. He coughed, and a torrent of blood poured out of him. He pitched forward and sideways, to land on his back at the edge of the platform. His head lolled over the side, his sightless eyes staring at the hysterical crowd.

THE REPORTER

All around me there was pandemonium when Gibson started shouting and pointing in my direction. I had been so fascinated by the tone of his speech, his identification with legend, that I had not begun to shout as I intended. He would have seen me earlier if I had shouted at him sooner.

But when he did see me, and pointed his accusing finger at me, I was grabbed at by hands on either side. They spun me around, so that my back was to the platform. As a result, I didn't see the Taoiseach being assassinated. But across the road, high on Clery's roof, I saw the man who shot him.

CHAPTER 21

JULY 16th - THE TWENTY - FIRST DAY

THE REPORTER

The people of Ireland went to the polls, and they gave Andrew Gibson's Party a massive majority. Only he wasn't around to enjoy it.

After the assassination, the Cabinet had met in an atmosphere of great crisis. Under the firm guiding hand of Bob Holloway, the Cabinet Secretary, their first decision was to make Sean Kelly Taoiseach. He might only be Taoiseach for a few days, until the full Parliamentary Party met after the election, but it was essential that there be a leader now. Their second decision was to order an enquiry into the security arrangements surrounding the rally, and in particular into how the assassin had got clean away. Their third was to announce that the election would go ahead, as scheduled, on Monday.

The new Taoiseach was sent on television that night to convey the decisions of the Government.

"My fellow citizens," he said, *"our nation is in mourning tonight, for the cruel loss of a great Irishman. He was a man that I admired above all others, as I know many thousands of you did too. It has fallen to me to take on the reins of Government in this unhappy crisis, and I must tell you that I am humbled by the task that lies ahead.*

My Government will pursue, with the utmost vigour, the killer or killers of Andrew Gibson. We regard it as a sacred trust to ensure that justice is done to his name. Our Taoiseach - your Taoiseach - will lie in state until Thursday next in Dublin Castle. He will then be accorded a State funeral, with full military honours.

But the most important thing, the thing we know he would have wished, is that the crowning glory of his life's work must be accomplished. He saw this election, due to take place tomorrow, as an opportunity for you the people to pass judgement on the Agreement that he negotiated and that he passionately believed in. It would be a truly tragic irony if his untimely death were to rob you of that opportunity. Accordingly, the Government has decided that the election will, and must, go ahead on schedule. We must mourn for Andrew Gibson. And we must not let him down."

It was, most people agreed, an effective and dignified address. There were only a small carping few who complained that Kelly had used the opportunity presented to him by Gibson's death to run an advertisement for the Party. As it happened, the drama and the tension caused by the incident in O'Connell Street would have brought people out in their thousands to vote anyway.

Many voted on their way to or from Dublin Castle, where they paid their last respects to Gibson's body, which had been worked on all night to try to remove the expression of terror from his face. For many others, that expression of terror was indelible, captured for all time on the video camera that Hanrahan had positioned in front of the platform, to relay Gibson's speech to both ends of the street. It ended up relaying Gibson's death to the four corners of the world.

In Kilkenny, even though he would never take his seat, seven thousand people voted for Gibson anyway.

Margaret and I were held overnight by the Gardai, under the Offences Against the State Act, which allows people to be held without charge for forty-eight hours. The Guards were so confused that they made no attempt to interrogate us. We were just locked up in separate cells, and left alone.

The following morning we were brought to the desk. Tim Hanrahan was waiting there for us. "I'm sorry," he said, "in all the confusion last night, I didn't even know that you had gone to the rally, let alone that you had been arrested."

Margaret shrugged, and grinned at him.

"Don't worry about it Tim," she said. "A night in jail under suspicion of assassinating the Taoiseach will do my career no end of good."

He blushed. "The new Taoiseach wants to see you," he told us. "I think he's prepared to put everything right."

Margaret insisted on being given an opportunity to freshen up before being driven to Government Buildings. I didn't care how I looked. Still, it was half an hour later before we were seated in front of Sean Kelly.

If a man can appear to grow in office overnight, he did. I knew him reasonably well, and had always regarded him as a pompous, self-important man, if reasonably decent and well-meaning. This morning he looked grave, and somehow more mature.

"Tim Hanrahan is a man to whom I owe a great deal," he began. "This morning he came to me and told me something of your story. I'd like you to tell me the rest."

I'd been through this before.

"No disrespect, Taoiseach," I told him, "but I thought I was reasonably experienced until three weeks ago. In the light of everything that's happened, I'd like to have a witness here."

He looked at me for a minute, then nodded. "Do you know Bob Holloway?" he asked.

"He'll do," I said.

Holloway was sent for, and introductions were made. Then we told them everything we had been through. Kelly interrupted once or twice, Holloway never said anything at all.

It took nearly an hour. When I had finished, Kelly started to say something, but Holloway put a restraining hand on his arm.

"Might I have a word with you for a moment, Taoiseach?" he asked him.

We got up to leave, but the Taoiseach motioned us back into our seats. "You stay there," he said. "We shan't be long."

So they left us sitting alone in the Taoiseach's room. A secretary came in with a tray of coffee and biscuits. I drank the coffee, Margaret wandered around the large room, admiring the pictures on the wall. After half an hour, Kelly came back alone.

"Your story is an incredible one," he said. "But I believe, in fact I know, that it is true in every detail."

He pulled his chair closer to us. "In confidence," he said, "I am going to tell you that we have all the proof needed to substantiate your story. Earlier this morning, the safe in Joe Stafford's office in the Phoenix Park was opened. These tapes were found inside, and these photocopies - together with a good deal of other information which will take a little time to sort out."

He smiled, ruefully.

"There are more than a few people in this town with skeletons in their cupboards, and Stafford seemed to have documentation about most of them," he said.

I opened the envelope he pushed towards me. There were two cassettes inside, and the photocopies of the McDonald letters. He held up a hand as if to restrain me from leaving.

"I'm giving you these things for two reasons," he said. "Firstly, I think you deserve them. You've been through hell and back to try to tell a true story. But secondly, my giving them to you is my way of asking for your trust. That story needed to be written, to prevent Andrew Gibson from being re-elected as Taoiseach of this country. But I am convinced it doesn't need to be written now. Andrew Gibson will never be Taoiseach again, and his crimes should go to his grave with him. In dying, he gave this country a hero, and we badly need a hero. If he's exposed now, now that he's dead, it will undermine the work that still needs to be done."

"I was taught that the people have a right to know," I told him, shortly.

"Even what they don't want to know?" he asked me. "Even a story as sordid as this one, that can now only damage the reputation of a dead man? Let me tell you something else, that I've never told anyone before. I know I have a reputation as a bit of a windbag, but I do have some principles. And one of them is an absolute belief that the person who occupies this office must be a person of absolute integrity. I've known, from my own experience for many years, that Andrew Gibson wasn't fit to occupy this office. He got here in the first place by blackmailing spineless politicians like me."

He held up his hand again, this time to prevent me from interrupting him.

"I won't be in this office longer than a couple of weeks," he said. "I don't have the integrity or the guts for it. I'm doing the job now because of my association with the Agreement, and because somebody has to get us over the next few weeks. But when the Parliamentary Party meets to elect a permanent successor to Andrew Gibson, I won't be a candidate. I'll be letting it be known well in advance that I believe Joseph Scally is the only man for this job."

"Why are you telling us all this?" I asked him.

"I'm telling you to try to convince you that this is an important office," he said. "The Irish people have a right to trust their Taoiseach implicitly. If all the facts about Andrew Gibson become known, the blow to national morale will be immense. The people will have lost a hero they badly need, and they will never trust their Taoiseach again. And whoever is in the job is going to need that trust more than ever in the next few years. It's going to be a difficult and a testing time for them and him.

"But the choice is yours," he concluded. "You have all of the documentation, you know my views, and you must do what you think is right."

I sat there. I couldn't give up the story now. Not after all I'd been through. I stood up, as Margaret spoke softly.

"Justice has been served, Jim," she said. "The man who killed my father is dead."

I stared at them both for a long time. It was the hardest thing I think I ever did, but I pushed the envelope back across the table to Kelly. He took it, and put it in a waste-paper bin beside his desk.

Then he stood up to shake hands. "By the way," he said, "if either of you have any trouble at work in relation to the last few days - or the next few, for that matter - you let me know."

At the door, Margaret turned to him and said, "I don't know whether it means anything to you, Taoiseach, but I think you've got both integrity and guts."

Hanrahan was waiting to drive us home, but I felt more like walking.

"What are you going to do now, Tim?" I asked him.

"I'm not sure," he said. "Kelly knows all about Stafford, and he's going to help me to work it out. And he's asked me to stay on for a while" - he glanced at us - "at least until some final arrangements are made. But I'm not sure" - another glance, accompanied this time by a crooked grin - "I'm not sure if I could cope with politicians who want to do everything by the book!"

Outside, in the warm sunshine of Merrion Square, even with Margaret's hand on my arm, it was hard to believe I had done the right thing. First and last, I'm a reporter. I had finally got my story. And I'd given it away.

Except I hadn't given all of it away. There was still one thing I knew that nobody else did. I knew the identity of Andrew Gibson's killer.

I hadn't figured out yet how I could write it without dragging in the rest of the story, but I would. And quickly.

The thought cheered me up. Margaret glanced at me when I started to whistle, and smiled.

"Would you like to go down to Kilkenny for a couple of days?" she asked me.

"You want to see your Mum," I grinned at her.

"Yes," she admitted, "and I'd like to show you a few quiet spots that only the natives know."

"I've got a better idea," I said. "Kilkenny is going to be in mourning for our late lamented Taoiseach for weeks. It's not really the place for us. Why don't you bring your Mum up here, and I'll show you a few places that you have to be born in Dublin to know."

"I'll ring her the minute we get home," she said.

We walked arm in arm all the way to Ranelagh. When we got to the entrance to Mount Pleasant Square, Margaret said, "There's nothing in the flat. I'm going into the village to get some bread and milk and stuff."

She looked at me, her eyes twinkling, and wrinkled her nose.

"You should go on up and get under the shower."

I can take a hint. I was still whistling when I turned the key in the door of the flat, but my whistling stopped at the sight of the devastation inside. The chest of drawers had been turned upside down, books were torn from the bookshelves, mattresses had been ripped open. What was worse was that the man who had done this ferocious damage was still there. He had been behind the door when I came in, and the same sharp knife that had ripped the mattresses was pressed dangerously close to my jugular vein.

"Sit!" he commanded, and pushed me towards the chair beside the kitchen table where only a few nights ago I had begun to write my story. My typewriter was there, a blank sheet of paper still rolled into it. I sat, and turned to face him.

It was Padraig Norton, Chief of Staff of the Provisional IRA.

"Where are they?" he asked me.

"Where are what?" I asked back. I wasn't trying to be brave, I just didn't have a clue what he was talking about.

"I don't have time for this," he snapped. "Where are my tapes?"

Suddenly, it was all clear - and so funny that, despite everything, I began to laugh. "Was that why you shot Gibson?" I asked him.

He was taken aback by my laughter. "What's so funny?" he demanded to know.

"What's funny," I told him, "is that you think I'm some kind of an agent of Andrew Gibson's. The truth is that I'm only a humble reporter, who found out some things about him that he didn't want people to know. So he made a deal with you to have me kidnapped, and then arranged for you to let me think I'd escaped so that I could lead him to some documents. I only stumbled on the tapes by accident on the boat, and he got them back when they captured me again."

He was dumbfounded.

"So you're saying you don't have the tapes? Is this the truth?"

I told him again. "As far as I'm concerned he got the tapes back by accident. Joe Stafford described it to me as a bonus. You probably thought he was in the process of double-crossing you ..."

"Oh, he double-crossed me all right," Norton said. "He made me double-cross two of my best people, and they're dead as a result. And I've not the slightest doubt, once he got those tapes back, that he'd renege on everything we agreed on."

He smiled at me, and there was nothing but menace in the smile.

"I shot him because I don't allow myself to be double-crossed," he said. He picked up a rifle that was just inside the door. The laughter was gone from his face as quickly as it had come.

"I'm going to have to leave now," he said. "And I'm afraid I have another principle as well. I don't leave witnesses behind."

As he raised the rifle towards me, a key turned in the lock behind him. Instinctively, he wheeled around, just for an instant. As hard as I could, I hit him on the back of the head with my portable typewriter. I've never been so glad of it as I was then.

He went down like a stone. His rifle, the one that I hoped a ballistics report would prove was the same gun that had shot Gibson, lay on the ground beside him. As Margaret stood in the doorway in shock, I tied his hands behind his back as tightly as I could with the belt from Tim Hanrahan's trousers, yelling at Margaret to ring for the police.

But she never moved. When I looked up at her, I saw that she was shaking uncontrollably, tears running down her face. I stood up, and took her in my arms.

"It's OK," I said. "It's OK. It's over now. It's finally over."